First Comes Love, Then Comes Murder

An Anthology Edited by
Teresa Inge and Heather Weidner

White City

Press

First Comes Love, Then Comes Murder

An Anthology Edited by
Teresa Inge and Heather Weidner

This edition published by White City Press
An imprint of Misti Media LLC
https://whitecitypress.com
Available in both Paperback and eBook Editions
1 2 3 4 5 6 7 8 9 10
Copyright Respective Authors © 2024
Paperback ISBN: 9781963479317
eBook ISBN: 9781963479300

Acknowledgements

The authors would like to thank Teresa Inge and Heather Weidner for their time and talent in editing the book. Their attention to detail in proofreading and editing each manuscript contributed to a well-crafted collection. Additional acknowledgement goes to the authors of *First Comes Love, Then Come Murder* for their creative contribution, and to Jay Hartman at Misti Media for publishing the book.

Contents

Introduction

First Comes Love, Then Comes Murder features nineteen juicy tales of revenge, betrayal, bad breakups, and a few *I dos and some I don'ts.*

Each short story takes ruthless relationships to an all-new level in all kinds of places like destination weddings, riverboat cruises, wineries, bachelorette parties, creepy stalkers, cheating spouses, and sneaky friends trying for their version of happily ever after. So, settle in for some love stories with a twist of revenge, infidelity, and murder.

Teresa Inge & Heather Weidner

Maid of Murder
Teresa Inge

"Welcome to the OBX Wine Shop." Lainey Gentry paused her task of pouring wine to face new customers entering her store.

"We're here for the wedding wine tasting," Alexa Rae, an occasional customer, entered the store with two women trailing behind her.

"There's a spot reserved for you at the tasting bar. I'll be right with you," Lainey said.

The women made their way to the bar by the other patrons. Lainey walked toward them.

"This is Tara Brooks, the bride I called you about, and Summer Prescott, her bridesmaid." Alexa waved her hand toward the women, then herself. "And I'm the maid of honor."

Lainey turned toward Tara. "When is your big day?"

"June twenty-second. I'm so excited."

"And will you be ordering the wine today?"

"Of course."

Lainey placed three sheets of paper, pencils, wine glasses, and a container on the counter. "We'll be sampling our most popular OBX wines." The OBX was the local vernacular referring to the Outer Banks, a popular vacation and wedding destination off the east coast of North Carolina.

"Plus, our customers will receive a discount on all wines purchased today. Ready to get started?" Lainey asked.

"Yes," the women said in unison.

"We'll start with white whites followed by rosés and reds. For each wine, I recommend swirling it in your mouth for flavor, then spitting it into the bucket." Lainey tapped the brass container on the counter.

"Sounds stimulating," Alexa purred.

"And don't guzzle it," a striking man with peppered gray hair added.

"Ladies, meet Erik Stewart, our resident wine critic," Lainey said.

"A real wine critic?" Alexa moved closer.

Erik swirled the wine in his glass. "My dear Lainey, must we always discuss my profession in front of novice tasters?"

"He only comes here for the free wine." Lainey set a bottle of Chardonnay on the counter and popped the cork. She placed one finger along the bottom of each glass and poured wine to reach the top of her finger. "As mentioned, our wines are from coastal North Carolina vineyards. This Chardonnay is known for its light taste."

The women swirled the wine and clinked their glasses together.

"Love the crispness," Tara said after she took a delicate sip.

Alexa gulped the entire contents and slid the glass toward Lainey. "Fill er' up!"

Noticing Alexa's slurred speech, Lainey asked, "Have y'all sampled other wines today?"

"Yes, but this is our last stop since we have our driver for only two more hours." Alexa blew a kiss to a man in a white shirt and black pants standing near the door.

Lainey nodded toward the driver and made a mental note to check on him later. "Chardonnay is great paired with salmon, fish, or chicken dishes," she continued.

"Needs more substance." Summer emptied her wine into the bucket.

"Seems I'm not the only critic," Erik rolled his eyes and sipped the wine. Rex Adler, one of Lainey's wine servers, greeted them and then welcomed a party of four to the bar.

Lainey grabbed a bottle of wine off the shelf. "There's bottled water on the counter to clean your palate and glass. And don't forget to rate each wine on the sheet I gave you."

The women rinsed their glasses and emptied the water into the bucket.

"Next, we have an excellent Pinot Grigio from coastal North Carolina. Summer, you may prefer this one for its medium-bodied texture."

"It's got a kick." Summer puckered her lips toward Erik.

"Too many of these will kick my butt," Tara laughed.

Alexa turned up her glass to empty the contents.

Erik tapped Alexa's arm. "Slow and steady to appreciate the aroma and texture." The "T" rolled off his tongue as his nostrils flared.

Lainey thought now might be a good time to offer more water and snacks. "Water to clean your palate?" She wiggled a bottle in front of Alexa and refilled the cracker basket.

Alexa guzzled the water.

The group next tasted a rosé.

"My fave," Tara said.

"Mine too," Lainey said. "It has a lingering fruitiness, melon flavor, and a delicate aroma."

Tara lifted her glass to salute the taste.

"Last, we have a charming Cabernet for the Cab drinkers." Lainey grabbed a bottle and poured the wine into the glasses.

"I love the complex flavors of dried fruit, tobacco, and subtle tannins." Erik held the glass just below his nose.

"You got all that from sniffing your wine?" Summer grabbed a cracker.

"Erik's sniffer is always on point," Lainey said, with a hint of sarcasm.

Erik winked toward Summer as she moved closer.

Patrons filled the shop, sampling wines. Lainey's idea to hold daily tastings to bring in more business had paid off. Sales soared after each tasting since customers purchased many of the featured wines. She prided herself on offering selections not available in grocery stores and other venues. She opened the shop on North Croatan Highway in Kill Devil Hills, a main corridor in OBX, after her husband passed two years ago. During their marriage, they had traveled to vineyards throughout the world educating themselves about wine. This location also brought in locals and tourists to the Outer Banks, making it a popular wine destination.

After pouring the last selection for Tara and Summer, Lainey grabbed Alexa's glass when the latter stepped away to the restroom and placed it behind the bar. She noticed the driver had moved from standing near the door to browsing the shelves. She grabbed a bottled water and walked toward him. "Care for some water?" She extended the bottle.

"Thanks." He twisted the cap and took a long sip.

"I'm Lainey, the shop owner."

"George Bordeaux. Great turnout on the tasting."

A group at the bar cheered as Rex uncorked a bottle.

"Yeah, sometimes too much." Lainey laughed.

"If you ever need car service, I'm available." He reached into his pocket and handed Lainey some business cards.

"Great. And if you ever need wine, stop by." She headed back to the bar to help Rex.

Alexa approached Lainey, Tara dogging her heels.

"Instead of removing my glass, you should be grateful I referred Tara to you." Alexa turned on her stilettos and walked away.

"Don't let her bother you. She has no filter when she drinks." Tara paused. "Is now a good time to order the wine for my wedding?"

"Sure. Let's head to the back where we can sit and talk." Lainey grabbed her laptop from the bar, and they walked to a table and chairs opposite a stylish couch.

"Have a seat." Lainey retrieved the wine and beer list to review with Tara. "What time is the wedding?"

"Four-o-clock. Reception is at six."

"I can provide bartenders at the reception for a nominal fee. And I have a portable bar to set up that morning."

"The portable would be great on the deck. Can I see it?"

"Sure. It's in the wine room. Where is the wedding taking place?"

"At my beach house in Nags Head by the pool." Nags Head is a popular beach town by Kill Devil Hills.

"Is there a backup in case of rain? You know the weather on these barrier islands."

"Yes, we can move into the efficiency apartment in my house and carport."

"Carport?"

"It's not what you think. It's spacious and will keep guests covered from the rain."

"Great. Our standard package includes a variety of red, rosé, and white wine, beer, two bartenders, a portable bar, and a set-up. And you mentioned you already have liquor, soda, bottled water, and mixers?"

"Yes, I have all of that."

"I require a fifty percent deposit today and the remainder one week before the wedding."

After Tara made the payment, the women walked to the wine room to view the bar and then headed to the front. Lainey eyed Rex talking to George and Summer still cozying up to Erik. Since it was closing time, patrons made their final purchases. After the last customer left, Rex locked the door, and he and Lainey began their cleanup.

"So, you know George?" Lainey asked.

"We used to bartend together." Rex pulled the trash bag out of the bin and twisted the tie.

"Does he still bartend?" Lainey grabbed empty bottles of wine and set them in a box.

"Yeah, part-time at OBX Bar and Grill, you know the one located in Kill Devil Hills."

Lainey nodded and placed wine glasses into the dishwasher while Rex wiped down the bar. She poured herself a glass of rosé and headed to her office to finalize the day's sales.

Thirty minutes later, Rex stepped into her office doorway with a bar towel across his shoulder. "How'd we do?"

"Here's to another successful tasting." Lainey raised her glass.

"Great. I'll lock the door behind me on my way out," Rex said.

Lainey closed the laptop, placed the daily cash into the safe, and locked the credit card receipts in her desk file. She grabbed her purse. While turning out the hall light, she noticed the back door was unlocked. She turned the deadbolt, wondering why Rex hadn't locked it. She stopped to close the wine storage door and caught a musky odor. Letting her nose lead the way, she stepped into the room, passing crates of wine. Slipping on a sticky liquid, she fell face-first on top of Alexa.

"Omigod!" She flailed at the sight of the corkscrew lodged in Alexa's neck and rolled off the body. She stumbled out of the room and dialed 9-1-1.

Within minutes, the shop was filled with EMTs, police, and officials in blue suits.

One of the suits approached Lainey in her office. "Ms. Gentry?" the man asked.

"Yes."

"I'm Detective Jax Barrett, with Kill Devil Hills Police. I'd like to ask you a few questions."

Lainey nodded.

"Do you know the deceased?" He pulled a pen and a small notepad from his jacket pocket.

"No. I mean yes…"

The detective's eyebrows knitted together. "Can you elaborate?"

"Her name is Alexa Rae. She was here for a wine tasting."

"Was she alone?"

"No. She was with a wedding group."

A uniformed officer appeared at the door. "There's a Rex Adler at the front door. He says he works here."

The detective turned toward Lainey. "Do you know him?"

"Yes." Lainey wondered why Rex had returned.

The officer escorted him to the office.

"Are you okay, Lainey? I saw all the emergency vehicles outside."

Rex studied her face.

The suit stepped in front of him. "I'm Detective Barrett. Please stay back. There's been an incident in the wine room."

Rex craned his neck. His eyes ballooned at Alexa.

"You know the deceased?" The detective stood with a pen poised to write in his notebook.

Rex ran his hand over his mouth. "She's a customer. What happened?"

"Looks like murder. We're trying to determine the cause of death. But from the corkscrew in her neck, it appears she bled to death." The detective paused. "Would you know her next of kin?"

Rex shook his head.

"I can pull her friend's phone number from the invoice today," Lainey offered.

The detective tapped his pen against the desk. "I'll take that."

Lainey jotted down Tara's name and number and handed it to the detective. He motioned for the uniformed officer to stand guard and stepped out of the room.

"What are you doing here?" Lainey whispered to Rex.

"I forgot my phone on the bar." He wiggled the phone in his hand. "Scared the crap out of me to see all the police cars out front."

The detective walked into the office. "Put the phone away and no posting pictures to social media. I have a hard enough time doing my job as it is."

"I didn't take any photos." Rex slipped the phone into his pocket.

"Did you contact Tara?" Lainey asked the detective.

"Yes, she gave me information on the victim. I'm curious though…she mentioned you argued with the deceased today. Can you provide details?"

Lainey frowned. "It wasn't an argument. Alexa had been drinking before she arrived, so I cut her off."

"What happened next?"

"She accused me of being ungrateful for the business referral."

"And?" The detective probed.

"I got busy with customers and never saw her again."

"You didn't call a cab for her?"

"No, she was riding in a limo."

"Do you know the name of the limo company?"

Lainey glanced at the cards George gave her. "By George Limo." She handed one to the detective.

The detective faced Rex. "Did you see Alexa get into the car?"

"No. I was serving wine all afternoon."

"What brings you to the store this evening?"

"Like I was telling Lainey, I forgot my phone and came back to get it."

"Do either of you know why Ms. Rae would be in the wine room?"

Lainey and Rex shook their heads. "It's not open to the public."

"One last thing. I need to view your security footage."

"Rex handles that," Lainey offered.

"Oh…Ms. Gentry. Once the forensic team is finished, you can resume business. I will be in contact if we have more questions." The detective stuck the notepad and pen in his pocket and exited the room.

*****

The next morning, Lainey stumbled out of bed, still shaken from the previous night. She showered and then gulped down bottled water before clicking on the television in her home office. The news flashed a reporter standing in front of the wine shop, which was decorated with discarded yellow police tape.

"Omigod! Everyone will think I murdered her." Her thoughts raced to Alexa's body in the wine room. Why would someone kill her? She rubbed her head. Everything was a blur.

*****

Later that morning, Lainey nosed her Jeep into a front parking spot at her shop. Why hadn't she asked the police to remove the crime scene tape when they cleared her to reopen the store? She gathered the police tape, unlocked the door, and headed inside. What was once a quaint wine shop was now a tainted crime scene. She would need to call in a specialty cleaner to remove the bloodstains and clean the room.

She had barely turned on the lights when three taps in quick succession led her back to the door. Lainey found Erik hunched and disheveled.

"I need to talk to you." He pushed past her and walked to the bar.

"Are you okay?"

"I know it's early, but I need something to calm my nerves."

Lainey walked behind the bar, popped a cork, and poured Erik a glass of wine, not bothering to measure her one-finger standard.

He guzzled the wine.

Lainey raised her eyebrows since Erik was all about drinking wine slowly and steadily. She realized he was shaken up. "What happened?"

"Someone tried to kill me last night."

"How?" Lainey poured more wine.

"During the night, someone entered my house and tried to strangle me." He wolfed down the wine.

"What happened next?"

"I fought back, and he took off."

"Did you call the police?"

"Yes, but they think it's related to a rash of burglaries in the neighborhood. They took a report but without a suspect, they can't do much."

"I'm glad you're okay." Lainey refilled his glass.

This time, Erik sniffed the wine. "One thing though…the intruder had a distinct scent of roses."

"Like in perfume?" Despite her efforts to learn more, Erik gave her no additional explanation of the events that had shaken him.

*****

No further news or incidents occurred by the time Lainey and Rex entered the OBX Funeral Chapel in Nags Head three days later for Alexa's funeral. After signing the guestbook, they slipped into a back pew next to Erik.

Rex twisted his neck for a better view. "I see George. Be right back."

He shuffled past Lainey and made his way to the front of the chapel.

Lainey slid closer to Erik. "How are you doing?"

"Haven't slept in days." He pulled a handkerchief from his pocket and wiped his forehead.

Lainey touched his arm. She glanced at Summer who sat two rows up. She wondered how long Alexa and Summer had been friends. She also wondered about Erik and Alexa. "Tell me, did you see Alexa after the tasting?"

"No, why?"

"Just curious. The police asked."

Erik's eyes bulged and his mouth started to open.

"I'm surprised to see you here." Tara stood at the end of the pew, dabbing a tissue against her swollen eyes.

"My condolences," Lainey said.

"I hope the police arrest you soon."

"I didn't kill Alexa."

"Everyone knows you had an argument with her and kicked her out of your store."

"That's not true."

"I personally will never go back there."

Rex approached the pew and pushed past Tara. "The service is starting."

Tara hurried up the aisle and squeezed into her seat.

"Don't let her upset you." Rex patted Lainey's leg.

Unable to concentrate, Lainey scanned the chapel during the ceremony. Do others think she killed Alexa as Tara suggested?

*****

Detective Barrett viewed unclear security footage with Rex. After he left, Lainey reviewed the weekly sales report on her computer. Since the news of Alexa's death, there has been a substantial lull in the business. She closed the file and thought of Tara's wedding. She had phoned her several times unsuccessfully. She glanced at the business cards on her desk and decided to pay George a visit at the OBX Bar and Grill.

Perhaps he could help her contact Tara.

Once inside the restaurant, she spotted George chatting to a customer at the bar. Lainey walked toward the counter and straddled a stool.

"What brings you here?" George dried a wine glass with a bar towel.

"Have you spoken to Tara?"

"Why?"

"I'm coordinating the wine for her wedding and can't get in touch with her."

"Let it go, Lainey."

"What do you mean?"

George slid the glass into the rack above him. "She thinks you murdered Alexa."

"But I didn't."

"That's not how she sees it."

Lainey turned and wiped her eyes. She needed to stay strong to clear her name. "Tell me, did Alexa ride in the limo after the tasting?"

George frowned and leaned in close. "Look. I don't want any trouble. Plus, I already answered that for the detective you sicced on me." He threw the towel on the bar. "But the answer is no. She stayed behind with Erik."

*****

Lainey and Rex stocked wine on the shelves. Business remained low with only a few tourists trickling in from the Outer Banks. She wondered why Erik had lied to her about not seeing Alexa after the tasting.

The doorbell jangled. Tara stepped into the shop. "George said you stopped by yesterday, so here's the deal. You can provide the wine since I signed a contract. But there's one condition…"

Lainey turned from her task, holding a bottle of wine.

"*You* can't come! Just send your staff, tell them to do their jobs, and leave." Tara threw a check at Lainey and exited through the door.

*****

On the day of the wedding, Lainey entered the wine room to box up wine for the reception while Rex and two staff members transported the bar to Tara's deck. Walking into the room brought Lainey much anxiety. She reached down to grab a box and noticed a tiny bottle of perfume under the shelf. She grabbed the bottle, sniffed it, and stuck it into her pocket.

An hour later, Rex entered the store. "Is this the wine for the wedding?" He peeked into the boxes on the counter.

"Yes. How'd it go?"

"We set up the bar and left."

"Was Tara there?"

"No. But Summer was directing people to set up chairs by the pool." Rex paused. "One thing though…she said to make sure you didn't come to the wedding."

That afternoon, Rex and the bartenders drove to Tara's to serve the beverages. Although business was slow, Lainey checked out two tourists who had stopped at the store. She looked at the clock. Quarter past three. She thought about Alexa and how she should have been at the ceremony instead of six feet under. Even though she didn't like how Alexa had behaved at the wine tasting she didn't wish her dead. Lainey slipped into her black bartender outfit, closed the shop, and drove to Tara's.

Lainey spotted Rex on the deck when she arrived. She made her way around ushers escorting guests to their seats by the pool.

"What are you doing here?" Rex asked.

"I'm here for justice."

Rex stood in front of Lainey as the groomsmen escorted bridesmaids along the outdoor red carpet. The wedding march began to play as Tara walked to the altar.

Lainey peered around Rex, hoping to catch a glimpse of Tara. Unfortunately, Tara spotted her.

"If looks could kill," Rex said.

"That's what I'm hoping for," Lainey muttered under her breath.

After the vows, the wedding party moved to the far end of the pool for pictures while guests flocked to the bar.

"We need more wine from the kitchen pantry," Rex said to Lainey.

As Lainey made her way to the barn, she saw George talking to Erik.

"Thought you were banned from the wedding?" George smirked.

"I'm re-stocking the wine." Lainey scooted past guests before entering the barn. She headed into the kitchen just off the doorway, passing hundreds of wedding gifts on the floor. She flipped the pantry light switch several times with no results. With a little help from the kitchen light, she ran her hand along the shelf to guide her through the deep, narrow room. Just as she spotted the wine at the rear, the pantry door closed. Lainey turned as footsteps approached.

"I knew you were getting close," a female voice said.

Lainey could not make out a figure in the inky darkness. "What do you mean?"

"Alexa deserved to die. She was always drunk and having affairs. I forgave her for taking what my cheating husband offered." The woman moved closer.

Lainey caught a whiff of roses and she thought of the perfume she found in the wine room and of Erik's intruder. "Summer?"

"But then she had to go after Erik. I told her at the tasting that I liked him, but she didn't care. The bitch."

Lainey tried to piece the story together. "You broke into Erik's house?"

"Had to. He was the last to see me and Alexa together as we walked to the wine room."

"You killed Alexa?"

"Yes, and now I'll have to kill you, too." Summer lurched forward, grabbed Lainey around the neck, and squeezed.

Caught off guard, Lainey couldn't breathe. If she didn't do something, she was going to die. She ran her fingers across the shelf, searching for a weapon. She wrapped her hand around a wine bottle and slammed it against the wall, then raked the broken ridges against Summer's arm. Summer screamed and her grasp weakened. Lainey pushed her away and ran out of the pantry tripping over a stray present. Summer appeared in the doorway, grabbed Lainey by the shirt, and threw her to the ground. Lainey landed on the presents, her head smacking against the door. Summer ripped a ribbon from a gift and wrapped it around Lainey's neck. As everything began to darken, Lainey knew she had only seconds to live. She spotted a broken wine glass on Summer's dress and grasped it in her hand, stabbing Summer's leg. Lainey scrambled to her feet and stumbled out the door, only to fall forward as Summer jumped on her back. Both women fell headfirst into the pool.

Lainey surfaced seconds before Summer, who was floundering, sputtering, and coughing.

Tara and her wedding party gathered around the pool. George, Erik, and Rex emerged from the crowd, followed by Detective Barrett.

Lainey pushed her wet hair off her face and looked at the detective. "What are you doing here?"

"Rex alerted me about additional footage of Summer and Alexa entering the wine room just before Alexa died." He pulled Summer from the pool by the back of her shirt and slapped handcuffs on her.

*****

Lainey popped a wine cork. Within weeks, business was back on track. She hoped to land more wedding contracts now that the publicity had faded. She promoted Rex to manager since he proved he could handle a crisis. She watched Erik at the bar sniffing his wine and flirting with a young woman.

Lainey turned as George tapped two fingers against the bar and handed her an envelope.

Puzzled, she opened the envelope as she spotted Tara outside waving from the limo. It was a Thank You card.

"She returned from her honeymoon in Las Vegas and wanted to make amends for suspecting you," George said.

"I'm sure you had something to do with that." Lainey smiled.

"Let me know if you ever need car service. I'll be around." George winked.

Dead Over Heels
Heather Weidner

Settling in behind the dented metal desk in the paper's well-used newsroom, Sylvia Richards blew on the cloud of steam from her vanilla latte. The desk phone buzzed out of sequence with the red pulsating voicemail light. Ignoring the mailbox that was probably full again, she scooped up the receiver. "What's up, Doris?"

"Morning, sunshine. There's a guest to see you in the lobby, and let's say she's determined to talk to you."

Sylvia was sure she rolled her eyes into next Tuesday. *Everyone thought they had the story I just had to write.* "Tell her I'll be down in a few." She skimmed her email inbox and took several swigs of coffee for fortification. Choosing the ancient elevator instead of the stairs, she jabbed the down button at least three times to make it move faster.

By the time the doors swished open in the lobby, Sylvia had checked her stocks and answered three emails. She strode past the greeter's desk, and Doris winked and pointed to the platinum blond in the barrel chair. "Mrs. Chadwick," she whispered, stretching out the last name to at least four syllables. "She'll tell you the deets, and that she's married to one of the commissioners for Henrico County." Doris cocked one eyebrow and turned to answer a call.

Striding toward the woman who jumped to her feet, Sylvia said, "Mrs. Chadwick, I'm Sylvia…"

"I know," Mrs. Chadwick interrupted. The petite woman in the crisp gray suit grabbed her hand with both of hers and her oversized jeweled rings dug into Sylvia's hand. "Is there a place we can talk in private? I desperately need your help."

"Right this way," Sylvia pointed to a conference room the size of a closet. "What can I do for you?" she asked after both women settled into orange side chairs that looked like they had been there since the days of Pet Rocks and mood rings.

"My daughter is missing. She's made no contact, and I usually hear from Cheri at least several times a day."

"How old is she?" Sylvia asked.

"Twenty-six. She works at a huge law firm downtown, and she's getting married soon. Something is wrong. The police won't take a report yet because they're not convinced she's missing. But I know something's happened to her."

"She's an attorney?"

"Uh, no. She's a lead paralegal who does very important work for the firm." Julia Chadwick rummaged through her oversized blue Coach satchel.

"When was the last time you heard from her?"

"Saturday. She called on her way to the bridal boutique. She was leaving work to go to a fitting with her bridesmaids. Cheri's been so busy juggling work and planning her wedding. She was looking forward to hanging out with her friends."

"And what happened on Saturday?" Sylvia prodded.

"The gals tried on their dresses, and Cheri got a call about work. No one's seen her since." Julia Chadwick stared across the table at the reporter. "And no one at her office saw her come back that afternoon. Here." She pulled out a large manilla folder. "This has the names and contacts of her fiancé who's an engineer, her friends, and her coworkers." The woman paused and stared at Sylvia with her dark eyes, heavily outlined in black. "I need people to listen. This is not like her."

Sylvia hoped the futility she felt inside didn't show on her face. But on the other hand, a runaway bride's story could make for interesting copy, especially with her father's political connections. "I'll see what I can do. I'll call you in a couple of days if I find anything."

"Good. I knew I could count on you. My number's on the folder. Call me the minute you know something. Her father thinks she's blowing off steam or having a fling." She made a harrumphing sound. The fifty-ish woman rose and headed out the door before Sylvia could reply.

This calls for more coffee. Picking up the two-inch folder, Sylvia hustled by Doris who stared at her computer screen with the phone receiver in the crook of her neck.

After almost an hour of perusing the Chadwick file, Sylvia convinced herself that it might be worth spending a little time on this story, and she texted her editor the lead. After packing her bag, she made a beeline for the nearest coffee shop and replayed in her head what she knew about the missing bride. Cheri had dated Rick Lancaster since college. From her social media presence, she seemed to be like any normal twenty-something who complained about being overworked while being obsessed with fashion and travel. She posted a lot about her grandiose wedding plans. But all activity on her accounts stopped on the day of the fitting. The last one showed Cheri and her six bridesmaids huddled around one of the displays at Happily Ever After, a bridal and formal shop in Richmond's west end. Cheri looked more like an overly thin teen in a baggy football jersey and red high-tops than a blushing bride. The rest of the gals showed off formfitting sheath dresses in several colors. The Rubenesque raven-haired friend looked out of place and uncomfortable in her straight-lined formal next to the crowd of rail-thin blonds.

After paying for her iced mocha and banana nut muffin, Sylvia took several bites and changed her morning plans. A quick detour to the bridal shop would give her some insight into what happened. *I still feel like she got cold feet, or maybe she ran off with someone that Mommy Dearest wouldn't approve of.*

Pulling into a strip mall, Sylvia parked in the first open spot in front of the boutique. Slipping a notebook and her keys in her purse, she hurried across the cracked asphalt to where a row of svelte mannequins made a rainbow of brightly colored gowns in the front windows. The door chimes, the mix of shiny dresses, and a blast of something vanilla-scented hit Sylvia's senses all at once. She hadn't seen that much colored taffeta and glitter since covering the drag festival last summer.

"Hi, it's a beautiful day to look stunning," a petite blond with corkscrew curls cooed from behind the counter. "How can I help you make your dreams come true?"

"Hi, I'm Sylvia with the *Times Ledger*. Were you working last Saturday?"

"Yes. I'm here most days. I'm Piper. Is there something in particular you're looking for? Wedding? Party?"

Several other staffers, also dressed from head to toe in black, hovered around the handful of customers pawing through the racks of dresses.

"There was a bridal party in here last weekend for Cheri Chadwick, and I had a few questions. I'm working on a story."

"Oh, yes. She's going to make a lovely bride in her Oleg Cassini original." Piper glanced around and lowered her voice. "Her mother paid extra so that no one else would buy the same dress this season. The bride's planning a fairy tale wedding, and her entourage will be in a mix of plum, magenta, and burnt umber, her signature colors."

"How was their fitting?" Sylvia pulled out a pen and her small spiral notebook.

"Everybody seemed excited. The bride was a little late, but her friends entertained themselves."

"Was everything okay with the bride?" Sylvia prodded.

Piper shrugged her shoulder and waved her hand dismissively. "I guess so. She's always so busy with her important job." The millennial paused and tucked a curl behind her ear. "You know, it was odd now that I think about it. She normally comes in dressed to the nines with perfect hair and nails. She came in wearing jeans, an oversized Patriots jersey, and a ball cap. It didn't look like her usual self, and then after two of the girls had a little spat about the dresses, she flew out of here."

"What was the argument about?"

"Don't put this in the story." A horrified look crossed Piper's heart-shaped face. "The bride's mother wouldn't like it." She leaned forward and lowered her voice. "But off the record, the one with the jet-black hair wanted to wear plum, but Cheri insisted that she wear the umber one. The purples and pinks were already assigned to girls with skin tones and hair more suited to warmer colors. Cheri and her mother had planned every detail, including matching the girls to groomsmen with the same type of look for the photos." Piper rolled her eyes. "Cheri insisted the maid of honor would wear the brunt umber one. Not sure her friend was too happy about it."

No wonder she looked cranky in the group picture. "Do you have any security footage from that afternoon?" Sylvia asked. "It would help me get a visual for the story."

"Uh, I guess it's okay. No one's ever asked before. Come with me," Piper waved the reporter down a hallway lined with sparking stilettos and spiky-heeled sandals. The beaded and sequined high-top tennis shoes were more Sylvia's style.

"Have a seat." Piper moved several folders from a guest chair and pushed it closer to a black lacquered desk. Tapping on the keyboard, she pulled up the footage and scrolled through the feeds. "It's a good thing you asked today. The system only keeps three days' worth of video. Okay, let's see. They came in after eleven." Piper clicked more keys and the images on the screen sped up and looked comical as the people zipped in and out of the store. "Those are three of her girls. And then two more." A few seconds later, she paused the image. "That's the umber-hating bridesmaid." After more fast-forwarding, Piper said, "And there's the bride." Cheri waltzed in with a large handbag over her shoulder.

Before Sylvia could comment, Piper tapped more keys. "See, there she is leaving. Hmm. She looks off in this shot and heavier…like she's dragging her feet. I wonder if we're going to have to adjust her dress. I probably should make a note of that. Sometimes, our brides stress eat. I hope she's not preggers." Piper's hand flew to her mouth like she was trying to keep any other comments from slipping out.

Sylvia stared at the grainy image on the screen. *The other clip was a quick look from the back. The gait and the demeanor didn't match. It looked like her shoes didn't fit.* "Can you make me a copy of those?" Sylvia rummaged through her purse and pulled out a thumb drive.

"Sure. I guess," Piper said. "Just don't reveal your sources. I'd hate for the owners to get mad at me. Do a nice plug in your story for the boutique. That'll make my boss happy."

While Piper downloaded the clips, Sylvia's thoughts darted through all the little pieces of information she knew about Cheri's disappearance. Hopefully, she could pull them together into some kind of story and figure out where Cheri went. "Thanks," she said, as Piper handed her the thumb drive. "Anything else you can remember about that afternoon?"

Piper shook her head, and her curls bounced around. "Nope. The girls were chatty and excited about the bachelorette party in Myrtle Beach."

Sylvia rose and tucked her notebook in her purse. "Thanks so much for all of your help. I'll try to slip in a plug for the store and its helpful staff."

Piper beamed and led Sylvia back down the hallway. "Let me know if I can ever help you with a fancy dress." The clerk who resembled a Disney pixie, batted her eyes. "I could make you look like a princess."

"Thanks," Sylvia said. Thoughts of her last boyfriend crossed her mind. After being stressed out at work, he decided that he needed a gap year from his career and decided to stay home and play video games. *Not my idea of Prince Charming.* Sylvia shook off the toxic feelings of Greg and eased into a sense of relief that she had sent him packing before she ended up as his babysitter.

After taking in all the bridal, prom, and cotillion fashions and the thousands of accessories, Sylvia headed for her car. On a whim, she turned and walked down the cracked cement sidewalk past a gift shop and a secondhand bookstore. Looping around the end unit, she spotted rusted doors and a beat-up dumpster. On the other side of the dumpster, the bright robin's egg blue door and glittery gold sign of Happily Ever After looked out of place. Two staffers stood under the sign and stared as Sylvia approached.

The taller blond puffed clouds from her e-cigarette and said, "Like I said. Ms. Gregorio was on the warpath. One of the designer gowns was found all scrunched up in a dressing room, and then one of the laundry carts was missing. She threatened to take it out of all our pay if we didn't find it."

The other gal with quite a collection of facial piercings wrinkled her nose. "She always makes a big deal about everything. It was only a stupid cart. It'll turn up."

Sylvia cleared her throat, and the pair halted their conversation. "Hi. Piper was helping me inside. I'm working on a story about wedding parties for the *Times Ledger*. Do either of you remember seeing the Cheri Chadwick party last Saturday?"

"Nah. I got lucky. I was off," the gal with the nose ring said.

"I was here. Like always," the woman with the ecig replied. "I was so busy with my clients. I didn't have time to pay attention to anyone else. Look at the time. We better get back before Mrs.-you-know-who blows a gasket." She snapped her purse shut and held the door for her coworker.

Bits of trash danced in the breeze across the worn asphalt. Sylvia walked to the edge of the pavement where the landscape dropped sharply down a wooded hill. Nothing in the dark woods looked out of place, but the setting sent a shiver down Sylvia's spine. Shaking off the eerie feeling, Sylvia hustled back to her car to figure out what to do next. *Is this worth pursuing or should I get back to my other projects? I need more than a bride with cold feet to make a decent story.*

Sylvia ate lunch at her desk and focused on another story about a sick little girl's wish for books for the children's hospital ward. After proofreading her copy, she sent it to her editor and pulled out her notes again. *Why does Cheri's story keep pulling me back like a magnet?*

*****

The next morning, Sylvia headed to Shockoe Bottom to visit Cheri's law firm. Inside one of Richmond's skyscrapers, the sterile smell of some kind of cleaner and the arctic blast of the air conditioning hit her as she opened the tall glass door. Sylvia's shoes tapped on the slick marble floor as she made her way to the security desk. "Excuse me," she said to the tall guard. His black uniform with gold and red patches stretched across his chest and arms, using almost all of the material's tensile strength. "I'm Sylvia Richards with the *Times Ledger*. I am doing a story on the disappearance of an employee of Marsh, Rich, and Kellogg. And I wanted to know if you could verify with the camera coverage when she entered and left the building on Saturday."

The tall guard stared down at her. "You'll have to contact my supervisor to get permission. We usually only provide them to law enforcement with a subpoena." He handed her a gold and red business card from the top drawer of the desk.

"I understand, but I need to confirm that she was here for a story on a tight deadline. She's a young woman who's getting married in a few months. Her family is frantic. She hasn't been seen since." Sylvia batted her lashes and tried for her best doe-eyed look.

"What time?" he asked quietly, sinking into the chair behind the computer screen.

"Between ten-thirty to eleven-thirty. She had on a Patriot's jersey with a ballcap."

"And she's one of the lawyers?" he asked, tapping the keys.

"Paralegal. She told her friends she had to work in the morning. Then she left the bridesmaids' fitting to come back here."

"When?" he grunted.

"Sometime between twelve and one," Sylvia replied, trying not to look impatient.

"You picked a good day. Not much traffic on Saturday. A couple of men with briefcases came in around nine. A woman in a pink suit took the elevators upstairs at ten-twenty, and the cleaning crew headed up at ten-thirty. Only the cleaning crew left between twelve and one. No young paralegal. No Patriots jersey. Sorry."

"That helps." Sylvia headed to her car. *Okay, Cheri. Where were you? Meeting someone somewhere else? Hightailing it out of town?*

Sylvia sat in her car and drummed her fingers on the leather steering wheel, trying to map out her next steps. She pulled out the manila folder and searched Julia's list of contacts. After six calls, two voicemails, and a handful of confirmations, Sylvia had an appointment to meet some of the bridesmaids for coffee at Sacred Grounds, a quirky coffee shop near the Virginia Commonwealth University campus. Maybe her friends would be willing to spill the beans on what the bride was really like.

About twenty minutes before her appointment, Sylvia found street parking near the coffee shop. She ordered a tall café Cubano and slid into a lavender wooden chair at a table recently vacated by a couple with backpacks and earbuds. With her back to the wall, Sylvia glanced up every few seconds from her phone to see if any of the gals had arrived.

The door opened and a group of college students shuffled in. Behind them, three women who at first glance could have been mistaken for sisters sashayed in and caused a few heads to turn.

"Sylvia? Hi, Sylvia," the one with the long blond locks said as she waved her friends over. "I'm Mindy, and this is Cindy and Petra. Rochelle and Mandy will be here in a hot minute. Stacie's still at work, so we're going to have to FaceTime her. Here," she said, handing her debit card to the petite blond next to her. "Iced soy mocha with a splash of low-fat caramel." Turning back to Sylvia, she said, "We're so glad you're looking into this. Not one of us has heard a peep from Cheri. That is so unusual. Something is definitely wrong." Her smile faded, and Petra nodded vigorously and took the lime green wooden chair beside her friend.

By the time Cindy returned with the three drinks, a svelte blond with perfect ringlet curls and the stockier dark-headed woman slid into the seats next to Sylvia with their drinks.

"Okay, we're all here," Cindy said. She pointed as she did a round-robin. "I'm Cindy. This is Mindy, Petra, Mandy, and Rochelle. Mindy, see if you can get Stacie. We all work downtown and could slip out, but Stacie's a second-grade teacher who's stuck in the classroom most days."

"Got it," Cindy said, tapping on her phone and setting it in the middle of the table.

"Hey, girl," Rochelle said when the video of another blond appeared on the screen. A chorus of greetings echoed from the other women. "Long day, but it's great to see y'all," Stacie said, brushing a long curl out of her eyes.

"Thanks for meeting me on such short notice. I'm Sylvia Richards, and I wanted to talk to you all about Cheri and last Saturday. Did she give you all any indication of what was going on?" Sylvia pulled out her notebook and flipped to an empty page.

"She's been out of sorts lately with work and planning this wedding," Cindy said.

"And Rick's been stressing her out," Mandy, the brunette, added.

"She can handle him," Petra said with a wink. "She's managed to hang on to him for this long." Mandy glared at her and took a sip of her coffee when she realized the others were staring.

Sylvia paused a beat and stared at each woman at the table. *Trouble in paradise?*

"Cheri's a strong one. She'll pull through. She needs to not be at her boss's beck and call all the time. I keep telling her that she needs to set some boundaries," Rochelle said.

"Why did she leave so suddenly on Saturday?" Sylvia added.

"Work, as usual. She said she had to take care of something." Mandy set her cup down. "She was trying on her dress again. She's in love with it, and she tries it on every time we're at the boutique. But I guess duty, or at least her handsome boss called."

"If I'm going to help, I need to know the whole story. Was she involved with anything she shouldn't have been? Any new people in her life?"

The gals across the table shook their heads. "She said someone at work was starting rumors about her and her boss," Stacie's voice echoed out of the phone's speaker. "She was having issues with a paralegal on her team who was vying for the partner's attention. Cheri felt she had to work extra hard to show up the wicked witch and not let her take credit for stuff."

"What's her name?" Sylvia asked.

"Scary Carrie something," Stacie added. "Wait, I have a text where she was ranting. "It's Carrie Spielman. Cheri called her the queen of snark and cheap shots."

"Anything else? Drugs? Creepy stalkers? Secret loves?"

Again, all the women shook their heads. "No. Cheri was a massive control freak. She was always on the straight and narrow, so she could point out our faults," Mandy said. "She had to be large and in charge at all times."

"And that's why we love her," Rochelle added, glaring at Mandy.

"Yes. We've all been friends forever. Me and Rochelle have been besties since our sorority days," Petra said. "And Cindy, Mindy, and Stacie go back to the days of gymnastics, cotillion, and cheer competitions."

"I met her in Mrs. Woodson's second grade class. We've been through a lot together," Mandy said quietly.

"Is there anything that jumps out? Why would she run off? Problems with her fiancé?"

"No, she and Rick were the perfect couple. They've been together since the sophomore spring formal. Stolen moments. Stolen boyfriends." Cindy giggled.

"We all remember the drama around that dance and that semester. Mandy, it's so good that you've moved past it. Rick wasn't right for you. You'll find your prince charming one day."

Mandy scowled and looked down at her nails. "I'm doing just fine. Thank you. Cheri and I sorted that out years ago. She didn't steal anything."

After a long, awkward pause, Sylvia continued, "Anything else?

There's got to be something."

"Nope. Nobody's heard a peep," Mindy said. "So unlike her."

"If you think of anything or hear from her, please call or text me." Sylvia handed out business cards like she was dealing a poker hand. The girls nodded as Sylvia rose. "Thanks for talking to me."

"I'll walk you out," Mandy said, hopping up and almost tipping her chair. She followed the reporter through a maze of tables and wooden chairs to the sidewalk outside. The breeze caught several strands of her hair and blew them in all directions.

Mandy stared at something across the street. "This isn't the first time she's taken off when she's been stressed out," she whispered. "All the girls are concerned about her, but she's run off before. She likes to stir up drama and make everyone panic." Mandy waved her hand dismissively and headed in the opposite direction before Sylvia could ask any other questions.

That was interesting. A sharp trill from her phone interrupted her thoughts about what she learned about Cheri.

"Hey, Ned. What's up on this fine morning?" Sylvia asked her editor.

"The police scanners are humming. Heard something you might be interested in. Henrico police found something suspicious." Sylvia frowned and waited for him to continue. "It's behind that bridal shop you mentioned."

A charge of excitement zinged through Sylvia. "Thanks. I'm headed over there. Any other details?"

"Nope. But it might be connected to what you're working on." He hung up before she could reply.

Sylvia retrieved her car and sped west. As she pulled into the strip mall, her phone alerted again with a number she didn't recognize. "Sylvia Richards," she said, clicking the button on the steering wheel to answer.

"Ms. Richards. This is Rochelle James. We met earlier at the coffee shop. I was thinking about what you asked, and I remembered something. Cheri video-chatted with me last week. She was so angry at her mom for making changes and cutting back on some of the entertainment for the reception. Cheri kinda felt entitled, and she didn't like when people told her no. She made some comment like she'd show her. I didn't think about it at the time, but now I'm wondering if she disappeared to get her way. Not sure if it'll help, but I decided to tell you anyway."

"Thanks for the update. If you think of anything else, let me know."

Sylvia found a parking spot, pocketed her phone and notebook, and locked her purse in the trunk. No one was in sight at the back of the building. *I hope this isn't a bust.* She walked past the dumpster. Several police cars and a forensic van sat at odd angles. Still not seeing anyone, she hiked to the edge of the asphalt. Down the incline, several people milled around a copse of trees and a large rock. Yellow crime scene tape fluttered in the breeze.

Sylvia blinked several times, trying to get her eyes to adjust to the dimness of the woods. It was hard to make out what was going on. Just as she was deciding whether to move closer for a better view, a tall woman in an orange running suit followed a pony-sized German shepherd up the incline. The woman wiped her eyes and nose with her sleeve.

"Are you okay?" Sylvia asked, approaching slowly.

"That's not what I expected to find on our run this morning. Zeus here got a whiff of something. I thought it was a squirrel, and he bolted, dragging me down the hill. He kept nosing at a pile of leaves. He uncovered a hand with blood red fingernails and a huge engagement ring. Who knows how long she'd been down there. Her eyes looked so sad with that empty stare."

"What else did you see?" Sylvia prodded.

"It was weird. When I kicked some of the leaves out of the way, she was wearing this Spanx thing. Nothing else and barefooted. What was she doing out here in her underwear? I guess it wasn't a robbery if they hadn't taken that ring. Zeus and I spotted an overturned canvas laundry cart thing and a pink scarf a few yards away." She pointed in the distance. "It's all so disturbing. I don't know if I'll ever get the image of that face out of my head."

"Can I get you anything?" Sylvia asked.

The woman shook her head as Zeus inched closer to Sylvia for a pat. "Nah. The detective in charge said he wanted to go over my statement one more time before I could leave. I hope they hurry up. I have an appointment at four-thirty."

The pair watched for any movement in the woods. More police arrived and hustled down the incline. After almost an hour of waiting, two officers climbed the hill. One dusted off his pants, while the other caught his breath. "Ms. Kelso," he said. "We'd like to get your statement."

Using that as her cue to leave, Sylvia nodded at the woman and patted Zeus on the head again.

As Sylvia clicked her key to open the car door, her phone trilled. "Ms. Richards. This is Mandy Delphino, Cheri Chadwick's friend. You said to call you if we heard anything. Uh, I got a text from Cheri."

"You did?' Sylvia said, settling in the driver's seat. "Is she okay?"

"She said she's fine and needs some space right now. We're not supposed to try to find her. She said she needed to think about things. About Rick. Like if she really wanted to marry him." The woman's voice trailed off.

"Thank you. It could help with my story. Do you mind if I meet you somewhere to see the exchange? My editor will want a picture." Sylvia's pulse pounded in her temples.

"Uh, sure. I've got plans later. I guess you can swing by here if you hurry. I'm near Willow Lawn," the woman said, rattling off an address that was a few miles from the bridal shop.

"Be there in a few." Sylvia disconnected and started the Honda. All kinds of thoughts ping ponged through her head as she drove down Broad Street. Did Mandy receive one of the last texts before Cheri died or is the bride's murderer trying to cause a distraction?

Sylvia slowed as she entered a street with seventies style townhomes lining both sides. Spotting Mandy, she pulled into the driveway behind a Kia covered in layers of grime.

"Oh, hi." Mandy waved with her free hand. She carried a pile of clothes, some in dry cleaner bags to the open trunk of her car.

"Do you need help with that?" Sylvia asked, stepping closer.

"No. I got it. Just cleaning out some stuff to donate," Mandy said dropping the load into the truck filled with several open boxes, ski boots, and books.

After a long pause, Sylvia said, "Could I see Cheri's text?"

"Oh, yeah. Sorry. It's been a busy morning. I'm so relieved that she's okay. Her mom's not going to like it, but at least we know nothing bad happened to her."

Sylvia surveyed the pale woman with stringy hair that looked like she needed a dye job on her dark locks. Deciding not to mention the police activity behind the bridal shop, the reporter played along. "That must be such a relief. Do the other gals know? What about the Chadwicks? Or the police?"

"No. I've been so busy trying to get this stuff cleaned up. It's next on my to-do list. I plan to swing by and see Mr. and Mrs. Chadwick after I drop this stuff off. Everything's going to be fine." A Cheshire grin crossed the woman's lips.

"What about her fiancé?" Sylvia asked.

"He's on my call list, too." A slight blush crossed Mandy's cheeks.

Deciding to poke the bear, Sylvia asked, "I heard from the other gals that you and he were very close until well, he and Cheri got together."

A flush rose from the young woman's neck to turn her cheeks bright red. "That's ancient history. We all go way back. Rick and I dated for a bit, but it was nothing." Something flashed behind her eyes, and Sylvia waited for her to continue. Mandy's countenance softened. "We'll have to see what the future holds now. Rick might be back on the market, and I won't have to wear that wretched dress. If you'll excuse me, I need to head out. Lots to do today."

"Thanks for calling me. Could you send me a snapshot of that text?"

Sylvia leaned forward to get a better look at the contents of the boxes in the trunk as Mandy tapped on her phone. A long blond wig stuck out from under a balled-up football jersey. "Oh, hey. Did you say this was all going to be donated? A Tom Brady jersey. Cool. Those red tennis shoes are super cute. Classic Chuck high-tops. And they look like my size. Do you mind?"

Mandy moved closer to block Sylvia's view. "That box is my sister's. Thanks again for coming by." Mandy slammed the trunk shut and headed back to the house.

A bolt of adrenaline rushed through the reporter. "Bye. I'll call you if I think of anything else," she said to Mandy's back as the woman lumbered inside. Sylvia snapped a picture of the license plate.

After a quick call to her police contact, Sylvia sent him the photos of the wig and Cheri's clothes. Now it was time to update the story from a runaway, moody bride to a deadly love triangle. Her contact promised her an exclusive as soon as they made an arrest for the murder.

You Can't Kill the Cat
Debra H. Goldstein

"You can't kill the cat!" Stella stared across the room to the overstuffed couch where her husband lay. "Wayne, make Benny stop talking like this."

Wayne raised his head and glanced in the direction of the man perched on the armrest near his feet. "Benny, stop talking about killing the cat. You know it upsets Stella. She thinks you'll really do it one of these times." He made himself comfortable again.

"This should be the time." Benny dropped a single sheet of paper toward Wayne's mid-section. Caught by a gust of air as the window air conditioner rumbled on, it fluttered to the floor. With a grunt, Wayne swung his feet off the sofa, then bent forward to pick the paper up. "Why is today different than any other day?"

"Look at the second line of the statement. The studio isn't going to be happy. The cat lost money."

"But only on promotional items," Stella said. "Ours are stale. If we created a new stuffed version in time for the holidays, I'm sure we could sell a lot of them."

Ignoring his wife's suggestion, Wayne peered at the statement before handing the sheet back to Benny. He turned his head to meet Stella's gaze. "Darling, the bottom line, which is the only thing that matters, is still intact. Now sweetie pie, don't you worry that pretty head of yours about creating any new merchandise. Leave that to me. With the new cartoon and what we've got in the pipeline, we'll do fine this holiday season. No need to rock the boat or, for that matter, to kill the cat." Wayne waved his hand in an easy circle. "The studio isn't going to forget that this is the house that cat built. Believe me, Frisky Feline will still keep us in kibble."

"Less than last year." Benny paced the room. "After eighteen years, the cat's old hat. Time to kill him off." He pointed to a framed blown-up picture of Wayne and Frisky Feline on the wall. "What is he? Dorian Gray? By now, you'd think his tawny fur would be sprinkled with grey."

"He uses the same hairdresser as my wife,"

Stella pursed her lips into a pout. "Very funny."

"Now, babe. Benny and I were kids when we created Frisky Feline."

Benny turned away from the Frisky Feline picture. "I wanted us to go with a dog. They're more interactive animals. I felt we could do more with a dog. But your husband was stubborn even then."

"The world already had Lassie and Rin-Tin-Tin. There were one or two cats, but nothing like Frisky Feline." Wayne stretched himself back out on the couch. "Thanks to Frisky, all three of us have had a pretty fine life and if we need a little more help in our golden years, he'll provide for that, too. For now, I'm going to shut my eyes and take a nap."

Benny's voice rose as he again leaned against the brocaded upholstery at the end of the sofa, worn thin by so many other times of being sat or leaned on. He stared at Wayne, whose eyes were tightly closed. "You don't get it. If we kill Frisky Feline now, we can enjoy the fruits of his labors and create something new."

"No thanks. You forget the nights when we didn't know where our next dollar, meal, or idea was coming from. Even if we make one thousand dollars less here or there, I'm content to muddle along in the style Stella and I have grown accustomed to. It's perfect. At this point, we only have to come to Hollywood once a month. Otherwise, we're happy staying in San Diego simply watching the waves from our condo or strolling by the palms on the Mission Beach boardwalk."

"That may be enough for you, but I'm not ready to retire in place.

I have bigger dreams. What do you feel, Stella?"

"Benny, what you or Stella feels doesn't matter. I'm allergic to change."

"I thought you were allergic to feathers." Benny picked up a throw pillow lying on the floor next to the couch and twirled it in his hands.

Wayne snorted. "Funny man, but not as funny as Frisky Feline. Stella and I own fifty-two percent of the cat and we're voting for the status quo."

Benny moved closer to where Wayne lay but stayed behind his sight line. He looked at Stella, who nodded.

In a graceful move that belied his fifty-plus years, Benny flipped himself forward and squashed the pillow against Wayne's face.

Wayne struggled as he inhaled the pillow. Amidst tortured gulps for air, he gasped, "My pen. Need my Epi-pen. Stella!"

"Not this time, dear. I'm casting my vote with Benny."

Having had her color touched up and her make-up professionally done, Stella knew she looked good at her husband's funeral. The severe cut of her black suit accented her pleasing shape and set off the highlighted hair cascading on her shoulders. Sitting in the front pew, with Benny at her side, she averted her eyes from the blown-up picture depicting Wayne and Frisky Feline. She'd arranged with the funeral home to slide the picture into the grave with Wayne. It would be one more thing she wouldn't have to dispose of.

Benny leaned over and whispered something in her ear about the cat and death, but Stella kept her gaze focused on the minister delivering the eulogy. She caught words like "a creative man," "a good soul," and "although he never had children, Frisky Feline was his child."

Some child, Stella thought. She'd wanted kids but they'd married later in life, after she'd gotten her two percent for coming up with the merchandising concept, and well, it never happened. Once she'd gone to a doctor who hadn't found anything wrong with her, but when the doctor wanted to see Wayne, he refused to go. Even then, Wayne assured her that Frisky Feline was all they needed to be happy. Benny had never agreed, but Stella had managed to keep him at a distance until now.

The headline in the newspaper two months later announcing Frisky Feline's remaining creator had secretly married his partner's widow wasn't set in as big a font as the one highlighting Wayne's death, but it still was large enough that Stella was sure tongues would wag. She didn't care. Benny and she were happy and that was what mattered.

Stella put down her breakfast fork and pushed a folded newspaper across the metal patio table toward Benny. "At least we didn't make the front page."

Ignoring the newspaper, he put down his coffee cup, rose, and came around the table to plant a kiss on her head. "And if we had? People are pleased we found each other instead of wallowing in sorrow."

This time, when he kissed her, Stella lifted her face until her lips met his. She let his linger longer than she would ever have let Wayne maintain a kiss. When Benny finally pulled away and returned to his side of the table, still licking his lips, she softly dabbed her mouth with her napkin. "So," she said, "what's next for us old married folks?"

"To see the world. It's time to kill the cat, lock this place up, and travel the world. You've never been to Istanbul or Paris, have you?"

"Benny, other than a trip or two to New York when Wayne and you received awards for those shorts about Frisky Feline, I've never been beyond California."

"We're going to change all that. I want to show you the things you missed seeing when you were married to that stick in the mud. You're going to love dining near the top of the Eiffel Tower and ..."

Stella recoiled. Her coffee cup clattered against the table. Brown liquid sloshed from the mug, but she held on to it, oblivious to what splashed on her fingers.

Benny stopped prattling. He grabbed his napkin, leaned across the table, and gently dried her fingers. "Stella, what is it? Are you afraid of heights?"

"No, Benny. That's not it. Remember, we promised we wouldn't speak ill of the dead."

"I'm not. I'm just telling you how life will be without that blasted cat controlling our every move."

She extricated her hand back from his napkin and placed it in her lap. "You called Wayne a stick in the mud. He was a sweet and good man."

"I didn't mean it negatively. Only that he didn't like to travel, and you deserve to see and experience everything."

Stella gave him a thin-lipped smile. "I guess I'm feeling a little sensitive today. It would have been Wayne and my twenty-fifth anniversary." Before Benny could say anything, she added, "But today is special. It's our twenty-fifth day of marriage anniversary."

He tapped the newspaper. "Time for us to make plans to celebrate our fiftieth-day anniversary in some faraway place."

"But how will we pay for the kind of trip you're describing?"

"Easy. We'll kill the cat."

"No."

"What do you mean?"

"We can't kill the cat."

"Yes, we can. Wayne's not here to stop us."

"But darling, I am. Remember, our pre-nup? I retained absolute control of Wayne and my shares of Frisky Feline. With me owning fifty-one percent, well…. Selling him now feels and would look wrong."

Benny banged his fist against the metal table causing their cups, as well as the glasses, plates, and silverware to jump. "Everything we did was so we could sell the cat."

"I thought we did it because we love each other. We acted irrationally out of passion."

Stella placed a hand over Benny's clutched fist. As she gently rubbed, he opened it. She pressed his fingers flat onto the table. "We'll go to Paris, but I think Istanbul will have to wait."

Twenty-five days later, Stella couldn't believe she was again wearing widow's weeds. As people came up to express their condolences, she murmured words of thanks. Periodically, she wiped away a tear with a black-bordered handkerchief.

A man, one of the studio honchos, approached her. He embraced her in a bear hug. She felt the tweed of his jacket rubbed against the bare part of her arm. Stepping back, he said, "I'm still in shock. Benny always seemed so healthy."

"He ate right and worked out every day," she said, "But, Benny had a minor heart problem that he never let stop him from doing what he wanted. Had I realized how serious it was, I never would have encouraged him to climb the two hundred and eighty-four steps of the Arc de Triomphe. I was waiting at the top, having taken the elevator, but he never made it. One of the guards had to come and find me."

As Stella sobbed and covered her face with her handkerchief, the man drew her to him again. "I'm so sorry," he said softly. "At least as close as Benny and Wayne were, I'm happy to think of them in heaven together."

One never knows, Stella thought." I'm sure they are. Thank you."

On autopilot, Stella made it through the rest of the funeral service and reception. Back home, as she hung her black dress in the closet, exchanging it for jeans and a red shirt, Stella couldn't help but let out a sigh. She wasn't sure if she'd stay in California or travel, but with the help of a little digitalis, she knew she was free to one hundred percent enjoy selling the rights to that damned cat.

There's Always Plan B
Grace Topping

"What do you mean you're in love with the girl next door? She's only eighteen!"

I stared long and hard at my husband of twenty-five years. Early in our marriage I'd discovered Henry was a bit strange, but in the last few seconds, he'd galloped from strange to deranged.

I almost felt sorry for him. Entering his fifties, he'd lost the handsome looks of his youth and some of his muscle tone—a polite way of saying he'd gained a paunch. What eighteen-year-old would be interested in him?

"Does she even know how old you are?" From the look on his face, I knew with certainty he'd had lied to her about his age. No wonder he'd started dying his hair.

"She loves me, and we want to be together—we've made plans." Henry looked rather sheepish but also a bit pleased with himself, like a school nerd who'd landed a date to the prom with the head cheerleader. "I'm sorry, but I think you saw it coming."

Saw it coming? When did I have time to see anything coming? After years of holding down two jobs to help put him through medical school and then working long hours managing his medical practice, I'd barely have enough time to think at all. Although there had been the day I came upon him standing next to a bikini-clad Tiffany as she washed her new Mercedes convertible. Foolish me had assumed he was lusting over the red sports car—something he had always wanted.

Then it hit me. I was about to become a cliché—the hardworking doctor's wife who gets traded in for someone much younger. Rage consumed me. I felt like a cartoon character with flames exploding from the top of my head and steam blowing from my ears.

"Tiffany would like to live in the house, so I thought a small apartment downtown would be ideal for you."

My vocal cords constricted, and I couldn't have said anything if I'd wanted to. Was he insane? Did he really expect I'd willingly move from our home with a fabulous view of the coastline to an apartment in the center of town?

He continued, obviously believing my lack of response meant I agreed. "Something near the office."

I couldn't believe my ears. He was trading me in for someone young enough to be our daughter and still expected I would manage his practice. Yes, he definitely was deranged.

Perhaps I could have understood it if the other woman wasn't Tiffany. We had watched her grow from a toddler into a voluptuous beach babe who'd barely made it through high school. If she had an ounce of intelligence, it was buried too deep to surface. Obviously, he wasn't attracted to her brain.

That's when I began to plan his demise.

My thoughts didn't say much for me, I know, but the memories of all the things I'd sacrificed over the years flashed before my eyes like a video on fast forward—the children we didn't have, the vacations I didn't get to enjoy while he went to medical conferences in fabulous places, the evenings I'd spent alone because he was supposedly seeing patients.

Stay calm, I told myself. I needed to make a plan and put it into effect before he cleared out our bank accounts. If he hadn't already.

I immediately ruled out cutting his brakes, especially since I wouldn't know how. I probably could have found a way on YouTube, but I didn't want anyone else to get hurt. Besides, he might be one of those survivors who escapes a mutilated car unscathed. Maybe sleeping tablets in his nightly Scotch or a gentle shove from the deck would do the job.

I plastered a smile on my face as though his news hadn't just turned my world upside down. "Let's not rush into doing anything hastily. We have things to work out—who gets the Lawrence Welk anniversary CDs your mom gave us, the stuffed animal heads from my uncle you wanted—important things like that." I didn't want to do or say anything that would prompt him to force me out of the house until my plans became firm.

"You can take what you want. Tiffany wants all new stuff."

My planning accelerated to warp speed.

"I'm meeting with my book club tonight at the library. Before I go, I'll make dinner and leave it for you—your favorite, beef stroganoff." Let him think I was the meek wife who would continue to toady to him even as he planned to evict me from my home.

"Sounds good," he said as he perused the mail. I could have said I was making grilled rattlesnake, and he wouldn't have noticed.

Stroganoff—with lots of poisonous mushrooms from our property. That would do the trick. Everyone knew I was allergic to mushrooms, so it was unlikely anyone would wonder why I hadn't shared his final dinner.

When Henry left the house, looking pleased that I'd taken his news so well, I slipped into the garage, grabbed my gardening gloves and a trowel, and pushed my way through thick shrubs in the tree-covered area of our property. Destroying angel mushrooms, one of the most poisonous mushrooms in the area, were at the base of some trees, hardly noticeable if you didn't know they were there. I wouldn't have been aware of them if a tree trimmer hadn't recently pointed them out to me. Not knowing how many it would take to do the job, I picked them all, which was probably enough to wipe out the whole community. To cover my tracks, I spread a thick layer of dead leaves over where the mushrooms had been.

Returning to the kitchen, I washed my hands, cleaned the mushrooms, and whacked each one with a meat cleaver. The cleaver was definitely overkill, but with each swing, I felt better.

Afterward, I buried the gardening gloves, mushroom trimmings, and the chopping board deep in a trash bag and carefully washed the cleaver. Only then did I wonder if I could absorb poison from the mushrooms by handling them. Too late to worry about that now, but I washed my hands several times to be safe.

Looking as casual as I could, I went outside and slipped the bag into one of my neighbor's trash cans. Fortunately, the trash collectors would be emptying them later that day.

Back inside, I laid my cookbook open to the recipe for stroganoff and went to work gathering the required ingredients. Once the dish was prepared and bubbling, I went upstairs to dress for my meeting, mumbling, *Bubble, bubble, toil, and trouble.*

I left a note for Henry near the cooling casserole dish, reminding him that I would be at my meeting and to have dinner without me. As extra insurance, I made a big show of backing out of the driveway, waving, and blowing kisses toward the house. Anyone watching would think Henry was lovingly seeing me off.

The book club meeting dragged on interminably. Even the discussion about one of my favorite books, *Maisie Dobbs,* couldn't hold my attention. To make the evening speed by quicker, I envisioned Henry dead on the kitchen floor. He never could resist taking a sample from a pot instead of waiting for a bowlful at the table or sitting on the sofa in the TV room. With any luck, it would take only a small taste to do him in. I winced at the thought of the mess he would make, and that I'd have to clean up.

When the meeting was over, I remained behind to chat with some friends for a few minutes, ensuring I'd have witnesses to my long absence from home that evening. I even told them about the stroganoff I'd made for Henry's dinner and how allergic I was to mushrooms. When they praised me for making him something I couldn't share, I cringed but remained resolute.

As I drove home, it began to unnerve me how quickly I'd plotted his death and devised my cover-up. A glimmer of regret came over me until I thought of the small apartment downtown and quickly shook it off.

Arriving home, I turned the key in the lock and pushed open the front door, listening for sounds in the house before entering. The fragrant smell of stroganoff hit me. It was then I realized I hadn't given any thought as to how I should react. Should I call 9-1-1, hysterically crying that my husband had been sick and was unconscious? Or calmly tell the operator that we needed an ambulance and give the address?

Which would be more believable?

When I could put it off no longer, I made my way down the hall and peered into the dining room. It was unlikely Henry would've had dinner there, but I thought I should check. I braced myself for what I might see, but there was no sign of him or any dirty dishes. Working up some gumption, I turned the corner into the kitchen, expecting to find Henry on the floor, convulsing, unconscious, or dead.

He wasn't there or in the TV room. Puzzled, I did a quick search of the house and on returning to the kitchen, lifted the lid covering the stroganoff. The casserole dish was still full. Henry hadn't touched it.

It was then that I saw his note. *Gone to have dinner with Tiffany.*

Drat! I seethed at how inconsiderate he was to ignore the meal I had so painstakingly cooked for him—even if it was intended to kill him. It was just like him to be so thoughtless. Too bad he hadn't invited Tiffany for dinner.

With Plan A being a complete flop, I poured the stroganoff into a plastic bag and made a second trip that day to the trash can. My frugal nature shuddered at the waste of good beef.

When I returned, I surveyed my cheerful kitchen, filled with items I had lovingly collected from antique fairs over the years. The thought of Tiffany blithely emptying it so she could fill it with decor from Ikea caused resentment to boil up in me again.

That's when it dawned on me. There's always Plan B.

I raced upstairs, pulled large suitcases from the cupboard, and began tossing my things into the bags. If my plan was to work, I needed to make everything go as smoothly and quickly as possible so Henry and Tiffany could be together.

Over the years Tiffany's mother had confided in me things about Tiffany I'd never revealed to anyone: her bizarre behavior, the powerful sedatives, and the frequent trips to psychiatrists. She often said she pitied the man Tiffany married.

Henry's life was about to become a living hell.

Closure
Maggie King

"My dear, your work simply vibrates with energy and enthusiasm. It's a celebration!"

The effusive woman and I held flutes of champagne aloft as we posed before my oversized orange abstract she had just purchased for twelve hundred dollars. The gallery's social media manager snapped a series of pictures.

"What inspired you to create this masterpiece?" The woman asked.

"My goal as an artist is to promote peace and happiness in our troubled world." She beamed. I beamed. Twelve hundred bucks sure brought out my pretentious side. What would she think if I told her the truth, that I painted using vibrant color to lift myself out of a years-long depression? Maybe she'd like the idea of a tortured artist.

My first show at the River City Art Center in Richmond, Virginia was already a success and it had started only minutes before. Twelve other local artists were featured in the center's latest exhibit. Moveable walls created "rooms" that showcased our work.

The place buzzed with conversation. Richmond's art enthusiasts, most dressed in head-to-toe black, had braved the cold of a January night to be part of the art scene. Some stopped to chat. Some slowed their pace as they walked by, scanning my work but avoiding eye contact. Servers carrying trays wove in and out of the crowd, offering avocado toast, shrimp, and that Southern staple, ham biscuits.

And then I saw them. Zach and Chloe Slater. As art professors at Central Virginia University, my alma mater, they were players in the local art scene and their appearance didn't surprise me. Still, I'd hoped to avoid them. I hadn't seen them in person in fifteen years, not since graduation. And that had been fine with me.

"Kate!" Zach boomed. "Kate Jenkins! How wonderful to see you again. Congrats on your exhibit!" Before I could stop him, he grabbed me in a bear hug. His mustache tickled my cheek. I kept my hands at my side, hoping I wouldn't spill any champagne. When he finally released me, Chloe swooped in for an even tighter embrace.

"Zach. Chloe. What a ... surprise." I pasted a smile on my face as I adjusted the neckline of my black sheath.

The two had changed little over the years. The track lighting caught the silver that now threaded through Zach's shoulder-length chestnut hair. He still stood tall and slim. I calculated his age at forty-five.

Chloe had maintained her tangle of curls, the color of rich dark chocolate, along with a shapely figure. She'd been the envy of the girls in our high school and college classes.

"This is so wonderful," Chloe gushed. "We were so distressed when you stopped painting."

Yeah, sure you were. I kept my thoughts to myself as I drained my champagne, wincing at the tartness of the bubbly liquid.

When the social media manager walked by, Zach rushed to grab her arm. "Get a picture of us with Kate here. She was my protégé!"

I would have tossed my champagne in his face if I still had any. A passing server took my empty flute. Zach and Chloe flanked me while the photographer took the pictures. I resisted the urge to make the sign of the horns over their heads.

A man drifted into my space, and, with palpable relief, I turned my attention to him. Zach and Chloe waved as they moved on, promising to be back. I half-listened to the man as he complimented me on my use of mixed media, a combination of paint, fabric, and recycled finds. I bit my lip to keep from laughing at his claim that my work revealed the mysteries of the universe.

I spent the rest of the evening chatting with art lovers about my work. We tossed around terms like complexity and visual patterns. Some carried small plates of finger foods, including mini eclairs and cheesecakes. One man munched on a chocolate chip cookie, leaving a trail of crumbs as he walked through my space.

A while later, Zach reappeared in my space, holding a plate stacked with mini pizzas and brownies.

"Let's you and I get together and relive old times. Just need to get rid of the wife."

"I'm not interested, Zach."

His brown eyes danced. "Playing hard to get, huh? You didn't use to play that game." He pressed a card in my hand and flicked my dangling silver earring. "Think about it, Babe." He clicked his tongue a couple of times, something men who think they're hot stuff do. "Love you as a blonde."

I made sure he saw me drop the card in the nearest trash can. Unfazed, he blew me a kiss.

Shortly before wrapping up for the evening, I turned to find Chloe sidling up to me. "Let's meet for coffee," she said. "Is tomorrow good for you? I'll make you an offer you can't refuse." She winked.

An offer I couldn't refuse? I had to admit that piqued my curiosity. "Okay, I have classes, but I can meet you about three."

"Three it is." We decided on Sweetbrew Cafe, a local coffeehouse.

*****

I sold four paintings that night. My face ached from smiling. A cold wind propelled me across the gallery's parking lot to my Prius. I shivered as I started the car and made my way to my home in Midlothian, a suburb of Richmond.

The aroma of the chicken I'd cooked earlier filled the house. My mother had died three months before after a brief illness, leaving a chest freezer full of chicken she'd bought on sale. As a result, I found myself eating chicken more often than not.

Mom also bequeathed me her estate that included this mortgage-free house, a collection of Twilight Zone shows, cookbooks, guns, electronic devices, and a closetful of clothes too big for me.

I kicked off my too-high heels and threw my purse and coat on a chair. My white leather recliner made a *whoosh* sound when I sank into it. It matched everything in this house: white walls, furniture, carpets, kitchen appliances. Mom thought the color would not only cheer me up but effectively showcase my art.

I scrolled through my social media posts, especially Instagram and Facebook. In photo after photo, I posed against a background of my "vibrant and inspiring" work. An Instagram star for the evening.

I would have loved to revel in my success, but my mind drifted to the unwelcome appearance of Zach and Chloe Slater.

Zach had been my art history professor at CVU. When he promised to recommend me for an internship at a prestigious DC gallery, I knew that strings were attached, and I grabbed the strings. But the internship was a nonstarter. Unbeknownst to me, Zach was making the same promise to Chloe Vanderloe, my best friend at the time. Chloe of the shining curls, pouty lip, mischievous blue eyes, and cleavage perpetually spilling out of snug tops. The gallery offered the internship to her, and Zach proposed. Three months after graduation, the two married.

Feeling like a fool, I managed to graduate but didn't pick up a paintbrush for years. I lived with Mom and took a job waiting tables at a local lunch spot. After messing up too many orders, I lost that job and found work as a stocker for a grocery chain. Counseling failed to lift my ever-present depression.

This dreary existence continued until I found a new counselor who encouraged me to return to my painting. To my surprise, and Mom's relief, I enjoyed it and landed a job teaching at a private school. Before Mom died, she made me promise to approach the art gallery about exhibiting my work. Tonight was the fulfillment of that promise. My future looked as bright as my paintings.

But tonight's encounter with the couple I credited with ruining my life, at least for a while, put a damper on all this brightness. What did

Chloe want? What was this "offer I can't refuse"?

*****

The next day, I arrived at Sweetbrew at ten past three. I pulled my jacket tighter against the blustery wind as I walked toward the coffeehouse. Heavy traffic rushed by on Forest Hill Avenue.

I had no trouble finding Chloe at a table against a brick wall, as she was the only customer. She jumped up and, like the night before, moved in for a hug. This time I dodged the hug.

"Sorry I'm late," I said. "My last class ran over."

She waved a hand. "No problem. Mine are forever running over. What can I get for you? My treat."

"Just a latte."

"Cookie? Scone?"

I shook my head.

While Chloe went to the counter, I took a seat at the table and looked around. Local artists showcased their work on the brick-clad walls. My own would replace them in February. Exposed pipes with bulbs for lighting added to the industrial decor.

Chloe brought our drinks and an oatmeal raisin cookie. She broke the cookie in half and waved at it. "Help yourself. I love the pastries here."

When I didn't comment, Chloe took a bite of the cookie and chewed. "So, Kate—it's been way too long. Tell me what you've been up to."

"Yes, well we both know why it's been way too long. You took my boyfriend and my chance at that internship."

"Yes, you're right, and I'm so, *so* sorry about that. It's one of the deep regrets of my life." Chloe covered my hand with hers. The black polish on her nails had chipped in several places. I'd forgotten how dramatic she could be. Her large blue eyes bore into mine. "Can you forgive me? Can you?"

"Um, well, yes, okay, I forgive you." Did such a grudging forgiveness even count? I snatched back my hand.

Chloe continued. "Believe me, I've paid dearly for my sins. You really lucked out. Zach cheats on me constantly, mainly with his students and his most recent conquest is another teacher. Apparently no one in that school has heard of the #MeToo movement. He thinks I don't know what he gets up to, guess he thinks I'm too stupid. He behaved the first couple of years, then it was all downhill. At least we don't have children."

Finished with her harangue, Kate munched on the cookie. "So does Zach want to get together with you?" she asked. "Reignite the flame?"

"Um, well—"

"That's a yes." She sighed. "Are you going to see him?"

"Hell, no."

Chloe gave me a measuring look, maybe trying to assess if I was lying. I didn't care about her assessment.

"Good," she proclaimed at last, and we sipped our lattes while we caught up on our lives. I learned about her work as an art history professor. I gave a highly edited version of my life, omitting my stints as a waitperson and a grocery stocker.

"I'm sorry about your mom," Chloe said. "I always liked her." After a pause, she went on. "St. Cecelia's is an excellent school," she said of the school where I worked, teaching adolescents the fine points of painting. "I've had some wonderful students from there."

I slashed my hand through the air. "Okay, enough with the small talk … what's this about an offer I can't refuse?"

Chloe laughed and gave me a coy look from under heavy brows. "Okay, you say you're not interested in getting back with Zach?"

"Absolutely not interested."

"How about helping me play a joke on him? I mean, he's wronged both of us."

"What do you have in mind?" I wiped milk foam from my lips.

"Invite him over for drinks. I saw him give you his card last night."

"I threw it away."

"No problem. I'll give you his number."

"I don't want him in my house. I don't want anything to do with him."

"Understood. But listen—" She leaned forward and lowered her voice. "I have some stuff that will put him out for a while. It's a date rape drug."

"Date rape!" I shrieked. Thankfully we were still the only customers. The young barista sat behind the counter, absorbed in his phone.

I closed my eyes and huffed a sigh. "Where—no. Don't tell me, I don't want to know where you got such a thing."

"All you have to do is put it in his drink. When he passes out, call me. I'll be close by. He'll be so humiliated that he'll never bother you again. As for me, the cat will be out of the bag and he'll know he can't fool me again."

"Why don't you leave him?"

"It's complicated." Chloe didn't amplify the catchphrase that many use to describe their relationships that were, well, *complicated*. "So whaddaya say, Kate? You up for it?"

"I don't know—why me? Why not one of his conquests at your school?"

"I was thinking of them, one especially. But when I saw you last night, I thought back on all the fun we used to have at school, playing tricks on people." Her eyes sparkled. "Remember the time we put a spider in Mrs. Cole's inbox? Remember how she screamed and danced around when it crawled on her hand?"

Despite myself, I laughed. "Yes, and I'm the one who got detention even though you masterminded the whole thing. Wasn't the first time I took the rap for you."

I grabbed the cookie half and took a bite. Chloe didn't take her eyes off me like she was hypnotizing me.

Did I want to take part in another one of her pranks? Especially if it involved having Zach in my house, passing out, and calling Chloe to collect him. But her practical jokes had always been fun. And, aside from Mrs. Cole's dignity, no one had ever been harmed. Besides, I'd always given in to Chloe.

I finished the cookie, took my phone from my purse, and said, "Give me his number." Chloe recited Zach's number and her own as I added them to my contacts.

"He likes bourbon, so get a bottle of that. You can pour the stuff in it and he won't notice. Oh, and be sure to act like you're interested. Wear something sexy."

I rolled my eyes. "I don't know about this, Chloe …"

"Oh, Kate, it'll be fun." She sounded like we were embarking on a Caribbean cruise. She stood. "Gotta go," she said as she pulled on her puffer jacket and a pair of suede gloves.

"Um, Chloe. What about the, um, stuff?"

"Oh! Almost forgot. Here's the book I told you about." She reached into her messenger bag and produced a hardcover copy of Ruth Rendell's short stories. "Don't open it now," she said *sotto voce* as she handed it to me. Aloud, she added, "I hope you enjoy it."

At home, I opened the book. Chloe had hollowed out some of the pages to hide a tiny Ziploc bag containing a white powder.

I called Zach and set up a date for the next night.

"I knew you'd change your mind, Babe," he said with a knowing chuckle.

I was starting to look forward to carrying out Chloe's scheme.

Call it closure.

*****

After a dinner of the inevitable chicken, I felt restless and found myself mindlessly web surfing. I googled Zach and Chloe, finding an obit for an aunt that listed Zach as her sole survivor. I perused LinkedIn profiles and student assessments—all glowing—but they yielded little of interest.

Zach arrived promptly at seven the next evening, reeking of cologne. "Hey, Babe," he greeted me with a mischievous gleam in his eyes. "Good to see you. Glad you called." He made that tongue-clicking sound again.

He took off his leather jacket, revealing a close-fitting silk shirt and tight jeans. He obviously spent time working out at the gym. I wore my painting outfit of an oversized denim shirt, paint-spattered jeans, and moccasins. So much for sexy. I hung his jacket in the closet.

Zach was already moving down the hall toward the bedrooms, studying my paintings that covered the walls. "Tell me about this one, Babe." He stood before one of my early works, depicting the James River as it flowed through Richmond.

As I moved closer, he grabbed my hand and pulled me close, mouth seeking mine. I backed into one of my paintings, sending it crashing to the floor.

"Oops. Sorry about that, Babe."

Did he forget my name? Maybe Babe was his generic name for all women. Less chance of mixing us up.

Zach grabbed my arm, ignoring the painting, and tried for another kiss.

"Zach, let's have a drink and chat before …" I couldn't finish the sentence. I knew I was supposed to appear eager to resume our long-ago bedroom activities, but the man repulsed me now. And I feared I'd gag at the cologne pong. "I have wine or bourbon."

"I'm a bourbon man," he said in a husky voice. "Neat."

"Make yourself comfortable in the living room." I winced at my choice of words. Zach would have no trouble making himself comfortable.

"Alexa, play Taylor Swift," I ordered the cylinder on the coffee table. The singer's soprano voice filled the air.

In the kitchen, I poured bourbon into a glass. I made sure Zach couldn't see over the pass-through as I doctored his drink with the white powder. My hands trembled.

"So, Zach … tell me what you've been up to for all these years," I said as I handed him the glass and sat next to him on the sofa, keeping space between us. He moved to close the space.

"I love those long golden curls." He stroked my hair like I was a cat.

I sipped my Chablis. How long would it take for this date rape stuff to take effect?

"Zach, I'm so happy you're here. I've missed you for all these years. But I have to ask: what about Chloe?" I took another sip. "How would she feel if she knew you were here?"

"Oh, poor Chloe," he said. "I don't know what happened, why I fell for her. Woman cast a spell on me, I guess." He took a sip of his drink. Then another.

"Casting spells sounds a bit dramatic, Zach." I resisted the urge to request "Witchy Woman" from Alexa.

"Now you, Babe … I never should have given you up."

His voice slurred over the words and his glass fell to the floor, making an amber-colored splotch on the white carpet. What had Mom been thinking, choosing a white carpet? Probably hadn't expected her daughter to be drugging her former lover. Zach clutched his throat and gasped for air before slumping into my arms.

Was this what Chloe meant by passing out, and going to sleep?

"Zach, are you okay? What's wrong?"

Zach obviously was not okay.

I needed to get to my phone, but Zach had me pinned against the arm of the sofa. I eased him off of me, propped up his head with a pillow, dashed to the kitchen, and grabbed my phone. My hands shook so much I could barely operate the device.

"Chloe, come quick. Something's wrong. Zach's having trouble breathing."

"I'm out front. Be right there."

Alarmed, I looked over at Zach, a bloody froth at his mouth, one hand twisted in his hair. He no longer gasped for breath.

"Oh, Zach, please don't die," I cried.

When I opened the door, Chloe rushed in and leaned over her husband. She checked his pulse.

"He's dead," she screeched. "You killed him!"

"*Me*? You're the one who gave me that stuff that was supposed to put him to sleep."

"What are you talking about? I never gave you any 'stuff.' Where did you get cyanide, anyway?"

"Cyanide?"

"Yes, cyanide. Can't you smell the almonds? You gave my husband cyanide!"

"No!" My desperation ratcheted up. "You gave me something you said would knock him out, put him to sleep." I stamped my foot like a toddler.

"Poor Kate. So delusional. I gave you nothing."

"You did!" My voice took on a frantic edge. "Yesterday, at Sweetbrew."

"Sweetbrew? I haven't been there in months."

I flashed to those Twilight Zone episodes Mom had left. Was I trapped in one of them? Or was Chloe gaslighting me? I suspected the latter. She'd framed me. Once again, Zach and Chloe were ruining my life. And this time I may not be able to rescue it.

"I'm calling the police and having you arrested," Chloe said. "I hope you have a good lawyer. You'll need one." She reached into her purse and let loose a string of expletives. "Where's my phone? I must have left it in the car or dropped it outside. Where's yours?"

"Oh—it must be in the kitchen." I gave a nervous laugh as I moved toward the kitchen, opened the cabinet under the sink, and grabbed one of the guns Mom had stashed around the house.

I can still hear her advice: "Katie, since you like to cook, you spend a lot of time in the kitchen. So if there's a home invasion while you're cooking, you'll have quick access to a firearm."

"But Mom, I'm a gun control advocate," I had said.

"Every woman should know how to use a gun."

I resisted Mom's efforts to convert me into a gunslinger and never accompanied her to the shooting range. But one day she insisted on showing me how to use the gun I now held. All I had to do was remember what she said--because I now faced a home invader.

"Where's your phone?" Chloe screamed.

"You really think I'm dumb enough to give you my phone so you can call the cops on me? Now who's delusional?"

"I guess I should thank you, Kate," Chloe said in a singsong voice. "With lover boy dead, I get his inheritance from his aunt."

It came to me in a flash, bits and pieces of information, conversation. "Oh, yes, the aunt who died and Zach was her only surviving relative. And you told me you couldn't leave him, said it was 'complicated.'" Not waiting for her response, I went on. "You staged this whole thing tonight, framing me, gaslighting me, just so you could get your hands on Zach's money. Nothing complicated there."

By now Chloe was in the kitchen, a menacing look on her face. Then she saw the gun.

Cock the hammer. Check. Aim. Check. Shoot. Check. There… I remembered everything. *Thanks, Mom.*

The gun dropped with a thud and I regarded the mess before me, the bodies of two people who had not only betrayed me but had betrayed each other.

What have I done?

No time for remorse. I had to get these home invaders out of my house, one that was no longer so white.

There was always the freezer.

Taylor Swift sang the heartfelt lyrics of "Closure."

Contract Accepted
Ellen Butler

"Well, Margot, I was right." She slapped the manila envelope on the table placing a Birkin handbag on the empty chair to her left. A ruby-tipped finger tapped the envelope. "It's all here in black and white. Or, I should say, in Technicolor. The PI made sure to get some juicy closeups." She folded her perfectly toned body onto the padded chair and deflated into a slump.

"Your wine, ladies." A tuxedo clad waiter placed two bulbous glasses in front of the women.

"I hope you don't mind, I ordered us the Rutherford Fumé Blanc."

Ashley gripped the glass, and, sinking lower in her seat, gave an offhand mutter, "You know best. I'm sure it's excellent."

Margot began her career working at a vineyard near the Hamptons, which is where she obtained her first husband. Ashley had learned early in their friendship to defer all wine decisions to Margot when she was around or else let herself in for a long-winded and officious lecture on why she'd made the wrong decision.

"Are you ready to order now, or shall I come back?" The waiter asked in deferential tones.

"We'll have the Salade Niçoise, with the salmon," Margot ordered, as if Ashley's agreement was a foregone conclusion, and passed the sturdy menus to the waiter.

"Actually," Ashley straightened tucking a blond lock behind her ear, "I'd like something more than rabbit food. After all, where has it gotten me?" She looked down at her body in disgust. "I'll have the *Duck à l'Orange* with the bread pudding. Stephen always raves about it when *he* eats here." Her lips twisted.

Margot's perfectly shaped and tinted eyebrows rose high, but she otherwise showed no other disapproval at Ashley's meal choice. "Thank you, Giovanni." She dismissed the waiter with a polite smile.

Giovanni melted into the background while Ashley gulped down the entire glass of pale gold wine in one go.

"You'd best tell me the whole of it. Before you get sloshed." Margot's silver bangles clinked as she laid the linen napkin in her lap spreading it across her shell pink Dior dress. "Shall I order you another?"

Ashley shook her head. "No. I need to keep my head on straight. I only sought to numb the pain a little."

Margot patted the younger woman's hand. "The first time is always the hardest."

You would know. Ashley didn't voice the unkind thought.

Margot had been married three times. Divorced from the first two and widowed by the third. If the rumors were true, her third husband's early demise was a blessing, as he'd made some exceptionally stupid investments forcing Margot to sell her villa in Tuscany to cover his mistakes. A villa she'd acquired in her first divorce—she was still bitter over the loss.

"Now—" Margo picked up her wine and sipped, leaving behind a hot pink slash of lipstick along the rim "—what's Stephen been doing?"

"Apparently, he's been *doing* the twenty-two-year-old receptionist at his club."

"What did the PI get?"

"All of it." Ashley slid the 8x10 glossies out of the envelope onto the table. "Here he is having lunch with her at Gino's. Must have been a Thursday—always Gino's and a Reuben on Thursday," she said with disgust. "Oh, and here he's kissing her hand. And here, he's flirting with her in the back corner of his tennis club. Here he is opening the car door for her. How solicitous. I can't remember the last time he opened the car door for me." She tossed each photo on the table in front of her friend.

"Is that all?" Margot picked up the picture. Her crystal blue gaze observed a lithe young redhead with porcelain skin and a pert nose. "Perhaps it's just a flirtation. If that's the case, I can tell you exactly what to do to bring him to heel."

Ashley delivered a side-long glance. "That's just the beginning. Here's Stephen helping her into the Cadillac. And here she is giving him a BJ. And the pièce-de-résistance, the pair of them doing the dirty in the back seat." She squinted rotating the photo that the PI had unkindly blown up ten times the size. "I'm surprised with his knee problems that he was able to manage the position at all."

"Hm … yes … I see." After a brief glance at the photos, Margot shoved them back into their casing and set them aside. "What do you plan to do about it?"

"If it had just started, I might consider giving him a second chance. However, the PI found a credit card that Stephen's been hiding from me. He's been getting hotel rooms across Manhattan for seven months. *Seven months it's been going on!*"

Margot glanced around the relatively empty restaurant. "Er, perhaps you don't want to broadcast it to the strangers in the barroom," she suggested.

Abashed, Ashley lowered her tone and hissed, "She's twenty-two. Can you believe it? *I* was twenty-two when we met." She stabbed a finger at her chest. "He's forty-one. He could be her father."

"Mm-hm. My second husband was like that. The first one was only nineteen."

"Her name is Kayli … with an i," Ashley said the last in a nasal voice.

"I believe the proper way to spell Kayleigh includes an i."

"Not that way. She spells it, K-A-Y-L-I."

Margot simply blinked and sipped her wine.

"You've been through this." The younger woman leaned closer to her seatmate. "Tell me what I should do."

"Well, I'd like to feed you a great line about forgiveness, counseling, blah, blah, blah." Margot signed, "But in my experience, honey, once a dog, always a dog. He'll stop for a while. But then, you'll have a fight, or he'll be traveling for work, and an opportunity will present itself. Only this time he'll know better, and be sneakier going about it, and you'll have to pay that PI for three times as many hours just to catch him in the act."

"This isn't who we are." Ashley shook her head in despair. "At least it's not who I wanted to be."

"Unfortunately, wealthy men in New York have easy access to a lot of beautiful young women looking for a Sugar Daddy. So, it's either divorce, or sucking up your pride, and forgiving him."

The women halted their conversation as Giovanni returned with their meals. "Salad for you Ms. Kalaverdi, and the duck for Mrs. Belvedere.

Once Giovanni disappeared, Ashley spread the linen napkin across her lap and asked, "What does divorce involve?"

"That depends." Margot dusted her salad with the vinaigrette dressing Giovanni left at her elbow. "Is there a pre-nup?"

Ashley nodded. "It's got a ten-year sunset clause." A thought occurred to her, and she gasped. "As a matter of fact, it expires, in two weeks, on April tenth."

"Doesn't matter. I assume infidelity is covered." She stabbed a piece of lettuce and added a tomato slice.

Ashamed, Ashely stared down at the table fidgeting with her napkin. "It only included infidelity on my part. Not his," she whispered.

The wind whistled between Margot's teeth as she sucked in a breath and laid down the fork. "Why on earth … how did you…"

Ashley's head bobbed up and down. "I know, I know. It was beyond stupid. I couldn't afford a lawyer at the time. My sister was in law school, and I gave it to her. She counseled me *not* to sign it because the document was so incredibly lopsided. But I was *in love*. Stupidly so, and I let it cloud my judgment. After all, if we divorced within five years of marriage for any reason, I'd get a million dollars. It went up to three million if we divorced before ten years."

"That's it? Stephen must be worth…"

"Net worth of over two hundred million. That doesn't account for the company stock portfolio or hard assets like the houses and his antique car collection."

Margot clicked her tongue.

"You have to understand, Margot," Ashley explained, "I had *nothing* when we met. I was trying to claw my way past the lowly rank of assistant, to the second coming of *The Devil Wears Prada*. Interviewing Stephen for the magazine was my big break. He doted on me from our first meeting. Never, in my wildest dreams, did I believe he'd be ready to upgrade to a newer model. At least not yet. I'm *only* thirty-two!" she cried.

"When I was thirty-one, Edgar, cheated on me with a twenty-nine-year-old." Margot said drily and picked up her fork. "I suggest, you wait two weeks before consulting the lawyer and hope that Stephen doesn't do so in the meantime."

"I don't know how I'll manage *that*. Right now, all I want to do is rip his eyes out."

She swallowed. "Go to your place in the Hamptons. Leave a note. Don't answer his phone calls. Avoid him. Ignore the anniversary, and hope he forgets." Margot counseled. "On the eleventh, I'll have my lawyer, Sidney, contact you about filing for divorce."

"Ugh. How can I do this? Everything will have to be split up. Who gets the house in the city? In the Hamptons? Aspen? The furniture? I spent hour upon hour designing the New York apartment to perfectly suit our needs." Ashley whined stabbing the duck.

"You'll get through it, we all do," Margot reassured her tablemate.

"I wish he'd choke on his fifty-year-old Highland Scotch and croak," Ashley said callously. "Seriously, I'd give a million dollars not to have to go through a divorce. It's so much easier when they die."

"Mm, Cooper's death certainly came at an opportune moment." Margot stared into her wine glass with a pained look. Her straight-cut, tawny bob curtained across her face, hiding her features.

Ashley, realizing her faux pas, pressed her fingers to her lips. "Oh,

Margot, I'm so sorry. I didn't mean it that way. I know you loved Cooper. He was one of the good ones. I'm a terrible person for having said that."

"I know you didn't mean it that way, dear." The older woman sighed pushing the hair behind her ear. "Sadly, it's true. If Cooper continued in the same manner, we might have had to sell everything."

"As bad as all that?"

"Not yet. But he was so headstrong and unwilling to listen to my advice. Too macho for his own good."

"Still, his unexpected heart attack was horrible. And you loved him."

Margot's eyes glossed over, and she blinked. "Indeed. I did."

The women discussed Ashley's options a little longer before moving on to other topics of discussion.

When the check arrived, Margot patted her lips with the napkin and said, "Ashley, dear. I know it's my turn to pay. However, the stupid receptionist at the hair salon forgot to return my AmEx. I would have stopped by to pick it up on the way over, but I was … running late … and … could you…"

Ashley snatched up the black bill presenter. "Of course! Don't give it another thought. You've listened to my woes and provided excellent advice. Lunch is most definitely on me."

In front of the restaurant, the two women shared air kisses. Ashley's driver held the door for her, while Margot asked the doorman to flag down a taxi.

"You're taking a cab? Where's Rinaldo?" Ashley asked with a furrowed brow.

"I have him running some errands," Margot replied in an offhand manner.

"Can I have Victor drop you somewhere? We're headed up—" Ashley's offer was cut off as a courier on a scooter practically ran her down, causing her to stumble and knocking her handbag to the ground.

"Sorry!" The young man called over his shoulder but continued to weave in and around the other pedestrians.

"Why I never…" Ashley sputtered.

"Oh, my goodness! Are you okay? They never should have allowed those scooters in the city!" Margot exclaimed, with annoyance.

"Are you alright, ma'am?" Victor held out Ashley's Birkin.

"Yes, yes. I'm fine." She assured Margot, and taking the handbag from her driver responded, "Thank you, Victor."

"Well, my cab is here. If you're sure…" Margot indicated the yellow taxi, and the doorman holding the rear door open for her.

Ashley, having forgotten her suggestion of a ride, simply nodded. "I'll call you."

Once inside the car, Ashley checked her bag to make sure everything was in order. Tucked next to the packet of photos, she found a small red business card with gold writing. In capital letters it read **CONTRACT ACCEPTED.**

"Contract accepted? I haven't made any contracts." Ashley frowned in confusion and crumpled the card in her fist. She tossed it in the lobby trashcan of her apartment building. On her way up the elevator, Ashley made a mental list of items she'd need to pack for the Hamptons, and called Josie, the housekeeper, to have her stock the refrigerator for her visit.

*****

"Ash, you left your phone in the kitchen, and it's been ringing constantly," Mitzi Grosvenor minced over carrying a hurricane glass full of red slushy liquid, and placed the cell on the table next to Ashley.

Ashley had been in at the Hamptons house for four days. In that time, she'd ignored three of Stephen's calls and three texts. Two of which asked if she knew the location of a watch and his gym bag. She'd sent one text suggesting he speak to Josie, about both items. Stephen still hadn't caught on that she was ignoring him. This call wasn't from him. Royce Hobson's face lit up the screen.

She let out a sigh and scooped it up. "It's Stephen's partner. I'd best answer it." Rising, she strolled away from the dozen people gathered around the fire pit. "Hello, Royce. What can I do for you?"

"Ashley? Where are you?" he asked in clipped tones.

"I'm at Mitzi and Bob's Thursday night soiree. In the Hamptons." Slipping off a sandal, she ran her toe along the top of the peacock-blue water of the pool. The underground lights flickered in the tiny wake. "Why?"

"I've been trying to reach you. There's been an incident."

"An incident? Royce what are you talking about?" Ashley frowned stepping further from the partygoers and the pool.

"Stephen … he…"

Her eyes narrowed, as she paused at the railing of the deck. *Is Stephen using his partner as a go-between? Did he finally recognize I'm angry with him?* "What about Stephen?"

"He was playing squash, and it seems … he … well, he collapsed on the court."

"Oh no! Was it his knee? Did it finally blow out? I've been telling him for months to get that surgery done, but he's been so busy with the merger." She spun around and headed toward the house. "What hospital did they take him to?"

"Ash, I'm sorry. He-he didn't make it to the hospital."

Ashley pulled up short in confusion. "What? What do you mean?"

"It-it wasn't his knee. The doctors are saying it was a heart attack. He-he's gone, Ash. They tried their best. But … he's gone," Royce said in a choked voice.

She couldn't catch her breath. Her ears buzzed and she spoke as if through water, "I don't believe it."

*****

"If one more person tells me, 'It was a lovely service,' I'm going to scream." Ashley snapped the door shut and kicked off her Manolo's.

The silence in the empty bedroom would have been deafening to some. To Ashley it was a blessed relief. The past week had been a whirlwind of funeral arrangements, condolences from well-intentioned friends, family members, and Stephen's business associates, and preliminary discussions with lawyers and financial advisors.

At the wake, Margot had asked about her plans, but Ashley couldn't see beyond the funeral. All she wanted to do was sleep and be free from all the decisions. "Maybe I'll go to Aspen for a few weeks. I don't know," she'd responded.

The women didn't utter a word about their last conversation, and Ashley planned to keep it that way.

She'd tucked away her in-laws and parents at the Four Seasons and given Josie the rest of the week off. Stephen's lawyer had requested a meeting at nine the following morning to go through the terms of the will. Ashley's feelings regarding Stephen's passing were mixed. While his death certainly made things easier when it came to dealing with his affair, Ashley truly grieved the loss. Though she'd been hurt and furious about his infidelities, she couldn't simply turn off ten years of the love she'd felt for him. The day before the funeral, she fed the PI's photos through the shredder.

Ashley drew off the vintage pillbox hat with veil and was about to toss it on the bed when the sight of a red business card in the middle of the white coverlet gave her pause. She scooped up the tiny placard. The gold lettering read:

CONTRACT COMPLETE

A white business card with the name and address of a bank in the Cayman Islands was stapled to the red card, and at the bottom was a handwritten routing and account number in block lettering.

"What in the world?" *What contract? And why leave the card on the bed?*

Ashley tapped the card against her palm. She'd paid the private investigator and included an extra $100 for his thoroughness. Was it the caterers for the post-funeral reception? She'd have to check with Josie next week. Tossing the card in the bedside table drawer, Ashley headed to the shower, dropping clothes in her wake.

Five days later, Josie stalked into Ashley's home office and slapped down the mail. "You've been in here for sixteen hours a day. You've barely eaten—" she eyed the untouched tray of toast, fresh fruit, and yogurt, "—and it looks like you haven't slept since the funeral. I'm making one of your favorite dishes for dinner, pan seared seabass with lemon garlic herb sauce. I expect you to eat it!" the tiny brunette declared.

Ashley gave the woman a wan smile. "It sounds like heaven, thank you. I had no idea how long it would take to wrap my arms around all of Stephen's financials." She waved at a stack of folders and random papers spread across the desk. "It makes my head swim."

"That's what lawyers are for. Pace yourself. Or you'll end up in the hospital." With that piece of advice, Josie left.

Inside the third envelope, Ashley found another red card. The gold lettering read

PAYMENT DUE, $1 MILLION

and was stapled to the same Cayman Island bank information.

Ashley gulped. *One million dollars? What on earth?*

Believing this had something to do with Stephen, Ashley picked up the landline and began dialing Royce. She paused as her gaze landed on the envelope. Her name and address were typed on it, as if someone had used an old-fashioned typewriter. There was no return address, and the postmark was NY, New York.

The red cards were clearly directed at her, not Stephen.

Ashley searched the internet for the number of the bank and phoned them. However, the bank manager refused to provide any personal information about the account holder. In a frustrated move, Ashley sent the envelope and cards through her shredder.

Instead of feeling better, as she'd hoped, an icky lump settled in the pit of her stomach. She glanced around her minimalist glass and chrome office searching for unseen eyes. The hair on the back of her neck rose, as a sharp memory returned.

What has she said? "I'd give a million dollars not to have to go through a divorce. It's so much easier when they die."

But Stephen had died of a heart attack. It's not as though she'd put a hit on him. Still … it was after that lunch when she found the first card.

Who left it there? Margot?

No. Surely not. Margot had plenty of money from her former husbands. Ashley shook her head and laughed at the thought of Margot in the role of assassin. Margot hired lawyers to take care of her problems.

Giovanni? The waiter who served the wealthiest clientele in New York. Was his side hustle contract killer?

Victor, her driver? He had three teenagers who would be headed to college in a few years.

What about the scooter kid who knocked the Birkin out of her hand? Who was he? She gripped her head trying to pull his face to mind. Did he play a part in the red cards?

Ashley's thoughts returned to one single fact—Stephen died of a heart attack. That's what the doctor put on the death certificate.

Squinting at the silent shredder, she hollered, "Josie! Pack my bags, we're heading to the Hamptons! Tell Victor I won't be needing him!"

*****

Unfortunately, returning to her waterfront Hamptons home changed nothing. The red cards began arriving on day two. By day six, Ashley came to dread the afternoons when Josie brought in the mail. She threw herself into the Hamptons social scene and tried to spend as much time out of the house as possible, hoping all the activities would wear her out. Every night she fell into bed dog-tired. And every night, somewhere around three o'clock in the morning, she'd wake, worrying about the missives.

Following a sunrise Pilates class, she found one of the hated cards sticking out of her gym bag.

"Join me for a goji smoothie?" Margot came up behind Ashley.

Ashley gasped, jamming the card back into the bag, and spun around. "Margot!"

"Anything wrong?"

"N-no, n-nothing. I-I didn't realize you'd come out to the Hamptons. Were you in class? I didn't see you?" Ashley glanced around the emptying room.

"Snuck in late. I was in the back corner." Margot squinted at her friend and asked solicitously, "How are you coping?"

"I … uh… am. You know." Ashley shrugged. "It's hard, but I'm trying…" Tears sheened her eyes.

Margot nodded with understanding. "Why don't I take you for a coffee, and you can tell me all about it?"

Ashley chewed the inside of her mouth. In the past two days, she'd been giving some serious consideration to simply paying the million dollars. It's not as though she didn't have access to that type of money. Stephen had left her a *very* wealthy woman. But she feared this could turn into blackmail, and paying once might lead to a lifetime of continued payments.

Margot was a woman of the world. Perhaps she would know how to handle it.

"Ashley?" Margot took hold of her arm. "You look pale. Let me drive you—"

"*No!*" Ashley pulled away.

Margot's mouth dropped with surprise and hurt.

"It's … it's nothing. I haven't been sleeping. I think I'll go home and take a nap. We'll get together for drinks. I'll … I'll call you." Ashley dashed to her Range Rover and zipped out of the yoga studio parking lot as if the devil was on her heels.

Back at the house, she added the card to the small pile collected in her bedside table drawer and contemplated doing what she should have done as soon as she received the first mailed envelope.

Contact the police.

After all, this is tantamount to harassment.

And for what? Stephen died of natural causes!

Didn't he?

Of course, he did!

Ashley shook off the spinning thoughts. With renewed determination, she found a plastic baggie in the kitchen, filled it with the cards, and stuffed them in her purse.

She'd parked in the circular drive and headed to the front door, only to find Margot raising a hand to ring the bell.

"Margot, I … what are you doing here?"

"Sorry to intrude, but I really feel we must speak."

"I was just on my way to see the police … there was … er … an incident at the neighbor's house," Ashley lied. "Can it wait?"

"It'll only take a few minutes. Besides, don't you want to clean yourself up before going out?"

"What?" Ashley blinked and stepped back to look in the front hall mirror.

Margot followed her into the foyer and closed the door. "Dearest, your mascara is flaking, your hair is sticking out of your headband, and your eyes are wild. I can see sweat stains on your shirt. Come now, you can't go to the police looking like a mad woman."

Her friend smoothly removed the purse from Ashley's hand. "Take a few minutes to run upstairs and clean up. Is Josie here?"

Ashley shook her head. "This is her day off."

"Don't you worry." She patted Ashley on the shoulder. "I'll make you a nice cup of coffee to settle your nerves. Go on."

Margot made a shooing motion and Ashley had no choice but to comply.

Thirty minutes later, Ashley returned to the kitchen to find a pair of mugs sitting on the island. The toaster popped up.

"Ah, there we are." Margot put the crisped bread on plates. "You're looking much better. There's nothing so soothing as coffee and toast. Shall we sit at the table or counter?"

Ashley's stomach rumbled, and she realized she couldn't remember when she last ate. Margot was right, it would be best to have a little something before braving the police department. "Table."

The two women took their plates and mugs to the round kitchen table in front of the bay window that overlooked the pool and ocean.

"Drink up."

Ashley drank deeply, swallowed, and released a deep breath.

Margot raised a brow. "Better?"

"Mm, yes. Much." Ashley sipped more of the coffee.

"Now, tell me what's going on? I haven't seen you since the funeral. It looks like you've lost ten pounds."

Suddenly, Ashley felt the tension from the preceding weeks slip away. As if the coffee and Margot's presence were a balm to her struggles. Initially, the story came out in little bursts. The red cards. The demands for money. The inability to sleep. Ashley began to feel floaty and detached as though separated from her body. The words simply poured out without control or thought.

"Yes, dear, I know." Margot finally replied when Ashley's monolog came to a halt.

The room began to shimmer around her, and Ashley blinked. "You know?"

"Of course, that's why I'm here. You see … when you didn't pay up. I realized you needed a little push."

"Pay for what?" Ashley found it hard to move her lips to pronounce the words.

"Why for Stephen's death, of course."

"I never—"

"You made it quite clear, at the restaurant, you'd pay a million dollars if Stephen simply died instead of having to go through a divorce. You said, 'I wish he'd choke on his fifty-year-old scotch'."

Margot's words came at Ashley as if spoken down a long tunnel.

"I'm sorry to say, it wasn't the scotch that got him." Margot shook her head. "No, it was the lunch he ate at Gino's. In his Rueben sandwich. Your husband was the epitome of habit. Every Thursday—lunch at Gino's. You told me so yourself." She winked. "He kindly invited me to join him when he saw me eating alone. The squash game with Royce was a stroke of good luck. Digoxin can take hours to do its damage. The squash game simply upped the timeline a bit. It couldn't have been more perfectly public."

Ashley strained to comprehend what Margot was saying. It's as though she witnessed the conversation from above, outside her body. She looked at her coffee. "Did … you … poison … me?" she slurred.

"Oh, no, dear. It's just a sedative. So, you won't remember after I leave. They call it a date rape drug, but it has other uses. You see, I couldn't let you go to the police, and I need your fingerprint to open your phone." Margot slid on a pair of reading glasses and placed Ashley's phone in front of her, maneuvering her right thumb onto the screen. "Just like that. Perfect. I remember when you put your banking app on the phone last year. How convenient, you've autosaved your password."

Unable to stop Margot's manipulations, Ashley labored to get out, "Why?"

"Sadly, Cooper made too many blunders, and even though I killed him off," she sniffed, "he left me with … unexpected debts. I need your million to get out of a tricky situation."

"Co-oo-oo-per?"

"Yes, dear. Same way as your husband. Amazing little plant, the Foxglove. A small amount can help the heart, but too much …" She made a silly sad face. "Cooper was my favorite husband. Delicious in the sack, but a complete moron when it came to money. He just about ruined me. I've had to let go of the car service, and that day at the restaurant—my credit cards were maxed out. I was on my way to sell some of my jewelry to pay them down."

"F-fooor m-m … m-money?"

"Of course, same as you. Now to put in the account number." Margot narrowed her eyes as she typed in the digits. "Ah, your bank conveniently texted a confirmation code for me to enter. And it's done. So painless." She wiped the phone down with a linen napkin.

"Now, let's get you up and over to the couch before you fall to the floor." Margot slung one of Ashley's limp arms over her shoulder and, with unexpected strength from the fifty-year-old, heaved the younger woman out of the chair. "There we go, right this way."

Through their own volition, Ashley's feet shuffled along as Margot transferred her onto the couch, gently laying her down.

"Now close your eyes and have a rest."

Ashley's eyes followed Margot's direction as a blanket covered her from toes to neck.

"Your husband left you a wealthy widow. No doubt the men will flock to you. In a year, you'll finish grieving, and you'll find a man who deserves you." She patted Ashley's thigh. "And when you wake, you won't remember a thing about today. Your bank statement will reflect your kind donation to an international charity feeding starving children. I'll even take these cards you've so helpfully gathered in a plastic bag for me."

Margot shook Ashley's arm. "Is this all of them?"

"Alllll…" Ashley slurred and drifted off to sleep.

Margot quietly closed the front door to the sound of Ashley's gentle snoring.

Cruise to Nowhere
Kristin Kisska

Take a European river cruise, they said. *It'll be fun*, they said.

They were dead wrong.

Who would *they* be? My brother and sister-in-law, Ryan and Tina, that's who. Don't get me wrong, I love them both. But a family reunion with everyone trapped on the same boat is more like a vacation to hell than an escape.

The whole charter boat idea sounded great at the beginning. Ryan found the itinerary we booked ~ *Private Boat Tour of the Danube*. It wasn't until we'd debarked from Budapest that we found out Ryan had long since been friends with Captain Andrej from his semester abroad during college.

What I didn't anticipate when we paid our non-refundable deposit for this luxury four-cabin super-yacht was the rain. Not just any rain, but the wettest and chilliest springtime southern Germany has experienced in decades. So much so the Danube is flooding.

Gone are the bright blue skies, medieval villages, and lush green pastures promised by my glossy trip brochure.

Instead, I've taken to standing with my feet apart to help temper our boat's rocking on the choppy waters. The unrelenting rain has taken a toll on all of our patience. I swear I heard arguing through our too-thin walls last night. This boat may be ours for the week, but it's still too small for drama.

Between the gray, overcast sky, the murky brown water of the Danube, and the tastefully appointed but beige cabin, my world has become monochrome. At least the fragrant bouquet of white roses and three lavender stems of bell-shaped foxglove on my room's bureau offers a burst of color to relieve the tone-on-tone drabness. It was a romantic gesture from my husband Charlie, purchased at a street market on our first excursion in Vienna, and I'm delighted they've stayed so fresh for this long. He did the same on our honeymoon trip to Paris a few years ago.

On the bright side, tonight is our last night of this godforsaken river cruise. Despite it only being afternoon, I crawl under the covers of my bed to nap until our daily happy hour. As I send up my little prayer of thanks, the boat's engine powers down. Grinding from the metal link chain announces that the anchor is dropping.

Oh, no.

We are no longer making forward progress upriver. Instead, we are being tossed about this way and that like some rubber ducky stuck in a wave pool.

After waking up, I noticed that my flowers aren't where I'd placed them, by the porthole. The bouquet is now on my nightstand. Odd. I feel disoriented. I wonder if the vase was in danger of tipping from the rocking of the boat, so Charlie moved them to a safer spot? Still, I can't seem to shake my unease.

"Get up, Vicki!" My sister Cindy's loud knock on my cabin door makes me jackknife into a sitting position. "Is Tina there with you?"

"No." I assume Tina must be upstairs kicking off an early happy hour. There isn't enough wine in Europe to help me survive this vacation. I know Charlie agrees. "Why?"

"Captain Andrej wants to speak to all of us. He called a meeting in five minutes."

*****

Six of the seven passengers—Charlie, Cindy, her husband Mark, our brother Ryan, our cousin Lisa, and me—take our seats in the boat's main salon. Gretchen, our private chef, and hostess has prepared a lovely charcuterie board of local Regensburg cheese, meats, and breads.

Her culinary tour of Bavaria has been the sole highlight of our week on the Danube. Behind the artfully displayed food spread rests a line of beer steins, each personalized with our initials—a lovely souvenir gift we each received from Gretchen as we boarded a week ago and doubles as our happy hour glassware.

Apparently, the choppy waters and rocking boat aren't causing Charlie any queasiness because his plate is filled with food.

Captain Andrej, Gretchen's husband, enters sporting a wet navy rain jacket and a walkie-talkie.

"*Guten Abend.* Good evening, my friends…" Captain Andrej nods at us, his face grave. "Unfortunately, I have disappointing news. The river's water level is too high for us to clear the Old Stone Bridge. I've dropped anchor, and we will stay here for the night. The river is expected to crest at midnight. If it recedes enough by morning, we can hopefully pass and continue our journey. There are several other boats in a similar situation, so we must wait our turn."

All of us passengers look around at each other, likely thinking the exact same thing. We are supposed to debark tomorrow for Munich and then fly back home to the States. Now, we're each in danger of missing our flights home.

I steal a glance out the windows on both sides of the yacht. A riverboat traffic jam blocks us on all sides. Crap. The river can't be very wide, and we are definitely not the only boat challenged by the high water level.

Charlie stops munching on a breadstick for half a moment. "Isn't there a drawbridge?"

"No, but the bridge behind us has a higher height clearance." Our captain's windbreaker drips on the Oriental rug. "To conserve power, I've turned off all noncritical services to power."

I thought this trip couldn't get any worse, but here we are without Wi-Fi and electricity to charge my now-dead cell phone.

"Why can't we turn around and return to our last city?" Of my siblings, Ryan was always the least patient. He's now stroking his stubbled chin, solving problems. He looks around. "Wait. Where's Tina?"

We glance at each other and shrug.

"She wasn't feeling well this morning, so I offered her a Dramamine pill, but she wouldn't take it." I shrug. This boat is small. I can't imagine there are too many places to hide. "Didn't she go to your cabin to rest?"

Ryan shuffles his feet but doesn't make eye contact.

Red flares from the sky outside brighten our lounge, reflecting off all chrome surfaces like Fourth of July fireworks. Despite the steady rain thundering against our boat's ceiling, we hear the squawk from a loudspeaker on the boat next to us.

"Man overboard!"

*****

Without rain gear on, everyone scrambles through the doorway and up the stairs to the deck. The crush of bodies partially shields me from the rainfall. Shouts from crew members of a nearby boat pierce the eerie hush from my fellow passengers as we press against the rail, watching them hoist a limp body up onto their deck.

No.

My heart sinks as cold dread washes over me. I recognize the peach chiffon scarf she was wearing this morning. We turn to stare at Ryan. His face has turned as gray as the choppy water beneath us.

"Tina!" He yells his wife's name, but he might as well have whispered it in the thundering deluge. In an instant, he climbs up on top of the railing. Thank God Captain Andrej has his wits about him and pulls my brother back down onto the slippery deck. "*Nein*. I'm sorry, Ryan, but you must not jump. Come back inside. We will wait for news."

"How? By smoke signal?" We follow Ryan and shuffle back inside the lounge, shaking off raindrops from our wet hair and clothing. "That's my wife over there!"

With no power on our yacht and the gray daylight dwindling, Gretchen lights a few candles and sets them in hurricane glasses. Her delectable charcuterie board is all but forgotten. We crowd around

Ryan, talking over each other with our voices escalating in volume and pitch. "When did you last see Tina? What was she doing? She knows how to swim, right? How could she have fallen overboard?"

My stomach twists into knots of worry. Despite my angst over this horrid vacation, I adore her. We all do. At least, I thought so. My sister-in-law is the glue that holds us together. I send prayers out to the universe that Tina can be revived.

"We've been seeing a couple's therapist for a while now. But this afternoon…" Ryan stands at the window, staring through the rain at the other boat, looking like he's about to throw up. I can hardly imagine the torment he's going through. Ryan takes a piece of paper from his back pocket and holds it up for us to see. "Tina asked me for a divorce."

Whoa. Everyone in the room grows deathly silent. We'd overheard his muffled arguing with Tina this past week—even a boat this size isn't private enough to mask that drama. But I'd assumed the problems stemmed from frustrations of feeling trapped on a boat with crappy weather and her seasickness, not marital problems.

Captain Andrej pushes his way back into the center of the salon. He grasps at the back of a chair as the boat bobs in the choppy water. "My friends, unfortunately, my phone is out of charge. May I borrow one of yours to ring the authorities and report the emergency about *Frau* Tina?"

Ryan reaches into his back pocket and then hands Andrej his cell phone. "Even with mobile data and roaming, I haven't been able to get any cell reception."

The clock is ticking. We need to figure out what happened to Tina before the police arrive, or Ryan will surely be the primary suspect. The husband always is, even without their impending divorce. How much time do we have? An hour? Less?

Could she have fallen? She couldn't have been drunk, and she's an excellent swimmer. Or, if Tina's fall wasn't an accident, then one of us on this boat pushed her. Unless she jumped. Ruling myself out leaves Ryan, my Charlie, Cindy, her husband, and Lisa. And I suppose we can't ignore that Captain Andrej and Gretchen were on board as well.

Our silence is replaced by a growing sense of panic vibrating as our exclamations reach a crescendo in the small salon.

"Everyone, please quiet down," I shout over the din. "We need to work together here. When was the last time we saw—or heard—Tina. And what was she doing?"

"Good idea, honey." Charlie squeezes me to his chest before addressing the group. "I saw her smoking a cigarette on the back deck in the rain. I asked her which of our cruise stops she enjoyed the most. She gave me a bitter laugh, stubbed out her cigarette, and said none. The only thing she wanted was to leave this floating hell hole. Coming on this trip was the biggest mistake of her life. Then, I assume she headed back to her cabin. I think that was around noon."

I cling to my husband and shiver. He admitted to me this morning that he felt the same way about this nightmare boat cruise as Tina. I couldn't disagree, especially now. "Was she acting any differently than normal?"

"No…" He pauses to consider my question. "Actually, the more I think about it, she wasn't herself. She was a bit wobbly. Like maybe she was seasick. Or tipsy. Her face was pale. But the boat was tossing all over the place in the choppy water, so I didn't think anything of it."

"She never showed up for lunch. That means we have about five hours unaccounted for." I lunge for a notepad and pencil resting on the bookshelf. "Who saw her this afternoon?"

Silence and shrugs follow my question. No one is even making eye contact with me.

"One of us must've seen Tina after Charlie did at noon. This isn't a big boat." I can't help myself, but I stare at Ryan. *C'mon, bro, I'm trying to help you.* But he just shuffles his feet.

What am I missing here?

Cindy nudges her husband's arm.

"I, uh, we…" Mark's furrowed brow betrays his reluctance to continue. Each of us is focused on him. He clears his throat. "Cindy and

I were together the entire day. We saw Tina around two p.m. or so. She was kneeling outside the door of her and Ryan's stateroom, but when we approached, she slipped a piece of paper under the door and then ran off. She seemed kinda upset. And then we, uh…"

When Mark wouldn't—or couldn't—continue, Cindy picked up the reins my brother-in-law dropped and stared Ryan down. "Then we went to our stateroom, which everyone knows is right next to yours, Ryan. The nooner going on in your room was loud, energetic, and clearly didn't include Tina."

"Nooner?" Jeez, my Dramamine must've conked me out if I hadn't overheard that illicit party. "Who was she, Ryan?"

"Not a she, Vicki." Cindy's voice was hushed. "Ryan was definitely not entertaining a *she*."

"Yeah, it was hard to ignore that party. I didn't think the boat could rock any harder than it did with the waves outside." Lisa spoke her first words in days.

Ryan has the decency to blush. I mean, he and Tina are technically still married. Maybe he didn't come on this trip with the intention of saving his marriage. The question is who was the guy he was getting lucky with. Chills race down my spine as I realize the only other man on the boat, other than Ryan and Mark, is my husband.

While I twist my wedding ring, one unsettling question after another collides in my mind. Charlie throws up his hands while stepping back, "It wasn't me! I was drinking beers right here in the lounge. Lisa was here too. She can vouch for me."

Oh, thank God. A wave of relief washes over me.

"Excuse me, I was *not* drinking a beer. Y'all know I frown on day drinking." Lisa crosses her arms. As our cousin, she shares our genes. But for whatever reason, she inherited all our grandmother's propriety, not leaving even a shred of manners for the rest of us heathen relatives, at least in her mind. "Gretchen brewed me a pot of herbal tea while Charlie drank his beer, but that's not important. The point is, neither Charlie nor I were at Ryan's little *tête-à-tête*."

"Then who was Ryan with?" But even as I articulate my question, it occurs to me exactly who he was with. There is another male on this stranded boat. I gasp. Then I recall the cruise had been Ryan's idea. "Captain Andrej?"

Interesting. Ryan's face turns a shade of purple as he averts his eyes. Busted.

It's not like we've moved a nautical mile since yesterday, and we've been moored right here for hours. Technically speaking, it hasn't been a demanding day for the captain of a charter boat. Yet, a passenger—my sister-in-law—ended up overboard.

Hmm. I sense this whole family reunion charter cruise idea had more of an underlying agenda than any of us had realized. Perhaps a different sort of reunion.

Ignoring the drama as Cindy, Mark, and Lisa accost Ryan, I walk over to the portside windows. Through the pelting rain, a small police patrol dinghy is moored next to the boat where Tina is. I hope and pray she survives and will recover.

"Charlie, do you mind going to the bridge and asking Captain Andrej and Gretchen to join us?" As he departs to do my bidding, I fight the impending doom. My brother is about to be arrested for murder—or at least attempted murder—whether or not he did it. How could he not be the leading suspect? Illicit affair. Tina's death would enable him to avoid a costly divorce settlement. Crap. This trip was even his idea.

As if he could read my mind, Ryan holds up his hands in surrender. "Wait. I know this looks bad—it *is* bad—but I didn't mean to hurt Tina. I love her. Andrej and I—we…" His shoulders drop as we fall silent. "We met while we were at university back during the semester I studied abroad in Munich. And even dated. We kept in touch over the years. I allowed my passions to take over. I'm as concerned about Tina as everyone else. You must believe me. I didn't push her overboard. I wasn't even with her."

"When was the last time *you* saw Tina, Ryan?"

"She said she was heading back to our cabin to rest during lunch. I went to check on her a couple hours later but found Andrej waiting for me instead. One thing led to another—"

I put up my hand to stop him. More information than I wanted. Did Tina know Ryan was bi, or did she figure it out during this trip?

"I probably saw Tina most recently. About an hour ago." Lisa chimed in. "She complained of being queasy, which makes sense. The water was pretty rough at that time. I offered to fetch Gretchen to get her some chamomile and ginger tea to help settle her stomach."

*****

After Captain Andrej walked in, he must've noticed the shift in our family's tone from worry to accusatory. Homewrecker. Two marriages now imploded, one wife fighting for her life. Reading the room, he sticks to concern for Tina's well-being. Wise choice. "I have good news from the captain of our neighboring ship. *Frau* Tina is breathing but is showing signs of sedation. A helicopter will transport her to a nearby hospital for medical treatment and observation."

We all breathe sighs of relief that she's still alive.

"Sedation?" My mind races. Could she have been drunk when she fell over? Or drugged?

Gretchen walks into the room, holding a pitcher in one hand and using her other to balance herself against the rocking motion against fixed surfaces. "Cocktail, anyone?"

Charlie lifts his stein to have her fill it. I hold up my hand to stop him. Something feels off. My mind races to figure out why.

I look over at the lineup of personalized steins that Gretchen gifted us as we boarded the boat a week ago. Each ceramic stein had our initials and the dates of our trip stamped on the bottom. It'd been helpful for keeping track of whose stein was whose. Each night, Gretchen would wash the tall ceramic mugs, and we'd start using them again the next day at happy hour. Each day, she featured a new cocktail, local beer, or wine.

Other than Lisa, who stuck with herbal tea, the rest of us have been drinking our fair share of alcoholic beverages to weather this trip, always out of our own stein. These days, since it's been too wet to venture off the boat, we've been in a near constant state of being tipsy. Suspended in a hazy time warp.

A gasp catches in my throat.

There wasn't just one jilted spouse in Ryan's dalliance. What if…

"Wait. Where's Tina's stein?" I race over to the buffet table, lifting each one and looking at the initials until I find hers. It's empty, clean, and dry. Tina didn't drink out of hers today. I glance at all the steins. But one is missing. Interesting.

"Vicki, what's going on?" Charlie's voice, already filled with concern, is now laced with notes of urgency as he glances out the plate glass window through the rain. "Look, the police are motoring over to us."

Whitecaps from the choppy water splash over the bow, tossing the small police patrol boat while its captain attempts to turn in our direction. Though their travel is slow-going, we only have a few more minutes before Ryan will be named the police's default prime suspect. To be honest, I'm not convinced he shouldn't be. But he can't have harmed Tina. My brother is the gentlest, kindest, most empathetic guy I've ever known, my own husband included.

Then again, I'd never have predicted he'd have an affair during a cruise with this wife, but here we are.

Captain Andrej turns to leave, presumably to greet the officers.

"Wait, darling." Gretchen stops him, nodding toward his belt. "I don't think it's smart to be armed as you meet the police."

He pauses, then nods as he removes a pistol from the waistband of his khaki pants, leaving it on one of the side tables.

Whoa. A chill runs down my back. Has Captain Andrej been concealing a weapon this whole trip? It's not like the Danube is known for roving bands of river pirates. Gretchen must notice our collective concern because she points out. "Not to worry. It's a flare gun for emergencies."

After he departs, the task at hand resumes its priority in my mind. "Lisa, when Tina drank her tea this afternoon, was she using a stein?"

"Yeah. She was sitting right on the lounge chair over here." She points to the chair in the corner of the room. "Gretchen brought us a pot of herbal tea. I poured for both of us. As she sipped hers, her nausea worsened. She seemed to be developing some sort of rash on her neck. She said she needed some air, so she left. That was about an hour ago. Do you think that's when she might have fallen overboard?"

"Maybe. Did anyone see her after?" I glance around at everyone in the room, who either shakes their heads or shrugs. "Cindy?"

"Not me. I hadn't seen her all day and even asked you about her when I knocked on your door."

"Okay. But what about her stein? Hers wasn't used, yet she apparently drank Gretchen's tea. So which stein did she drink from?" I pick up the teapot, which sits cold and mostly empty on the buffet table, waiting to be collected the next time Gretchen came through cleaning.

"I poured it from this pot into her stein, but…I swore she drank quite a bit of it."

"Could she have drank from someone else's cup by accident?" On the buffet table, all the other steins were lined up, clean and empty. All except one was missing. After a quick scan of the engraved initials on the bottom, I know what we need to do. "Ryan, where is your stein?"

Flustered, Ryan looks around while running his hands through his hair. Then, he dashes towards the door. "Hold on…"

As we wait for Ryan to return, I remember my unease earlier at the misplacement of my bouquet in my stateroom. Not only was it relocated, but now I recall why it looked off. Charlie had given me three stems of lush, raspberry-colored foxglove along with a dozen white roses. When I woke from my nap, there had been two, which means someone must've taken one of my stems.

And could that person have used my foxglove blooms to poison the tea Tina drank? Crap. That would make Charlie and me suspects.

Noises from the stern suggest that Captain Andrej is helping the patrol boat tether to ours with ropes. Given the rocking of the boats, it must be a difficult task.

Ryan bursts back into the main salon, holding his stein aloft. "It was half full, but I swear, the last time I saw it was last night when I finished my beer. I didn't touch it today."

"What's in it?"

He glances in the ceramic mug, then smells. "Tea. It's cold now, but it's chunky. I guess the teabag must've broken because loose tea leaf fragments are floating on top."

I recognize the telltale bits of raspberry-colored petals skimming the surface of the now-cold tea.

Foxglove.

The person serving us food and beverages this entire voyage has been our endearing, gracious hostess, Gretchen, always with her omnipresent smile and good cheer.

And the wife of her cheating husband, Captain Andrej.

"Gretchen? You couldn't possibly have…" I sputter, realizing what had happened.

Her smile disappears as her brow furrows. She lunges towards the table and grabs the flare gun, pointing it at me. Shrieks erupt from all of us.

"Don't shoot!" I put my hands up. Flare or real, I'm staring down the barrel at close range. "Put the gun down."

Charlie swoops in front of me.

"*Polizei*, arrest her." Gretchen yells over her shoulder at the door as the police officers enter the salon. "This woman—Vicki—poisoned a female passenger with the blossoms, then pushed her in the water."

Who, me?

"She's lying!" My head is spinning as I defend myself in a twisted game of she said-she said while trying not to get shot. "I was asleep. Gretchen had access to all the cabins to clean and make the beds while we were eating. She knew I had the bouquet because I asked her if I could borrow a vase the afternoon Charlie gave me the flowers. They'd already been moved by the time I took my nap."

"Gretchen cleaned our room this morning. I saw her holding the flowers." Charlie, the love of my life, comes to my defense.

"No, wait…I…" Gretchen sputters. Then, her shoulders slump as police officers surround us, taking possession of the flare gun.

"She poisoned Ryan's stein." I let my hands slip down, my voice calmer. "She'd intended to murder Ryan the next time he used his stein…probably right now during happy hour. Unfortunately, Tina drank from it first. The choppy water must've sent her overboard."

"Gretchen?" Captain Andrej's face turns crimson. "How could you?"

"Check her fingers for foxglove residue." I motion to the police officer who is holding her arms. "And please notify the medics immediately so they can administer the antidote to Tina."

"…I never meant to hurt Tina. She and I were both victims." Tears well in Gretchen's eyes as the officers handcuff her and slip bags over her hands to keep her from wiping them. "We both realized our husbands were… were…intimate. Tina told me she'd left a note for Ryan asking for a divorce. But a divorce was too kind for such an insult. For my husband, losing his paramour would be punishment enough. I'd do it again. My only regret was that my friend must've gotten confused and drank from the wrong stein…"

Poor Tina. She was the collateral damage in a desperate act of jealous revenge. She and Ryan organized this river cruise up the Danube.

But instead, Gretchen, our personal chef and hostess, ended up working on a cruise to nowhere—nowhere but prison.

For the Love of Virgil
Shawn Reilly Simmons

Mallory wondered if the heat would make their hangovers worse. Maybe it was nature's way of helping, providing the environment to sweat out the previous night's excess.

Why do they do it? These packs of women that come and stay at her resort. They arrive looking Instagram-perfect, having spent the day all in a row at the beauty parlor getting scrubbed, buffed, brushed, waxed, blown, polished, plucked, and sprayed, only to end up by the end of the night hanging over a toilet bowl, makeup smeared, regurgitating the expensive liquids they bought in mass quantities, literally tossing their money down the drain.

This was the second bridal party for this particular bride-to-be. Same cabin, same sweaty month of August, different year. Same hens, different groom. Last summer must have been a practice run, a starter marriage that never got started. This time, they didn't make the mistake of running out of beer and having to give Mallory an extra twenty to make a run to the nearest store for them, thirty minutes away. There aren't any convenience stores out here on the river. Convenience wasn't a consideration when her granddaddy built this resort, a string of cabins he named the Far Away Inn way back when he was a young man. He was more about living off the grid, back before that was a thing wannabe hipsters started saying to sound cool. "Unplugged" was code for attempting spiritual depth. But Mallory knew most people started bugging out after a day on the river, begging for the Wi-Fi password.

This time, the hens had stocked up on the alcohol, hauling in three cases of beer, a bottle of tequila, and some gas station brand sparkling wine. That stuff is the kicker. You can roll with a few too many beers on occasion without much physical consequence, but that sugary fizz thrown on top will have you praying to the god of porcelain within the hour.

They had finally quieted down around midnight, thank the lord. The Far Away Inn was popular for these kinds of gatherings because folks could be as loud as they wanted. No motel cop was going to come in and break up the party. They'd hired a male dancer, and that's when the music really started cranking around ten. Mallory could hear them hooting at him from the back porch of the main cabin as she sat out and read her book. He ended up crashing in the smallest cabin at the end of the row, having thrown back a couple of shots with the gals, paying in advance of his arrival. The road back to town was hard enough to navigate while sober, much less when you've had a few. Or even one. Mallory admired his responsibility. He was definitely a grown-up. He was old enough to be everyone there's father.

Mallory knew the bride, Olivia, from back in school, although they hung with two very different crowds. If you can call one other person, Mallory's best friend who left for college somewhere in Oregon, as far away as she could get right after graduation and never came back a crowd. Mallory had always preferred her own company anyway. Books and fishing off the dock with her dad were all she'd needed. He'd be surprised, had he survived his heart attack a few years back, how well she'd done on her own, running the family business. She had guests all summer long and had steady bookings most of the other seasons, too. He'd be surprised by a lot of things, she figured.

The sun was just beginning to reflect off the water. Mallory stepped into her sandals and took her chipped coffee mug down to the dock, like she did every morning, to breathe in the air and talk to her dad. She knew he couldn't really hear her, but she figured just in case he could, it didn't hurt anything to keep him updated on things. She'd stopped asking him for advice a year or so back. These days, she'd just tell him a funny thing that happened with one of the guests or tell him what she was planning on picking up that week in town or at the farmers market.

"Mornin', Dad," Mallory said as she stepped onto the dock. The water lapped gently against the pylons beneath her as she inspected a split board. "I wonder if those gals in cabin four are having déjà vu." She sipped her coffee and made her way to a pair of faded Adirondack chairs at the far edge. A few rowboats were tied to the dock for guests who wanted to venture farther out on the water to fish. "They're in the same cabin as last summer. The bride requested it, which seems—" Mallory stopped short as she got closer to the edge. Long red hair floated on the surface of the water, flowing gracefully out from beneath the boards, brushing the side of one of the boats. Mallory leaned over carefully. "Oh no," she mumbled. Her arm went limp and fell to her side. Coffee splashed across her toes.

Olivia, the second chance bride-to-be, was floating face down in the water, tethered to a pylon by a thin piece of rope around her ankle, a slipknot dug into her bluish flesh.

*****

The sheriff's car crawled down the dusty lane toward the main cabin. Mallory stood on the porch and pulled a faded cardigan over her shoulders. She shivered despite the increasing heat of the morning.

"What you got, Mal?" Sheriff Hammond said as he stepped onto the porch. Mallory's lips felt rubbery as she spoke, explaining what she'd found in the water. The sheriff sighed and put his hands on his hips, studied the tip of his boot for what felt like a full minute.

"Alright then," he said finally. "Let's take a look."

"I don't want to go back down there," Mallory said. She was surprised by the tears that threatened to surface.

"Okay, that's fine," he said. "You just sit down here. Collect your thoughts. You're going to have to tell me everything you know, everything you remember, hear?"

Mallory nodded, her head loose like her muscles had forgotten how to hold it up.

The sheriff walked back slowly from the dock twenty minutes later, his phone pressed to his ear, his mouth set in a grim line. He nodded at

Mallory and made his way over to cabin four. Mallory knew those hens were going to feel like she did soon, a mix of fear and dread. This was a day none of them would ever be able to put out of their minds again.

*****

The hens sat on the front porch of cabin four, looking sick and miserable as the sheriff began asking them questions. Cassie, Olivia's best friend and maid of honor, stood up suddenly and threw up over the railing. Mallory reminded herself to throw some sudsy water on it later to keep critters away from the cabin. They were attracted by anything out of the ordinary on the ground. She'd gotten over the worst of the shock and had managed to pull herself together enough to join them.

Cassie gripped her stomach and sat back down, closing her eyes, and taking a deep breath. Becky offered a supportive shoulder rub, then put her hand to her mouth as if she might be sick too. Sarah stared straight ahead, looking pretty green around the gills herself.

"Try and remember, ladies," Sheriff Hammond said. "When did Olivia leave the cabin? Who was the last to see her? Why did she leave? Anything you can remember will be helpful."

Cassie spoke first, her red-rimmed eyes glassy with tears. "I didn't hear her leave. I went to bed first, up in the loft. I had my earplugs in, you know, because I can't sleep otherwise…it's just…what happened to her?"

Sheriff Hammond nodded and looked at the other two.

"We were all pretty hammered," Becky said, her plump cleavage threatening to spill out of her thin tank top. "It's kind of a blur after we did those shots with the stripper."

Sarah snorted, then bent down to put her head between her knees, her long black hair spilling around her ankles. Mallory hoped she wouldn't get sick on the porch. She'd have to haul more than one bucket of soapy water out here, most likely.

"Okay, so none of you heard her leave? She didn't mention to any of you she needed to get some air? Was she meeting someone down at the docks?"

Cassie shook her head. Becky stared past him, the shock settling in. Sarah remained bent over, her body rocking as she heaved. Cassie stood up suddenly and threw up again, in the same spot as the first time. Mallory was grateful for her consideration.

"I was passed out," Becky said. "I drank way too much."

*****

The ambulance bounced down the lane, followed by Virgil's cherry-red Mustang. Olivia's fiancé rushed out of the car and stumbled over to cabin number four, panic etched across his face. He was handsome in a rough kind of way, with a thin, pointy face and tattoos scrawled down his wiry arms.

"What's going on?" Virgil said, his eyes darting from one hen to the other. "Cas? Where's Olivia?"

"In the water," Sarah said. "Drowned."

Cassie started weeping in earnest, then let out a wail. Becky came back to reality and joined her. Sarah sat back in her chair and covered her eyes with her hand. She had a thin band with a small diamond on her ring finger Mallory hadn't noticed before now. She hoped her hen party would go much better than this one.

"I assume you can verify your whereabouts last night, Virgil?" Sheriff Hammond asked him.

"What are you trying to say, Sheriff? That I snuck up here and drowned my fiancée? What kind of shit is this?"

"Now, calm down," the sheriff said.

"I was down at Shooter's, alright?" Virgil spat. "With Tommy and Bryce. Playing pool till close. You can ask them. I wouldn't hurt Olivia. I loved her."

"Don't you bring Tommy into this," Sarah warned from beneath her hand.

Cassie's cheeks flared red. "Virgil was nowhere near here, obviously," she said, standing up. "You need to go do your job and find out who did this."

Mallory walked down the steps of the porch and eyed the small cabin at the end of the row. The dancer for hire was squinting at them from the front window. He wasn't wearing a shirt, and she could only hope he'd changed out of his thong or whatever he'd been wearing under his tear-away pants. Mallory caught the sheriff's eye, then glanced at the cabin. He followed her gaze and sighed again, making his way over.

"Howdy, sir," Sheriff Hammond said. "Wait…Frank? What are you doing out here?"

Dr. Frank Gillespie stood on the front porch of his cabin shirtless, thankfully wearing sweatpants.

"I didn't know you…" Sheriff Hammond seemed to struggle to find his words, "did this kind of…work?"

Dr. Gillespie was a dentist up in town, had an office on Main Street right next to the police station.

The dentist shrugged and gazed into his coffee mug, his bare toes gripping the wood beneath his feet. "Things have been…difficult recently, since the divorce, and…well, you know, my son dropped out of dental school and moved away. Money down the drain. We're in a gig economy. The extra cash is nice, and I can still hold my own. I know the moves." Dr. Gillespie shifted his hips slightly and flexed the bicep of the arm holding the coffee mug.

Mallory grimaced, then reminded herself to schedule a checkup and cleaning.

The sheriff paused for a long moment, then said. "Okay, so…when did the party break up?"

The dentist shrugged again. "Around twelve? They'd been going all day and were pretty lit up when I got here. I ended up partying a little longer than usual with them, but that's what I recall."

"Who hired you…the bride or…?"

"Becky did," Dr. Gillespie said, motioning his mug toward cabin four. "Olivia was very surprised when I showed up, that was pretty clear. It was a real big surprise." He chuckled under his breath, then pulled his mouth back to a frown.

"You normally drink with your…clients?" the sheriff asked.

"Not always, but I've known these girls for a long time."

Mallory cringed and looked away. Dr. Gillespie had known them all since they were girls. He'd been friendly with her dad. Why would Olivia, or anyone from their…generation…want to see him with his clothes off?

The sheriff cleared his throat and shook his head. "How did Olivia seem to you? Did you have a sense of how she was feeling?"

Dr. Gillespie shrugged again. "She seemed fine. A little on edge. Maybe something was bothering her…maybe seeing me in a place she didn't expect, you know, someone she knows showing up to dance…it can be awkward."

"You run into a lot of patients doing this?" the sheriff asked, scratching his jaw.

"Sometimes," Dr. Gillespie said. "Doesn't bother me none."

"Mallory and your son used to go out, didn't they?" Mallory said from behind the sheriff. He turned and looked over his shoulder at her, his eyebrows raised.

"Briefly, in high school. Didn't last. But who hasn't Mallory gone out with?" Dr. Gillespie said. He took another sip of coffee. "She likes a guy with a fast car these days, I guess."

"I remember he was pretty broken up when they split," Mallory said.

Dr. Gillespie shrugged. "He moved on. They were kids. I told him getting dumped early on is good training for the rest of your life."

"What's your boy up to now?" the sheriff asked, crossing his arms over his chest.

"He moved away, up to New York. Finding himself, he says. Dental school isn't for everyone."

"It didn't make you feel…awkward? Dancing for your son's ex-girlfriend?"

"It's just a gig, Sheriff. I wasn't trying to date the girl. Although, I'm on a short list of guys who haven't."

Mallory looked at the ground, feeling a tug of sadness for Olivia, who was on the verge of hopefully finding her happily ever after.

"How else did she seem to you? Did she say anything?"

"Not really. Seemed to be having fun. Maybe she had some pre-wedding nerves. But once the music got going and she had some champagne, she was in the chair, and I was doing my thing."

"Your thing?"

"You know, lap dance stuff." He took a sip of his coffee, and Mallory suppressed the urge to add to the piles of barf.

*****

Mallory made her way back to cabin four. The ambulance crew had retrieved Olivia's body from the water and were rolling a stretcher up from the dock.

Virgil sat in Cassie's chair. She stood next to him, rubbing his shoulder. He looked away as the ambulance crew passed, squeezing his eyes shut and dropping his head in his hands.

The sheriff stepped up behind Mallory, finishing up a phone call. "That was Skeet, bartender down at Shooter's. Old friend of mine. He says you were there till close, Virgil, but he can't recall seeing you for at least an hour at one point around midnight. It was a busy night with a pool tournament going on, but he noticed your group slowed down on ordering pitchers of beer around then."

"So, because I was drinking responsibly, you think I'm a murderer now?" Virgil said with an indignant snort.

The sheriff eyed him carefully. "Skeet also said he saw your Mustang wasn't in the same spot when he took out the trash around last call at two. Said you must've moved it."

Virgil dropped his head into his hands again and began to cry, surprising everyone.

"Okay," Virgil said. "I'm a bad person, okay? But I didn't kill Olivia."

"Shh," Cassie said, tightening her grip on his shoulder. "Don't you say that."

Mallory noticed she didn't say it in a comforting way, as if he wasn't a bad person, but more in a threatening way, as in you better keep your trap shut.

Cassie's eyes were clear as she glared at the sheriff.

"You're not hungover," Mallory said, glancing at the other two hens on the porch, who looked worse now than they did when they woke up.

"I'm lucky like that," Cassie said, a warning edge to her voice.

"You're pregnant," Mallory said, looking down at the top of Virgil's head.

Becky stood up in her chair and squealed. "Pregnant! Wow! Congratulations!"

"Sit down, you idiot," Sarah said from beneath the hand over her face. "Virgil knocked up Olivia's best friend."

Becky slapped a hand over her mouth.

"By the way, we're not planning a baby shower for you, Cas. And, Becky, please don't hire my dentist for my bachelorette party next month."

"He was cheap," Becky whispered, her hand falling back to her side. "He gave me a flyer with his prices at my last cleaning."

*****

The sheriff pulled Virgil's hands behind his back and linked up the cuffs despite his protests and Cassie yelling about false arrests.

"Boy, you can do whatever you like between the sheets, with whomever you like. But this isn't the way to get away with knocking up your bride-to-be's maid of honor. Funny title, that. Not much honor involved with what you two have been up to. You messed up, son. Big time," the sheriff said. "Maybe you were in on it together. Don't you worry, I'll find out."

The ambulance pulled away as Sheriff Gilespie eased a stunned Virgil into the back of his patrol car. The sheriff walked back toward cabin four, his phone pressed once again to his ear. Cassie had grabbed the keys to the Mustang out of Virgil's pocket before he was led away so she could follow them to the station and was inside the cabin, throwing her things into a suitcase.

"You knew this the whole time?" Becky said to Sarah. "About Cassie and Virgil?"

"I guessed it last night," Sarah said. "I saw Cassie pretend to throw a shot back, but she missed. It dribbled down her chin. I thought it was because she was so drunk, but she did it two more times. And she threw up yesterday morning at the salon too. Said it was food poising."

"Why would Virgil wait until your girls' night to…" Mallory began.

"He came to see me, if you have to know everything," Cassie said huffily, back out on the porch, her overnight bag bumping against her thigh.

"Seems like he's been seeing way more of you than he should have been," Sarah spat at her. "How could you do this to us? Did you help Virgil drown her also?" Her nostrils flared as she stood up and covered the space between them in two strides, their noses almost touching.

Cassie cowered slightly but stood her ground. "No. He didn't do it. I texted him and told him I was telling Olivia everything, that it was time she knew the truth. I told him I wasn't going to watch them walk down the aisle, that I was going to do the aisle walking, not her. He came over and convinced me to hold off telling her. That was it. He left. He didn't kill her."

"I didn't hear a car last night," Mallory said. "Definitely not a Mustang motor."

"He parked down the road and walked up. Duh," Cassie said.

"Tell it to the judge," Sarah said. Becky just sat and shook her head silently.

*****

Dr. Gillespie had gotten dressed and was sitting on his porch, lacing up his boots. Sarah and Becky were inside cabin four, packing up their things. The sheriff had eased the patrol car away, with Cassie following close behind in the Mustang.

Mallory took a deep breath and walked over to the smallest cabin, pausing at the bottom of the steps.

"Checking out?" she asked, watching him lace up a boot.

"I thought I'd head down to the dock, try and catch a fish or two," he said, winking at her. "It's really peaceful down there, especially at night."

Her eyes dropped to his fingers as he looped the lace between his index and pinkie finger, then pulled the slack through in a slipknot. Her stomach dropped as she eyed the knot.

"You have to be careful down there, though. I imagine it's easy to fall in. Even harder to get out."

Be careful," Mallory whispered, then turned and walked away.

"I will," Dr. Gillespie said. "You too."

Stabbed in the Heart
Marilyn Levinson

"Cool, isn't it?" The voice itself was cool with a sliver of amusement.

I turned from the dagger I'd been admiring to study the man beside me. He was imposing, his tall, fit physique elegantly turned out in black pants and a black silk turtleneck under a gray cashmere jacket. Judging by his graying sideburns he was in his mid-forties, perhaps seven years older than me.

"It is," I agreed. The dagger was magnificent! Made in Toledo, Spain, centuries ago, it had retained its original condition. Though cabochon rubies and sapphires adorned the filigreed silver handle, its blade was forged and tempered of the finest steel. This was no ceremonial weapon. I wondered how many lives it had ended in the hands of its various owners.

"I bet it could cut a loaf of bread in one fell swoop," my companion joked.

"Or decapitate a victim just as quickly," I quipped then wished I hadn't.

"In which case, it's a good thing the dagger is safely enclosed in its vitrine." This time the amusement was evident in a broad smile that revealed a perfect set of teeth.

Vitrine. A word only people familiar with displays of precious items would use. But before I could decide how to phrase a comment that might give me a clue to his background, Ridley approached on my other side and slipped an arm around my waist.

"Thinking of bidding on it?"

I felt a thrill of pleasure as I smiled at my handsome fiancé. "Why not? It's a beautiful work of art."

"A weapon belongs in a museum, not in our new home. Why don't we check out the furniture and decorative items? Maybe we'll find a painting we like. Or a hand-blown vase."

"Sure. That's a great idea," I agreed.

I allowed Ridley to draw me away from the dagger in the clubhouse lobby because I knew he was eager to select a few items to bid on. His country club was holding the auction to raise money for an orphan disease that the club's president's youngest daughter was suffering from. The fundraising committee had hired a prestigious auction house to fill the mansion's downstairs rooms with articles of furniture, paintings, jewelry, carpets, and home décor pieces. To my untrained eye, they'd done their job well.

"The preview's over in fifty minutes. Let's start in here and do it methodically," Ridley said when we were in the smallest meeting room where lamps and decorative pieces were on display. He kept up a running commentary on the history, manufacture, and value of many of the articles.

"I can't get over how much you know about so many of these pieces," I said.

Ridley shrugged. "We used to have a lot of this stuff in our homes. My mother and Gran used to tell my sister and me about our so-called treasures ad nauseam. I never listened carefully, but somehow it stuck in my head."

"It's too bad you lost most of it," I said.

Ridley's mouth formed a tight line. "Thanks to my father's gambling and poor investments. Racehorses and the stock market ate up most of the money my mother's father had amassed. At least we were able to save the house in Connecticut."

Where his sister lives and pays little upkeep, I thought, then forced myself to focus on the present moment. Our new home was being built in the upscale Westchester community where Ridley had grown up, a few miles from the country club. Most of the homeowners were from old money. I was determined to fit in with my new neighbors, and to this end I tried to learn as much as I could about home furnishings of quality.

Ridley knew almost everyone attending the auction and exchanged pleasantries with people in passing.

"This is my fiancée, Adele Brightstone!" he was happy to announce to club members I was meeting for the first time. While I knew he was proud of my pretty face and fab figure, he was even prouder of my Brightstone family line, one I'd created some years ago. Brightstone was a rich and powerful name in Nevada where I came from, but my only link to them was Randy Brightstone who was in my class in elementary school.

"What do you think of this desk?" Ridley asked.

We'd moved on to a larger room filled with furniture. The desk looked puny. It had spindly legs and a rolltop.

"It's French," Ridley said. "We had one like it in our Westchester house."

"Did people actually write on it?" I asked.

Ridley laughed. "At one time they did. I think it would look great in a corner of the living room. It would give the room a," he waved his arm, "*je ne sais quoi* feeling of class. Establishment."

I swallowed. I knew where this was leading. "How much do you think it will go for?"

He shrugged. "Four thou. Four thousand five hundred the most."

"You want me to bid on it." It wasn't a question.

Ridley smiled his beautiful smile. "It would make me happy to own it."

"Then of course I will," I said, trying to match his smile.

Ridley didn't like to discuss finances. He made a good living as a financial advisor in a well-respected company. Much of his salary went to his apartment in Manhattan where we lived and to the construction of our new home, whose costs seemed to increase with every passing month.

I had offered to pay for our furnishings, not realizing what I was in for. Ridley had expensive taste and only wanted the best of everything. I'd told him I'd inherited three million dollars when my father died. Actually, I'd stashed away four mil from my earlier career. Good thing, too. The antique dining room set with twelve chairs and matching breakfront we'd bought had cost close to three hundred thousand dollars.

But I was done with my old life and determined to start my new one on a high note. Meeting Ridley in that bar seven months ago had been fortuitous. He was taken with me and I was madly in love with him. I kept my hair perfectly coiffed and dressed with care. I was taking a gourmet cooking course so I could prepare delicious meals. I couldn't wait to move into our new home and take on my new role as Mrs. Ridley Fielding.

We moved on to other rooms. Ridley found a few more items he wanted me to bid on. I liked the baker's rack. He said it would be fine for the kitchen, so I added it to our list. They now included the desk, a vase, and the baker's rack.

When we reached the last room, I noticed my earlier companion studying a large ceramic Chinese horse. He winked at me and smiled.

"Who is that?" I asked Ridley.

Ridley turned. "Who?"

But the man had left the room.

Roger Harrowgate, the club's current president, announced over the PA system that the auction would open in ten minutes in the Georgian Room. "Make sure you have your bidding paddles."

There was a buzz of anticipation as we climbed the stairs to the ballroom on the second floor. We were well over one hundred in attendance as little Danielle Harrowgate was a darling child, and everyone wanted to help the six-year-old who was suddenly unable to walk and now resided in the pediatric ward of the local hospital.

Ridley and I found seats in the third row. I felt a twinge of excitement as the bidding opened. I'd only been to one other auction, and that was three years ago. I was there to keep eyes on a mark, so I'd paid little attention to the bidding or what was being sold. When the mark left, I'd followed him to his dinner appointment and offed him as he was about to enter his apartment building hours later.

Phil Paxton, the auctioneer, acted as though he'd been hired to entertain us, which in a way he was. A man in his early sixties, he had a full head of white hair, a matching mustache, and a pot belly. Phil described each lot in detail in his gravelly voice. When the bidding flagged, his humorous comments encouraged laughter and usually managed to bring life back to competing bids.

"He sure knows how to raise the stakes," Ridley mumbled.

"That's not good," I said.

"Not good at all."

I noticed that before he opened the bidding of each lot, Phil conferred briefly with an attractive young woman with a mane of blond hair stylishly cut. She wore a white short-sleeved blouse, a black pencil skirt and very high red heels, all of which served to show off her dynamite figure.

The novelty of watching people bidding against each other wore off by the time the fourth item—a large oil painting featuring a rural setting—came up and I found myself observing the people around me. Who was nervous? Who looked shifty? Who noticed me? Nothing to worry about, I reminded myself. But old habits died hard.

And so, I found myself studying Blondie, now seated to the side of the auction block. Her eyes scanned the audience. When they reached Ridley, she flashed a smile.

I glanced at my fiancé. Did he just wink at her? I couldn't be sure, but hadn't I detected a movement? A flutter?

Now she was gazing up at the ceiling, a blank expression on her face.

"Who's that?" I asked.

"Who do you mean?"

I pointed discreetly.

"That's Phil's daughter, Valerie."

"What is she doing up there?" I whispered.

"She's studying to be an auctioneer. He's giving her pointers as he calls up each lot," Ridley whispered back.

The bidding for the painting grew heated until it was sold. Down came Phil's hammer and his comment on what a good deal the bidder had gotten.

"Some deal," Ridley scoffed as the painting was removed and a large vase took its place. "It went for five hundred more than the three thousand it's worth."

"Pretty, isn't she?" I said as I watched father and daughter confer.

Ridley put his arm around me and pulled me close. "Not as pretty as my Adele," he whispered.

"Thank you, my love." Then I asked, "How do you know she's going to be an auctioneer?"

"Phil must have mentioned it."

I shot him a look of surprise.

"When I went to the auction house with the Harrowgates to check out their inventory."

Despite Phil's attempts to raise the bidding on the vase, only two people vied for it. And since their bids were below the reserve price, it was removed from the auction block.

"When did you go to the auction house?"

Ridley grimaced. It wasn't like me to nag him.

"I'm just curious," I said, my BS radar kicking in. This was the first I was hearing about a visit to the auction house.

"A few months ago. Back in August, I guess. Look what's up next."

My pulse raced as the rolled-top desk was set on the auction block. Phil read its description and provenance out loud. He spoke briefly with his daughter. Then he opened the bidding.

"Wait." Ridley stopped me from raising my paddle.

A man in a green polo shirt and an older woman with a blue streak in her hair bid on the desk. Then I raised my paddle and raised the amount five hundred dollars.

"Twelve hundred dollars for this lovely antique rolled-top desk," Phil said. "In mint condition."

"Fourteen hundred," the man in the green polo called out.

"Two thousand dollars," I said.

Phil repeated my bid then began his spiel. Green polo increased it to twenty-two hundred. Phil tried to raise it to twenty-six hundred dollars. I waited till he was going to call it at twenty-two hundred.

"Twenty-five!" I shouted.

There was no rebuttal. The desk was ours!

"Good girl! You pay over there." Ridley pointed to the alcove off the ballroom. I was exhilarated as I walked over to the skinny young man in a black turtleneck sweater sitting at a desk. I was surprised when he quoted me an amount well over three thousand dollars.

"Tax I get," I said," but what's the rest?

He grinned at me. "Hey, we have to make a living too."

I handed him my charge card and agreed to pay even more to have the desk shipped to our apartment. This was running into more money than I'd figured.

I bid on the vase and got it for what Ridley said was a fair price then let the painting go to another bidder.

"You should have raised it two thou," he said.

"It was getting expensive," I said.

"That artist's work goes up in value every year. We'd get three times the cost if we sold it in seven years. Even five years."

"Really? His colors are garish."

"Maybe you should take a course in modern art instead of poetry," Ridley said.

I ignored his comment, but I was in a funny mood. Restless. On edge. Wary. It couldn't be because of that girl Valerie, could it? Just because she'd smiled at Ridley. He was handsome. She probably was trying to flirt.

Except later I ran into her in the bathroom. She was washing her hands at the sinks when I came in. No smile for me. In fact, if looks could kill, as the saying goes, hers would be a stiletto knife straight to the heart.

*****

The dagger was the final lot of the day. It was past six when a worker carried its glass case up to the auction block.

Ridley stood. "Let's go,"

"I want to see this," I said.

He frowned. "I've had enough. I'll be in the room outside the dining room when you're ready."

Fewer than fifty of us had remained. As they'd done with the smaller items, a worker carried the glass case along the aisle while Phil started up his patter. I stopped the young man as he approached my row. "Please open the case so I can examine the dagger."

"Be careful. It's very sharp."

He removed the dagger and placed it in my hands. I felt the heft of it, its perfect balance. Gingerly, I touched the edge of the blade.

I smiled as I handed it back. The dagger was going to be mine.

Three people got involved in the bidding. I waited a while then I jumped in. A man in a striped shirt upped me five hundred dollars. The two other bidders didn't respond. Phil tried to raise the price one hundred dollars. I raised it two hundred dollars.

Striped Shirt and I went higher and higher. We parried back and forth to nine thousand dollars. My opponent, his face flushed, raised his paddle. "Twelve thousand dollars."

Phil looked at me. I didn't move. I didn't speak. As he raised the hammer, I called out. "Twelve thousand five hundred."

My opponent shook his head.

The hammer fell. "Sold."

"Congratulations," a male whispered in my ear. "I'm glad it's yours."

I turned to the man I'd spoken to hours earlier. "Me, too."

He extended his hand. "Alec Dalton."

"Adele Brightstone."

He winked, and I got the feeling he was mocking my made-up name.

But all he said was, "I look forward to running into you again."

*****

The words came to my lips as I paid for the dagger. "A surprise gift for my fiancé," I said as I handed over my charge card, this time to an older man dressed in a sports jacket and shirt.

"He's very lucky to have such a thoughtful fiancée," he answered.

I was about to take the wrapped parcel, then decided to have it sent, and gave him the address to my apartment. "Less to carry," I said with a little laugh as I handed him back my charge card to pay for the shipping and insurance.

I walked across the hall to the room crowded with club members and their guests. I looked around for Ridley. A shot of adrenaline flashed through me when I saw him standing in the far corner talking to Valerie Paxton. They were laughing at something one of them had said. I hesitated, then made a beeline for them, determined to put an end to their tête-à-tête.

"Oh, there you are!" Ridley said as though he'd been waiting impatiently for me to show up. Still, he slid his arm around my waist as I came to stand beside him.

"Adele, this is Valerie Paxton, Phil's daughter, who will soon be an auctioneer. Valerie, my fiancée Adele Brightstone."

I put out my hand. "Nice to meet you."

Valerie barely grazed my fingers as we shook. "A pleasure," she murmured. She swung her hair around, missing my face by inches. "Nice chatting, Ridley."

She flashed him a smile and took off.

"What were you two laughing about?" I asked.

"Valerie was telling me a funny story that happened at an auction last week."

"Does she go to all her father's auctions?" I asked.

Ridley shrugged. "How would I know?"

We were saved from pursuing the subject because Dick and Sarah Preston were approaching. I liked the Prestons. Both were warm and down-to-earth. Ridley and Dick had known each other at college. They were never close friends until a year ago when the Prestons moved to Westchester, close to where we were building our new home.

Dick was a hedge fund manager. Ridley had grumbled more than once that he'd be making Dick's salary if *his* father were Colin Preston, CEO of T and P. I knew Ridley was considering approaching Colin Preston about working at Tarkington and Preston, but he wanted to run it by Dick first.

"How was the auction?" Sarah asked.

"Pretty good," Ridley said. Two loveseats facing each other suddenly became free and we hurried over to grab them. "We bought a beautiful antique desk, a vase and a baker's rack, didn't we Dellie?"

I smiled. "Yes, we did." The warmth in his voice told me we were back in a good place. Now wasn't the time to mention the dagger.

"Nice additions for your new home," Dick said.

"I'm sorry we missed it," Sarah said. "I bet we could have picked up a few items."

Dick turned up his palms. "What can I say? Kids come before auctions. You know how much Matt wanted us at his meet."

"I know." Sarah sighed dramatically. "It's just that with three teenagers going in three directions, I sometimes wish I could be in two places at once."

The announcement came over the PA system that dinner was being served. Ridley and I walked into the dining room; our arms wrapped around each other's waist. We had reserved a table with the Prestons and two other couples. Robby and Alita Klein were both radiologists, and John Fuller and Margo King lived together and worked in the same law firm.

We were all at least ten years younger than most of the other members, which bonded us as good dinner companions. I enjoyed taking part in the stimulating conversations that changed topics as suddenly as the weather. The men played racket ball together on Sunday mornings, which led to a lot of bantering and teasing.

As I expected, Ridley made a point of talking to Dick about finances, but every so often he'd turn to me to say something romantic.

"Having fun?" he asked as they cleared the table to serve dessert.

"I am."

"I'm glad. Your happiness is important to me."

I leaned over to kiss his cheek. "I like everyone at the table, and I love you."

"I love you too, Dellie."

Sarah stood and announced she was going to the bathroom.

"Think I'll join you," I said.

We walked out to the hall and down a narrow corridor to the bathrooms.

Sarah put her arm through mine. "I can't wait till you guys are living in your new house."

"Me, too."

"Do you know when the work will be done, and you can move in?"

"There seems to always be some new delay, but Ridley hopes we can move in in May, a month before our wedding."

Sarah squeezed my arm. "Your wedding. You must be so excited."

"I am. I wish it were next month. Not seven months from now."

As we approached the women's bathroom, Sarah said, "Dick says you're a wonderful influence on Ridley."

"He does?" Sarah seemed on the verge of saying more. "Come on," I coaxed. "You can't leave me on tenterhooks."

"Actually, Dick didn't think much of Ridley when they were in college. Ridley was dating a good friend of Dick's. She found out he was cheating on her the whole time they were together."

"Really?"

"But that was eighteen years ago. Ridley's grown up. I see how he looks at you. The man adores you."

Sarah opened the bathroom door and I followed her inside.

*****

That night Ridley and I made passionate love. Afterward, I fell asleep immediately. I had a strange dream. Alec Dalton and Valerie Paxton were in it. They both were trying to tell me something, but I couldn't make out their words. It didn't matter, I told myself when I woke in the morning. It was only a dream.

Ridley loves me. We're planning our life together. There's no reason why I should be jealous of a woman who's attracted to him. Then I remembered the shabby way Ridley had treated his college girlfriend. But that was many years ago, and it was only Dick's take on the situation. Besides, hadn't Sarah commented on how much Ridley adored me?

I got dressed and went to my cooking class. We made a delicious chicken and pasta dish with a creamy sauce. As we ate our portions, I mused this was the perfect meal to serve if you planned to poison someone. I'd made use of a few tasteless poisons before I retired. But why was I thinking about poison?

Ridley called as I was leaving class. He sounded excited.

"I just talked to Dick. He's going to sing my praises to his father and arrange an interview. He said they have a very strict hiring procedure, but he's pretty sure his dad will bypass it for me."

"I'm so happy!"

"We'll celebrate tonight!" Ridley mentioned an expensive restaurant we'd been wanting to try.

"Okay. I'll skip my poetry class," I said.

"Oh, Dellie. I forgot about your class."

"No, this is more important. It's about our future."

Dinner was wonderful, and so was the following day when the desk, vase, and baker's rack were delivered to our apartment. I made the chicken cream dish for dinner and Ridley loved it.

Wednesday afternoon, Ridley left work early, and we went to see how our new house was coming along. We arrived just as the contractor was leaving. Ridley had words with him while I walked around the half-built rooms to check on the progress.

I went into the great room and imagined the dagger hanging over the large stone fireplace. I realized with a start that I still hadn't told Ridley that I'd bought it. I'll tell him tonight.

I heard shouting. Ridley and the contractor were arguing. I heard cursing. Something about money. An ultimatum, then the contractor left.

"What was that all about?" I asked.

"The SOB claims I owe him thirty thousand more for the small changes we made."

"Is this the first time he's mentioning it?" I asked as we headed for the car.

"He said it would be more, but never that much more."

"Maybe we should cut back—"

"I don't want to talk about it. It will all work out." Ridley started the car.

I knew from the few times he'd gotten angry that nothing I said would change anything. He'd get over it in a few days.

Ridley drove home well over the speed limit. We'd planned to bring in something for dinner, but when we got to the apartment he headed straight for the drinks trolley and poured himself a stiff Scotch. Then another. When I finally mentioned ordering in, he said he wasn't hungry, but I should go ahead and order what I liked. I made do with some leftover chicken and pasta then watched TV in the bedroom. I finally fell asleep, so I had no idea when he'd come to bed. When I awoke the next morning, he was fast asleep reeking of liquor.

Ridley woke up while I was in the shower. He apologized profusely for the night before. I made light of it, but I was growing concerned. I thought Ridley was comfortably well off. As far as I knew, he didn't owe money aside from the home equity loan he'd taken out for the new house. And I'd never seen him drink like that before.

He must have sensed what I'd been thinking because, as I poured him a cup of coffee, he told me why he'd gotten so upset. His sister had just hit him for twenty thousand dollars for repairs in the Connecticut house. "If I'd known the cost of those changes, I would have told Brenda she'd have to live with the old windows. At least for a couple more months."

"When does the contractor want the money?"

"Next week. I'll stop by the bank and increase our home equity loan. Or...." He looked at me.

"Or what?" I asked, playing dumb.

"You could lay it out, and I'll return it with interest in a few months."

I waved away his offer as I knew he'd expected. "I don't want your interest."

"Can you swing it?"

"I'll check my accounts. I've been spending a lot these past few weeks—"

"This is for the house," Ridley said coldly.

"I've been buying things for the house," I said softly.

Ridley shot to his feet. "Gotta go. See you tonight."

I was too upset to finish my breakfast. Since I had nothing planned for the day, I decided to stop by my apartment where I hadn't been in weeks. The dagger was scheduled to be delivered sometime today. Besides, I needed to bring more winter clothes over to Ridley's apartment.

I taxied to the West Side and greeted Tim, the doorman. My building was old but well kept, and the doormen and custodians were honest and reliable. Six years ago, I'd bought a one-bedroom unit intending to upgrade but never felt the need to. Ridley had been after me to sell it and put the money into the house, but for some reason I was reluctant to sell it before we married. Besides, I kept important records and items here in a well-hidden safe. When I sold the apartment, I'd have to find a secure place where no one would find them.

The apartment smelled stale, so I opened the living room and bedroom windows. I pulled out sweaters from my bureau and pants and long-sleeved blouses from my closet, then decided to go through my wardrobe. I made a big pile of clothing I never wore to donate to charity. I needed to buy dressy clothes to wear to club functions and business dinners that Ridley wanted me to attend.

The unpleasantness of our morning's spat was fading. I could easily afford the thirty thousand dollars Ridley seemed to need so desperately. There was no reason to argue over something we both wanted for our house.

Around one o'clock, Tim called to tell me I'd received a delivery.

"Thanks. Could you please bring it up now?"

"Certainly, Miss Brightstone."

As soon as Tim left, I unwrapped the packaging and set the dagger on a table in the living room. It was a beauty! I decided to have lunch at a nearby pub, return to collect my suitcase of clothes, then cab back to Ridley's apartment.

The pub was dark and cozy, and half-filled with customers. I ordered a burger and coffee and leaned back in the comfortable club chair. My phone rang. It was Ridley.

"Hello, Adele."

"Hi."

"Listen, I'm sorry about this morning."

"Me, too. I think I can manage the thirty thousand."

"You can? That would be wonderful! You're the best, Dellie."

I smiled. "We'll talk about it over dinner. Anything special you'd like me to make tonight?"

"Actually, that's why I'm calling. A client showed up unexpectedly, and I gotta wine and dine him." Ridley groaned. "He's a big drinker so I'll be home late tonight."

"Oh." I suddenly felt bereft. Like a child who'd been told her birthday party was canceled. "I'm near my apartment. Maybe I'll stay over tonight."

"Sounds like a good idea. I'm really sorry about this evening. Talk to you later."

My hamburger arrived. It looked delicious, but I'd lost my appetite. I pushed the plate away and sipped my coffee.

"You're not going to let that go to waste, are you?"

I looked up, into the smiling face of Alec Dalton.

When I didn't answer, he asked, "Upset about something? Someone?"

"My fiancé." The words tumbled out on their own volition.

"Ridley. Philip. Fielding."

I nodded. Alec Dalton moved a chair close to me and sat down.

"I'm afraid Ridley isn't the man you think he is."

"How would you know?" I asked.

Alec's voice dropped to a near whisper as he told me that Ridley's finances had hit rock bottom, and he was close to being arrested for embezzling clients' money."

My eyes widened in shock. "But how can that be? We're building a house. He gave the builder a hefty down payment."

"Half of what they wanted. And now they're wanting more."

I closed my eyes to think. "Thirty thousand?"

"Three hundred thirty thousand, actually. Ridley's hoping that giving them the money you agreed to put up will give him a chance to beg for more time."

"How do you know all this?"

"It's my job to investigate."

"You're tapping my phone!"

That earned me a wink. How dare he! But I was too furious with Ridley to deal with the outrage that this man had been spying on me.

"You can't mean he's marrying me for my money?" I scoffed.

"I'm afraid so."

"But I'm not wealthy! Where did he get that idea?"

"He knows you have secrets, which he interprets that you're hiding assets, assets he plans to get his hands on soon as you're married."

I remembered Ridley's questions about my finances. The repeated innuendos that now was a great time to sell the condo. My face flushed with rage and humiliation. I, whose job it had been to eliminate marks, was Ridley's mark.

"Anything else I should know?"

Alec cleared his throat. "That young woman you saw him talking to, Valerie Paxton?"

"They're involved."

Alec nodded.

I sat back and absorbed the bombshells he'd dropped on my head. These past seven months I'd been living a fantasy. I'd wanted my life to change, and so I let myself believe that what was happening was real when in fact someone was playing me for a fool! I was the fool for taking Ridley Fielding at his word and not checking his finances, his police record, nor his social background as I would anyone I'd worked with or worked for in my past life.

"What do you want from me?"

Alec, who'd been sitting quietly drinking a cup of coffee he'd ordered while I was digesting his news, seemed amused by my question.

Irritated, I asked, "Do you work for a branch of the law and expect me to act as a witness against Ridley? Because I know nothing about his finances."

"We know that."

The fury I'd been experiencing now turned to fear. "Who is *we*?"

"An agency that would like to hire you and make good use of your talents."

I stared at him. *He knows!* I stood. "I have to go!" I opened my pocketbook and threw two twenties on the table.

Alec placed a hand on mine. "I didn't mean to frighten you, Adeline." His voice was gentle.

"How do you know...?"

"We know quite a lot about you and your career, and we're hoping you'll work for us. Please hear me out."

I sat down, never taking my eyes from his as he told me about the special government agency he worked for that needed my expertise for assignments abroad. "They'll come every few months or so, and you'll have free reign as to how you complete your assignments. Meanwhile, you can live here in the city and collect your monthly checks.”

He quoted a salary that made me gasp. “Tell me more.”

And he did. When he finished, I asked, “How do we know I haven’t lost my skills?”

Alec’s eyes sparkled. “You can always test them out before deciding.”

I grinned. “Is Ridley planning to spend the night with Valerie?”

“They’ll be at her place.” Alec glanced at his phone and read out an address.

“Thanks.” I thought for a moment. “And I’ll need your number and address. You’re going to be my alibi for the entire evening.”

Alec grinned. “It will be my pleasure to be your phantom lover. Besides, after you’ve completed your test we’ve much to discuss about your future.”

He winked and reached for both our checks, while I reached for my hamburger. It was cold but I was suddenly ravenous. I took a bite and began to plan exactly how I was going to deal with Ridley and his girlfriend.

I felt a thrill of excitement in anticipation of the familiar ritual of studying a mark’s terrain. I had to memorize the layouts of Valerie’s street, her apartment building, and her unit. Locate all streetlamps and CCTV cameras. I had to be ready for all contingencies to make this operation a success.

An epic life change was in store for me. It involved working abroad, something I always wanted. And there was Alec. I felt the connection between us and hoped he wasn’t married.

I reentered my apartment, pausing to admire my beautiful dagger. How I longed to sink it into their cheating hearts, but that would make me a suspect. Instead, I’d use the strongest, sharpest knife in my collection. I hummed as I sat down at my laptop and got ready for the evening ahead.

Straight to the Heart
Sandra Murphy

I was late for work. It was only by a few minutes, but Morgan demanded punctuality. If I wasn't there to make her morning coffee, plate a warm scone next to a spoonful of clotted cream and one of jam, and have her opened mail on her desk, I'd hear about it. She'd never been one to hold back, even when my lateness was because I had to run an errand for her. The job paid well, but she was a pain in the neck.

Who am I trying to kid? The pay wasn't great and she's a non-stop pain in the more than just my neck. I often wondered, how much stress does it take to develop an ulcer?

When I walked in the front door, Jasmine, our unpaid intern, was on the verge of frantic. "Oh, Miss Sherry, thank goodness you're here. I didn't know what to do." Jasmine started to ramble before I had both feet across the threshold. "Mr. Nelson called and demanded to talk to Miss Morgan, urgent he said."

"Calm down, it can't be that bad." I put a grocery bag with kid sized bottles of orange juice on the desk. "Nelson panics. She'll talk him down."

"Remember when we did orientation? You said, Miss Morgan is a punctual lady."

"Yes, I remember. She's been yelling because I'm, um," I glanced at my watch. "Eight minutes late? I'd blame rush hour traffic but in a town of only 4,500 people, there's not much need to rush. I'll go calm Her Highness."

"No, no, you did say she tends to yell a lot but this morning," Jasmine gulped loud enough for me to hear. "It's been dead quiet. I heard her go into the office from the house. I knocked but she didn't answer. Mr. Nelson, he was real mad."

"She must be in a snit." I crossed to the office door and reached for the knob. "It will disrupt her schedule, but I'll tell her to call him."

"I tried, it's locked, Miss Sherry." Jasmine looked like she was about to faint. "It's going to be my fault."

"Jasmine, this is an intern job and unpaid. She's not going to fire you." Under my breath I muttered, 'She'd make me do it.' I tried the door. Yep, locked. "I'll take care of it. Go to your desk, put your head on your knees, and take slow breaths."

I knocked. "Morgan? It's me, open up. It's scone time." No reply. I knocked harder. Nothing.

"Are you sure you heard her go into the office?"

Jasmine was rattled enough she wasn't sure it was daylight and she spoke English.

"Look, she might be in the kitchen to fix her own coffee, just to make a point. I'll walk around back and look. If she's not there, then we'll panic, okay?" Our only access to the main house was through Morgan's office. I went out the front door before Jasmine could stammer a reply.

The windows down the right side of the house brought zero results. The bedroom drapes were open to show a neatly made bed, the room, empty. The bathroom door was ajar, not there either. There was no sign of Morgan in the kitchen. The back door was locked. With a sigh, I walked to the other side, where there's no sidewalk but plenty of uneven ground to trip me up, glad I'd worn tennis shoes. Heels would have impaled the lawn with the first step, leaving me stranded or clomping barefooted.

A glance into the living room showed me Morgan wasn't there. I dialed Morgan's cell. Voicemail. Twice. Two more windows proved to be as much help as the first, that is, none. The office was the final stop. If I didn't see her at her desk, ear buds blocking our attempts to get her attention, I had no idea where she could be.

The ground sloped so I couldn't walk up and look inside. I was at least two feet short. I hoped Mrs. Foster, the next-door neighbor, wouldn't call 9-1-1 to report me.

I ran, rather, walked fast, to the back patio, grabbed a sturdy chair, and one of the bricks from the edge of the flower bed. As I dragged my burdens across the lawn, I used all the colorful language I knew. If I went to this much trouble, got hot and sweaty for no reason…

I paused to catch my breath and tested to make sure the chair was level, then hoisted myself up by hanging on the windowsill. The curtains were drawn but through a two-inch gap, I saw Morgan at her desk, slumped to the right. I tapped the glass, but she didn't move. The window was locked.

I jumped down, picked up the brick, and regained my position without falling. I shielded my face, took a deep breath, and then wham! Glass shattered and for the most part, fell inside. There were small shards and one big piece that hung like a stalactite from the upper frame. I pulled my summer sweater over my head and wadded it up on the sill to protect my hands to bash the glass from the frame. It worked, mostly.

I could grip the inside ledge of the sill and with less grace than Spiderman, walked my feet up the wall and flung myself into the room. If the sound of my landing and yell of, "Ouch! Damn it!" didn't get Morgan's attention, nothing would.

I touched her face, and she didn't flinch. Her empty little juice bottle was on the table. It had been the last one. Buying fresh blueberry scones and more orange juice was what made me late today.

I unlocked the door. "Jasmine, I can't wake her. Call an ambulance." Jasmine sat there, stunned. "Do it!" She managed to pick up the phone and dial. I went back to Morgan.

"Miss Sherry, they're on their way. What should I do?" Jasmine stared at Morgan, her eyes huge.

"Go direct them to the office, not the house, and hurry!"

The heavy door swung shut. I tried to pull Morgan's body upright to no avail. I shifted the cushion she used for back support to get her better seated, scooted the chair away from the desk so the EMTs could check her. I heard sirens in the distance. They'd be on scene in less than a minute.

I glanced around the room. Everything looked as usual.

*****

As I thought, Morgan was dead but Josh and Todd, the EMTs, didn't have the authority to give an official verdict. They called their office who phoned Doc Scofield. In his day job, he's a podiatrist and the least likely to have emergencies to conflict with people dying or dead. As city medical examiner, he's the only one who can act in an unattended death. We sat in the outer office, left Morgan alone but within view.

While we waited, Todd cleaned the cuts on my hands, asked when I last had a tetanus shot, advised me to get one, and applied a couple of Hello Kitty bandages over the deeper cuts. I made coffee and set out the juice and blueberry scones.

Doc took one look at Morgan, listened with his stethoscope, and announced time of death, 9:17. Josh asked, "Can we take her? And where?"

"To the funeral home. I can do an autopsy there. The hearse is occupied, taking Ethel Brownlee to the cemetery." At 102, Ethel's death was not what you could call unexpected. I heard she was in the middle of a ninety-minute Zumba class where she mostly did jazz hands and waved her arms, when she wobbled, sat down, and said, "I gotta go." Then she did.

Josh said, "It's my turn for the shoulders. You did the last one." Todd made a face but didn't protest. Not anxious to see them put Morgan on the gurney, I turned toward the front window

"What the hell? Doc, come look!"

Todd had leaned over to pick up Morgan's feet.

"I didn't want to put her back and make things worse. Can you see or do you want me to move her forward?" Josh's face wasn't as tanned as a few minutes ago.

"Ease her back to the way you found her. Everyone out of the room." Doc sighed. "This was *not* natural causes. I'll call the police."

*****

Jasmine went bonkers when she heard Doc. Todd administered a mild tranquilizer Doc prescribed. She would never have made it through police questioning otherwise. Detective Ben Ackerman talked to her first, then had a uniformed officer drive her home.

"So, Miss Sherry, tell me about your morning." Ackerman sat at the other end of the small sofa in the office. "Josh and Todd fix up your hands? They run out of bandages?"

"I should have asked. Would you like a coffee or orange juice? I think the juice is room temperature." I started to stand but he motioned for me to remain seated. "My morning? I've had better. My boss is dead, I ruined my favorite sweater, and I guess I'm unemployed."

"How was she as a boss? What is it you do here?"

"We broker deals, introduce people who have money, to people who need money."

"You didn't answer the part about your boss. I'll need a list of your clients, anyone who's been unhappy with your services, who lost money. It can wait until after the autopsy and we know what we're dealing with." He made a few illegible marks in his notebook, not that I was looking.

"Morgan as a boss…she was a pain in the patoot, exacting, anal down to the color of ink in our pens. She made money for everyone who listened to her. Some didn't and wished they had. As a person, she lacked social skills. That's what she had me for."

"Talk me through a usual day."

"This is not the kind of business that has usual days." I stood. "Sorry, I was too athletic this morning and feeling it."

"Walk me through this morning, a reenactment of sorts. I could use a stretch too. Any idea who inherits or who her lawyer is?"

"No, yes, and I'll give you his number."

"Start with what time you were supposed to be here and what time you came in, step by step." He was next to me as I stood near the front door, pretended to talk to a now invisible Jasmine, put Morgan's juice on my desk, and knocked on her door.

"Okay, now the fun part, let's take a stroll. The girl says you can't get into the house from the outer office, right?"

"The girl's name is Jasmine, and she's a young woman and yes, access to the house is through Morgan's office or the front and back doors to the house. The back door was locked, I didn't check the front."

"It would be a short cut, why not?"

"Morgan rarely used it herself because the door sticks. It stays locked. I walked around on the sidewalk to look in the kitchen, then to the other side of the house to look in the rest of the windows."

"I don't suppose you have witnesses?"

"Mrs. Foster, next door. She writes down everything and everyone she sees. I've seen flashes of light from her windows so I'm pretty sure she takes photos." We reached the rear of the house. "I saw her curtains twitch so she's on the case. She's gonna love to meet you."

"Women do. It's my affable nature." He grinned as we walked on.

"I didn't see anything out of place, no Morgan. The lawn slopes and here's the office. I went back to the patio, grabbed this chair and a brick. I'm sure I gave Mrs. Foster quite the show. I was not graceful."

"Want to reenact it?"

"No! Only the on the chair part, not the through the window fiasco." I double-checked the stability of the chair, climbed on. "I could see Morgan, tapped on the window but she didn't move. I stepped down, got the brick, managed to get back up here, then broke the window. Some glass was still in the frame. I used my sweater to protect my hands and then cleared as much glass as possible. I went in, splat." I managed to step down from the chair without a splat this time.

"The curtains open or closed? They were open in the rest of the house."

"Closed except for a gap about two inches wide. Morgan said if they were open, it felt like Mrs. Foster could look over her shoulder."

"How'd you tear your blouse?"

"Where? Oh, damn. I guess I missed a piece of glass. Am I bleeding? I can't see. It doesn't hurt." I turned in circles, tried to look over my shoulder to see the damage.

Ackerman took a closer look. "Nope, just a rip in the fabric. Let's go in and you can show me what happened next."

"The cuts on my hands are from landing on broken glass on the floor. I'm glad my knees didn't find any. I checked Morgan, told Jasmine to call for an ambulance, moved Morgan's chair so Josh and Todd could examine her."

"You shouldn't move the body at a crime scene."

"Crime scene? What do you mean?"

"It's an unattended death of a suspicious nature. Until proven otherwise, we treat it as a crime." He walked around the room. "You'll know better next time."

"Next time?! Thank you very much, once was enough for me. Until Doc said he would call you, I didn't think, of course, you'd assume natural causes, wouldn't you, coming upon a body? Maybe not you, but the average person. The door and window were locked, she was alone."

"It's a puzzle, all right. I'll figure it out. By the way, you don't strike me as average." He sketched a diagram of the room as he walked, pacing off the dimensions. "What was with doling out coffee, juice, and scones?"

"Jasmine was so jittery, I thought doing a normal thing would calm her. I picked up the scones and juice on my way in this morning, used our coffeemaker, not the one here."

"Did it work?" Ackerman stared at the desk. "Was Morgan face down on the blotter, regular distance away, or tight against it to prop her up?"

"No on Jasmine. Morgan, not face down, not propped, regular distance, slumped to her right enough I could see her head and arm from the window."

"Okay, pretend I'm Morgan. From the moment you picked yourself up off the floor, what did you do besides move the body, put your bloody handprints on every surface, and generally contaminate the scene?" Ackerman moved Morgan's chair to one side, dragged the visitor's chair into its place, and flopped down. "Why didn't she have a chair with wheels? Scoot me into position, tilt me like Morgan was."

"This was the desk chair her father used. Tradition, she said." I held back a smile. "She tried a regular office chair. The second day she had it, she bumped into the chair as she started to sit, it rolled back, and she landed on the floor. I inherited the chair."

It felt weird to remember how I'd approached Morgan's chair from behind, touched her wrist for a pulse, then her neck, both sides.

Even on a live detective, I couldn't zero in on a heartbeat, just the five o'clock shadow he had by 10 A.M. Despite the stubble, I could tell he didn't use her expensive brand of moisturizer. His skin was a degree or two warmer than Morgan's had been. The smell of his aftershave, Brut, brought back memories of the '80s, not necessarily a good thing. At least it wasn't Old Spice.

To get away from the Brut, I ran to the door, pretended to call Jasmine, gave the instructions to meet the ambulance.

At the desk, I stood behind the chair and tried to move it. Peeling back his eyelid was the worst part since unlike Morgan, he could, and did, look back.

"Morgan's shoe caught on the chair mat and almost fell off, so I came around and pushed from the front. I checked her eye, but it was blank. She was gone. I looked to see if there was a clue as to what happened. Everything looked normal. By then, the EMTs were here. They came in, Jasmine and I waited in the outer office. Doc called you."

"Did you kill her?" Ackerman looked up at me, just with one eye, the one I'd opened.

"Oh, sure, did I leave that part out? I told you what I did." I left him there and went to my office. He was right on my heels.

"I gotta ask the awkward questions. Is there a copy of her will here?"

"Don't know, don't care. Call her lawyer. I've never seen it." I stood.

"Are we done? I've got someplace I'd rather be."

"Where's that?"

"Where you're not."

"What about my affable nature?"

"I must have missed it. Gotta go, people to see."

"Would 'people' be the woman in the photo on your desk? Who's she?"

"Lila."

"You haven't called her to tell her what happened?"

"No. She's not well, no need to upset her. I'll tell her when I get home." His eyebrow went up, but he didn't ask about our living arrangement.

"How did you two meet, you and Lila I mean." The notebook was out of sight. I think he was making a cop's version of small talk.

"We beat up Tommy Decker. It was a bonding moment."

"There's a story I want to hear. I will take coffee and a scone if the offer still stands."

Lila was the delicate one, a wisp of a woman, looked like she should wear floral maxi dresses in pastel colors, and run in slow motion through fields of wildflowers.

"Lila and I met in kindergarten. Tommy was a bully who made sure everyone knew the swing sets were his territory. Miss Andrews, fresh out of college, herding twenty-seven five-year-olds, didn't pick up on it.

One day, Lila walked straight to the swings like she had a plan. I watched, fascinated this skinny girl in floral overalls, lace-edged ankle socks, and red leather Mary Janes, was either so stupid or so brave, she'd take on Tommy Decker.

He let her swing enough to get some height, then walked behind her. She knew he was there. On the fourth backswing, he gave her a mighty push. I saw the moment she let go of the chains, sailed through the air, and landed on her hands and knees. Tommy stood in front of her, ready to lecture about ownership of the swing set. Until I ran at him full tilt and punched him in the nose.

He landed hard, flat on his back, knees bent and wide apart. Lila stood, looked down at him, and said, "The swings are for everyone." Then she raised her foot, and with her left red Mary Jane, stomped him right in the inseam. We've been best friends ever since."

"I'd like to meet her but keep my distance at the same time." He'd crossed his legs, a reflex of protection.

"You know, it's kind of weird your friend died, and you aren't more upset." He had his damn notebook out again.

"She was my boss. We were friendly enough here, but it didn't extend past the front door, by mutual consent." I scribbled a note with the alarm code. "I updated the voice mail to say the office is closed today. Here's the spare key and alarm info. Lock up when you leave."

I backed out of the driveway and headed for the deli. Today's soup was corn chowder. I bought enough for two and hoped I could convince Lila to eat.

*****

"Six bites of soup, two crackers with cheese, and half a slice of toast with honey before bed. Final offer." It was a fair, if skimpy on calories and nutrition.

"Four bites of soup, one graham cracker, and at bedtime, a small scoop of the black cherry ice cream you stashed behind the Brussels sprouts. Final counteroffer." Lila whistled under her breath. She had me and she knew it.

"Agreed, on one condition. The ice cream is eaten on the patio."
Lila nodded. "Deal."

*****

I continued to go to the office to answer calls from frantic clients, close out accounts or arrange transfers to another broker. Most said Morgan was irreplaceable and put their money in safer, long-term assets.

Ackerman's team was on hand for the first few days. By the end of the week, they'd gathered every stray hair, dust mote, and minuscule piece of broken glass possible. Ben dropped by about four to tell me he released the office. "Morgan didn't have any relatives. The house, car, everything goes to her alma mater and charities. Let the attorney know how long you need to shut it down; he'll work with you. Do you have any questions?"

"Have you found the cause of death or is it too soon?"

"Yeah, I pretty much knew the day she died. I just had to wait for the official report. She was stabbed."

"Stabbed? But, how? I didn't see any blood or a knife."

"There was a spike thing, like used to be on desks, you know. Papers the boss was finished with were stabbed onto the gizmo for the help to file later."

"Ah, okay, the mail spike. It belonged to her grandfather. He founded the company. It was always kept on a shelf where she could see it." I shook my head. "Such a shame this happened."

Ben gave me a long look. I wondered what was on his mind. Then he said, "Got any coffee? Maybe a scone or two?"

I did. He stayed for about forty-five minutes. We talked about things we had in common. Morgan's death didn't come up.

*****

Lila napped after lunch if you could call the small amount of food a meal. I worked around the house in the mornings, got her settled with books, the remote, and snacks she ignored, and went to the office until four or five. We had international clients and the schedule worked with their time zones. If I were truthful, it gave me a much-needed break from Lila too. Not her company, of course. I could listen to her talk, wait for her laugh, or just sit and be happy. No, it was watching her die that made the office a haven.

Ben dropped by for a coffee and to talk about cases he'd worked in the past, never Morgan's. It's what they always say on television, no discussing an active investigation although with Morgan's odd death, I wasn't sure how active it could be. I didn't ask. Sometimes ignorance is not only bliss but the wisest choice. Besides, he brought jelly donuts.

*****

I sensed he was behind me. There was no mistaking the smell of Brut. "Sit. At least under the canopy, it's shady."

Ben sat and patted my hand. After so many mumbles of sympathy, awkward hugs, and well-intentioned promises to keep in touch, I welcomed the silence.

"Are we keeping them from their work?" I nodded toward the funeral home employees. "Do they want us to leave so they can get on with the job?"

Ben gave me one more pat and walked over the uneven ground to speak with the two men who stood under the shade tree. I think money exchanged hands. They left and Ben returned. "They're taking a long lunch today. We can stay as long as we like."

"Thank you." I was quiet for what seemed like a long while. "You've been very kind, you know. I appreciate it. I've enjoyed our talks. I'll miss them."

"So, try to break any noses lately?" At my surprised look, he laughed. "A couple of days after Morgan died, I stopped by your house, thought you'd be there. Lila gave me her version which was bloodier than yours. I take it she didn't apologize?"

"Nope. Teacher told her to. Lila looked at poor Miss Andrews and said he had it coming. Much later in life, we heard Miss Andrews was asked to renew her contract for a second year but told the principal, hell no, went to secretarial school instead. She was here today, said we were memorable, and she wanted to see what we'd become."

"Poor woman. You two know a lot of people, big crowd today."

"It was all Lila. She had the look of a delicate flower, the heart and soul of a leather-wearing biker babe, and the ability to make everyone she met feel special. I stood by and observed."

"There was a lot of wailing and many tears. You aren't crying."

"Toward the end, she told me not to be sad she was gone but to be happy we'd had so much time together. Besides, she wouldn't be far. I like to think it's true. At least, for now."

"Who was the guy who blew his nose right as the minister said, 'let us remember the sound of her laughter'?"

"Oh, wasn't it awful? Her Uncle Jim. For a little man…" I couldn't finish the sentence, trying to hold back a laugh.

"It sounded like a cow farting." Ben paused. "After eating six cow-sized servings of refried beans." He gave me a side-eyed look and lost it, me right with him.

"Oh, Lila would love this, us sitting graveside, laughing our asses off." I wiped my eyes. "She liked you a lot."

"You knew?"

"The hospice nurse ratted you out. Plus, there was a lingering smell of Brut in the house. How is it you use aftershave but always look like you have a three-day beard? Anyway, I felt better about hiding out at the office, knowing you were there."

"I was hiding too. You ran *to* your office; I ran *away* from mine. I had a few hard decisions to make. She helped." He took a deep breath. "There was nothing doctors could do for her?"

"If she'd been able to get treatment sooner, the odds would have been a lot better. She worked weird jobs that paid more in creative satisfaction than cash, no insurance plans. I tried to get Morgan to hire her so she could be on our plan, but Morgan refused. Lila would have brought in tons of business. I tried everything I could think of but there was no way to afford treatment." I was quiet for a few minutes. "We were out with gay friends one night and the subject came up. One of them said, hey, same sex marriage is legal now, get hitched, put her on your insurance as your spouse. So, we did, I did, and it was too late."

"Why didn't you take family leave when it got worse?"

"I asked. Morgan said no, we weren't a real family, weren't a real couple."

The silence stretched on as the sun began its descent. Ben didn't look at me when he asked, "Is that why you killed her?"

"She refused to help in the beginning, refused to give me time off at the end, and threatened to turn me in for insurance fraud if I didn't work a full schedule. If I quit, she'd withhold my benefits, profit sharing, pension, everything. We might have had a marriage of convenience, but Lila was my family, and no one was going to keep me away when my friend needed me most." I paused. "How did you know?"

"Two things. Who else could have done it? You had a few minutes with her when Jasmine was outside. When you reenacted with me as Morgan, I felt your breath as you checked my pulse. You whispered but I couldn't hear what you said."

"I told her, 'it wouldn't have killed you to have shown some compassion.' Morgan didn't like the taste of orange juice. Every day at closing, I opened a bottle and added honey to it. The next morning, she'd shake it up and drink it all at once. She didn't notice I'd spiked it with a heavy dose of antihistamines. I gather your people found those?" He nodded. "I took the long way around the house to make sure the pills had time to knock her out. When Jasmine ran out to flag down the ambulance, I leaned Morgan forward, took the spike and inserted it through the seat cushion so I could aim, then sat her up and gave her a good shove. I told you the first day, I did it."

He looked surprised. I guess he didn't know as much as he thought. "You asked if I killed her. I said, oh sure, did I forget to mention that? You had a confession then. And another now. What's next? Handcuffs, fingerprints, mug shot, orange jumpsuit? I gotta say, orange is not my color."

"One of the things I talked to Lila about was my job. I'm tired of the politics, the deals, some guy gets backed into a corner and goes to jail while guys who did worse walk free. As of this week, I'm retired. I no longer have the authority to arrest you. Never had the desire to."

"They'll send somebody else to do it."

"Actually, no. There isn't any evidence, the room was locked, the pill bottle was in her desk drawer, the spike was held in position by the cushion. The coroner ruled her death a suicide. No charges, case closed. You're free to do whatever you want. Although I have an idea."

"Are you blackmailing me?"

"Sending people to jail is to convince them not to do the crime again. You were pushed to the limit in a volatile set of circumstances. You're a one and done kind of criminal. You'll be more beneficial as a free woman." He turned to face me. "I'm going private. I can pick and choose my cases, take only clients I like. Lila thought you might want in. I agreed because everyone knows, a good PI needs two things—a fedora and a leggy looker in the office. Or as a partner."

"Leggy looker?" I thought it over, took all of three seconds. "I'm in. Provided you buy me dinner tonight. I'm not ready to face an empty house just yet."

"You drive a hard bargain but okay, as long as refried beans aren't on the menu. Hey, I meant to ask, whatever happened to Tommy Decker?"

We walked back to our cars, the last two in the lot. "Didn't you know? He's the minister who married us and who said we should remember the sound of Lila's laugh."

I swore I heard that laugh float over the still summer air.

Bridesmaid #1
Mary Dutta

Amber noted the time of the call on the first page of her wedding scrapbook: 5:42 PM. So thoughtful of Kayla to allow her time to get home from work before calling to give her the good news. But then, that was Kayla.

A wave of dizziness swept over her. Amber wasn't sure if it was due to the thrill of starting on the wedding journey, or to the diet she had started the day Kayla had posted a picture of her diamond solitaire with the caption "I SAID YES!!!" She wanted to get a head start on losing weight so she would be ready when the inevitable call came inviting her to be a bridesmaid.

Amber kept a close eye on her social media feeds. Nine women had posted about how thrilled, ecstatic, and honored they were to be Kayla's bridesmaids. Nine. Amber knew Kayla would never have an odd number of attendants. It would mess up the photos, for one thing. Kayla liked things to be perfect, and Amber liked making things perfect for her.

Saving the best for last, Amber assumed when Kayla finally called. But just because she was number ten in order of invitation did not mean that she wasn't the number one bridesmaid. There was no *official* maid of honor, of course, but she knew that Kayla secretly considered Amber her best friend. The bride's childhood pal Devyn had actually gotten the first invitation to be in her bridal party. But where had Devyn been when Kayla needed someone to write a term paper for her the night of their sorority formal? Or when some other girl had foolishly decided to run for class president when Kayla had already sort of suggested that maybe she might do it? Of course, by the time the challenger returned from her sudden, semester-long medical leave, the election was over.

But Amber's bridesmaid adventure was just beginning. And whatever Devyn had to offer in long-term friendship; Amber would one-up it in sheer devotion. She would make sure that she was the first down the aisle at the wedding, Bridesmaid #1.

By the time they all gathered for bridesmaid dress shopping, Amber put herself at a solid seven in the attendant rankings. Some of the girls in their group chat had been less supportive of the bride's choices than they should be. If they didn't want to shell out for a bachelorette weekend just because they had been laid off or wouldn't at least *consider* some minor gastric surgery to slim down for the wedding, then they shouldn't have accepted the honor of being Kayla's bridesmaid. Amber forwarded some of the messages to the bride, so she would know who was working toward ensuring her perfect day and who was not.

One of the girls actually failed to show up at the bridal salon. Like her grandmother even knew who was at her side when she died. Amber murmured along with everyone else over the heartbreak of it all, but mentally reassigned the missing girl to the tail end of the wedding procession. She herself happily struggled into every sample bridesmaid gown with undiminished enthusiasm, the rainbow pile of rejects spilling onto the dressing room floor. After all, the more indecisive Kayla was, the more time they spent together.

The bride only made a decision when her fiancé, Blake, arrived to pick her up. "It's just a dress, babe. Pick one already," he said. "You said you would be done half an hour ago."

Just a dress? Didn't he understand that every detail of Kayla's special day had to be perfect? The wrong bridesmaid dress could ruin the whole visual aesthetic. Just like the wrong groom could ruin the whole wedding.

"You're right," Kayla said, twisting her diamond ring.

Amber barely managed to stop herself from shouting that he was not. She glared at him instead, but Blake's eyes were fixed on Devyn's ample cleavage.

The childhood bestie gestured at the halter dress she was modeling, the one most flattering to herself, the one that made Amber look like a linebacker. "I think we have a winner, don't we?" she said.

"Definitely," Blake said, and winked.

Amber bit her tongue so hard she tasted blood. She was fine with the unflattering dress in the color that washed her out completely. This was about Kayla's perfect day. She supported whatever Kayla wanted. Even if it was Blake.

She did her best to ignore him. She never let Kayla's significant others come between them. As if they could. Their friendship was too special. She focused only on Kayla as she accompanied the bride and groom to tastings at various vendors, congratulating herself on jumping on the one task that would keep her in Kayla's company more than any other bridesmaid duty.

Amber listened eagerly to her friend's opinion of each sample, echoing her every *mmmm* and *uh-uh*. So, what if the very smell of tuna tartare made her nauseous? If raw fish would make Kayla's day perfect then Amber would choke down a boatload of it. Not like the bridesmaid whose refusal to consume a stuffed mushroom containing a few measly chopped walnuts had ousted her from tasting duties. Wasn't that why she carried an epi-pen, for god's sake?

Blake sighed dramatically through every possible menu item, gobbling everything without seeming to taste it. "It's just an appetizer, babe," he said at only the second caterer. "Pick one already." He pushed back from the table and headed for the restroom.

"I guess we're done," Kayla said, and stood to follow him. "Do me a favor and make the notes on the sample menu, okay? I think Blake really liked the puff pastry things."

Trust Kayla to find such a subtle way of saying that she admired Amber's handwriting. Another bridesmaid had already messed up the place cards with sloppy calligraphy. Kayla knew she could rely on Amber to keep things exquisite for her.

Amber slipped her own copy of the menu into her purse to add to her scrapbook, musing over just the right washi tape to use for a border around it. She would choose it with as much care as she had the scrapbook itself, a custom creation with "Wedding Memories" on the cover in glittery pink script. Pink was Kayla's favorite color, and hers too, naturally. Amber had special-ordered extra pages, so there would be plenty of room for every memento she had been collecting for herself as the wedding planning progressed.

With the menu safely tucked away, Amber picked up Blake's phone from where he had left it on the table. His background was a picture of him and Kayla she had never seen before. It would be perfect for the slideshow she was working on for the reception. Another bridesmaid had promised to put the show together but had dropped the ball and subsequently dropped in the rankings. Amber just knew that Kayla had wanted her to do it all along, but a bride had to give even her less-favored bridesmaids tasks to make them feel important. When she texted Amber "U need to do the slideshow," Kayla didn't come out and say that Amber's artistic sensibilities were far superior to those of the other attendants, but of course she was thinking it. Amber could read between the lines. Even when there was only one. And she was happy to take on the additional task if it put her closer to the #1 position.

She guessed Kayla's birthday as Blake's phone passcode, surprised to find it actually worked. He seemed more likely to use his own. Still, his paltry birthday tribute dimmed next to the birthday bashes that Amber had thrown Kayla over the years. People still talked about the helicopter.

Amber didn't care to know what was taking Blake so long in the bathroom, or more likely the bar across the hall, but it gave her time for a pretty extensive search through his photos. She sent quite a few to her own phone, figuring she could crop him out of most, and congratulated herself on her ingenuity in finding a way to avoid having to deal with him directly.

Avoiding Blake would be easy on the bachelorette weekend, to which he was blessedly uninvited. Amber packed and repacked, agonizing over the perfect outfit for each scheduled event. She was good to go for the clubbing, having confirmed what Kayla would be wearing and choosing something just shy of identical. The spa provided matching robes, but brunch still had her stomach in knots. Devyn had said something about a sundress, but what if Kayla deemed that too casual? She soothed herself with the knowledge that the weekend's organizer had knocked herself down several rungs in the bridal party hierarchy by originally suggesting a camping weekend for their celebration. As if Kayla did dirt or plaid shirts. Amber felt confident that she was top three.

The weekend went even better than Amber could have hoped. For once, Devyn didn't glue herself to Kayla's side. She actually begged off of brunch, claiming illness, which was plausible given the miles they had put on the Pedal Pub the night before. Kayla furrowed her brow at the news, which was enough for Amber to volunteer to check on her rival. Kayla would not be getting any wrinkles on her watch. And Amber was feeling generous. Missing such a crucial activity just made Devyn's climb to the top of the bridal totem pole that much more slippery.

Devyn wasn't answering her phone, so Amber had to head back to the hotel to check on her in person. She knocked loudly on Devyn's room door, hoping the banging would exacerbate the hangover the other woman was surely nursing. Served her right for putting speed bumps on the road to Kayla's perfect day. When she got no answer, Amber considered asking housekeeping to let her into the room but decided that the more time Devyn was out of the mix, the better. Let her sleep it off and reap the attendant consequences.

If she hustled, Amber could make it back to the restaurant and slip into the seat next to Kayla before the mimosas ran out. She ignored her own pounding headache. It was a small price to pay to ensure flawless festivities for Kayla. Hurrying through the lobby, she saw Devyn push through the front door in the same outfit she had worn the night before, only significantly more disheveled. Her "Bride Tribe" sash trailed behind her.

Amber's heart soared as she snapped a picture. Surely this would knock Devyn out of contention for Bridesmaid #1, should things come down to the wire. Not only had she abandoned Kayla at the bachelorette brunch, but she had also used the occasion to hook up with some rando. Amber watched the other woman toss her bridesmaid sash into a trash can and head for the elevator. She pushed the up button, but Devyn was definitely on her way down.

Amber held the picture close to her vest but left it out of her scrapbook. It had no place among the layouts she spent so many happy hours designing and constructing. Soon, though, she would add her lovingly crafted creation to the closet full of similar keepsakes chronicling her and Kayla's friendship. Because Kayla's wedding day was, finally, almost here. The dress alterations were done. The out-of-town guests had been notified of all the arrangements. She and the bride and groom just had one last tasting, to pin down the seasonal menu items. Amber couldn't stop time, and as much as she treasured the journey with Kayla, she couldn't stop the wedding. Kayla deserved her perfect day.

The wedding day dawned sunny and breezy. Just the perfect, perfect day Kayla deserved, Amber thought as she took her rightful place at the front of the bridal procession. Bridesmaid #1. She tossed her hair, the highlights faultlessly matched to Kayla's, and cast a triumphant smile behind her at the nine losing bridesmaids. She gazed around the church. Colored light streamed through the stained-glass windows. The heady scent of the flower arrangements perfumed the air. Everything was perfect except for the woman in the third pew who wore an unconscionable shade of puce. If only Amber had seen her sooner, she could have done something about it, but the organist had begun the processional music. She stepped forward, secure in the knowledge that she had done absolutely everything in her power to give Kayla the wedding she deserved.

She imagined she could feel Devyn's impotent glare boring into the back of her head. Pretty ungrateful, considering Amber had graciously decided not to expose her bachelorette antics once Kayla announced the procession line up. Of course, Devyn didn't know that any more than Blake knew that when Amber looked through his phone for photos, she had found some very recent, very incriminating shots of the groom with other women who were very much not Kayla.

He also didn't know that at every tasting after that she had added a little something to his plate that, accumulating in his system, would work together to kill him. She doubted he would make it back from the exotic honeymoon he had been so keen on. Odds were the authorities would chalk his death up to ciguatera poisoning or some other tropical toxin whose effects she had worked so carefully to mimic.

Amber had promised herself that Kayla would have a perfect day and she had delivered it. Someone as wonderful as Kayla would easily find another husband. And then she and Amber would begin another wedding journey together. Amber looked forward to giving her friend a perfect day all over again. She already bought the scrapbook.

Best Laid Plans
Diane Fanning

Emily's foot dislodged a rock, and she slipped ten feet down the hillside. Adrenaline pumped through her bloodstream making her heart pound. *Did he hear?* She froze while she listened for approaching footsteps. She saw a twisted branch and "rattlesnake" raced through her mind. She was wrong but now every stick looked like a threat.

Slowing down, she was careful not to place a foot on any loose stones or bang her shins on the boulders that erupted all over the property. She hadn't gone down the driveway because she knew anyone in the house would have a clear view of her descent. Finally, the post-modern cabin her and Frank built two years ago was in sight.

Emily loved everything about this parcel of land except for the damn snakes. The views of the mountain terrain were incredible. When the leaves changed color in the fall, the colors were glorious and almost blinding. The serenity of the vacation home tucked deep in the lot, far from the road felt like heaven. Since it was located at a ski resort, she did get tired of telling people she met at shops and events that she didn't ski—that was her husband's thing. Still, it hardly dented her joy of being nestled into her cabin with a view of the world stretching out in front of her.

Hiding behind a clump of wild raspberry bushes, she stared at the deck where a couple danced to what sounded like a Barry White song. When it ended, they walked through the open glass accordion door and into the living room. She heard their voices but could not understand any of the words.

Spotting an open window, Emily crept in closer until she could reach out and touch the round logs of the structure. She was close enough to hear them, but she couldn't see them without exposing herself. She heard her husband Frank's voice. "I've told you. We will not need to go through with the divorce proceedings. She will not be able to blame you privately or officially. She does not know your name yet. I will take care of her before that happens."

"Take care of her? The only way she is not going to embarrass me, take your property and your money is if she is dead."

"Exactly, Christine."

Emily gasped and threw a hand over her mouth. She plastered her back against the wall, praying they had not heard her. *Dead? He wants me dead?*

"And just how are you going to manage that without ending up in prison?"

"Emily and I might be separated but I still have a key to the house. I will hide in there when she is at work."

"And scare her to death?"

"No, I already went into the house a couple of nights ago and searched until I found her gun."

"You can't just shoot her."

"I can if I make it look like a suicide."

"You think you can pull that off?"

"Easy. I'll do it tomorrow. I'll type a suicide note on her computer, print it out and leave it beside her body. Everybody knows she's been depressed lately."

"But everyone will say she is depressed because you left her."

"Baby, I don't care." Frank swept her into his arms. "It is worth any amount of scorn to spend the rest of my life with you."

"I love you, Frank."

In the silence, Emily imagined the embrace and the kiss, and it sickened her. She feared if she stayed any longer, she would vomit on the spot. Footsteps sounded on the oak treads leading to the loft bedroom. The large

French doors of the balcony on the side above her head would give them a more open view of the rugged path she used in her descent.

Emily edged past the deck, keeping under the overhang to shield herself from view. Again and again, she reminded herself to breathe. *Dead. He wants me dead.* Just past the house, she saw a rattler sunning on a boulder. Her adrenaline rush flared even brighter. She made a broad circle around it and behind the house returning to the path she'd taken on her downward trek.

At her car, she fumbled with her keys, dropping them once, before finally opening the door and sliding inside. Her hands shook so hard she could not get the key to slip into the ignition. Slumping forward in defeat, she laid the key ring in her lap, and focused on breathing. Inhale-one-two-three-four-five, exhale-one-two-three-four-five. Within three minutes, her shaking had subsided enough that she was able to turn on the car and pull out onto the road.

She drove down the mountain, pushing Frank's words out of her head only to have them replaced by the sickening sweet music of the Broadway hit, "Tomorrow." Just what she didn't need when tomorrow meant she might be dead.

Reaching the highway, she pulled over at the first coffee shop on the route. Inside, the fragrance of the grounds washed over her like a calming stream. She ordered a whole milk, caramel latte and found a table in the far corner. She needed to make a plan. Her first thought was to leave town, but she had a job. She couldn't stay away forever. And she couldn't leave Romeo in the house without food and water. He'd have to come with her. But where could she go? Who would welcome a 110-pound Great Pyrenees into their hotel or home?

No matter if she did find a place to hide, Frank would find her and eliminate her in some other way. *He wants me dead. Frank always gets what he wants.*

She couldn't count on Romeo to protect her. He might be my dog, but he'd recognize Frank in one sniff and allow him free rein in the house.

She needed a steel-trap plan—one that would scare Frank off for good. *Restraining order? No.* Eavesdropping on a private conversation was not grounds for that. Besides, people violate them all the time and she was sure Frank would do just that. *I could change the locks, but it was impossible to find a locksmith who would come out to the country on a Sunday evening.*

Finishing her coffee, Emily went back to her car with no solution reached. She needed to scare him. How? What could she do? Buy a shotgun and when he opened the door, blast away. *But do I really want to kill him?* In the darkest shadows of her heart, she knew that would permanently make her safe. In those deep depths, she yearned to end his life. But the memories of how much she once loved him penetrated the darkness with bright light and she flinched away from that possibility.

Emily stood outside the door of her home, staring at the knob. *What if he decided not to wait until tomorrow? Am I walking into a trap?* She took a deep breath and jerked the door open. Romeo's little happy barks told her he knew she was home and was glad to see her. She smiled for the first time that day.

She ruffled his neck, attached his leash, and they bounded outside, down the steps and into the woods for a walk. All summer long, she'd widened the deer paths and kept them clear. She looked forward to the colder weather when the paths would need little to no maintenance, when she and Romeo could stomp through the leaves and frolic in the snow.

A tree had fallen in the path. Romeo leaped over it with ease. It was more of a scramble for Emily. She made a mental note to return after work tomorrow with a chain saw and wheelbarrow to clear it out and haul the firewood back to the woodpile.

When Romeo stopped to raise his leg, she noticed the electric fence that ran along her neighbor's cornfield. She froze in place. Electric current was the answer. I need to find a way to give him a severe shock—big enough to make him fear for his life.

The first thing that came to Emily's mind was a toaster in the bathtub. *Good heavens! How would I get him into the bathtub? And what was it I read about the newer toaster safety features?* Romeo tugged at his leash, ready to be on the move again.

When they exited the forest, Emily went into the shed to check that she had fuel for the chain saw. The jerry can was nearly empty. She grabbed it, pulled out her keys and opened the trunk of her car. As she set the container inside, she saw her jumper cables. *I could use those, couldn't I? But how?*

She carried them into the house in hopes that their presence would inspire her thought process. Mindful of the need to make a plan that night, her eyes caught glimpses of the cables on the table, every time she walked by. A half-formed idea flickered through her thoughts prompting her to pick up them and carry them to the entrance to her home.

She allowed the jumpers to dangle in her hands as she stared at the door. *He would use his key, causing him to contact the knob. I could attach one cable to the back of the knob.* She opened the jaws and fastened them there. *The other to…to…to… ah ha! The hinge.* She clipped the other one on there.

The power source? To the right of the door, an electric outlet. Emily hurried to the junk drawer in the kitchen and scrummaged around for a screwdriver. Then she stepped into the utility room and turned off the electricity.

Emily unscrewed the cover plate and examined the plug, studied the connecting wires, pulling them towards her. She'd have to disconnect the wires from the plug. She tried removing one to be certain of what was needed, then reconnected it and pushed it back into the cavity before lightly fastening the cover. Now, she knew what to do in the morning.

But the car. It can't be parked here when he arrives, or he'll know I'm at home. "C'mon, Romeo, we're going bye-bye-car." Romeo jumped to his feet, eager for another walk and the ride. Emily drove a mile away to the country grocery store and parked behind the dumpster. She left a note on the windshield. "Lawrence, I hope you don't mind but I need to leave the car here for a day or two. Your neighbor, Emily."

She walked with her white furry friend back to her house. The walk calmed her a bit, but soon, her heart resumed its ardent tattoo in her chest. She tried to read, to watch TV, to listen to music—but nothing lowered her stress levels.

At least I can get some rest. Emily climbed into her king size bed and patted the space beside her for Romeo to join her. She lay flat on her back, focusing on one part of on one part of her body after another, starting with the toes, willing the muscles to relax. By the time she reached her knees, Romeo's feet were moving and his chest heaving as he chased something in his dreams.

She smiled and her thoughts turned to living a life without the presence of Frank—with not having to see him ever after the divorce was final. Hundreds of options were open when she did not need to account for her time or her actions to anyone, well, except for her employer. She drifted off into a pleasant space where the sun was always shining, spring flowers were in bloom, and the quiet susurrations of a lake caressing the shore never stopped.

Emily woke in a near panic as the first light of the morning cast its faint glow into her room. She glanced at the clock and instantly relaxed. It was dawn, Frank would not come to her house until after he was certain she would have left for work.

She chugged a cup of coffee, took Romeo outside to do his business, then went inside and turned off the electricity. She removed the cover plate and the plugs and connected the red wire to one of the clamps and the black wire to the other. Then, she attached the other ends to the doorknob and the hinge. Not wanting Romeo to accidentally trigger the contraption, she used an ottoman and a couple of dining room chairs to barricade the front entrance on the inside.

Flipping the electricity back on, Emily grabbed another cup of coffee and a chew bone for Romeo and plopped down on the sofa. Romeo reclined at her feet, chewing away on his treat. She stared at the door with relentless concentration. Romeo heard the arrival of a car first. He jumped to his feet and barked. Emily grabbed his collar and ordered him to sit. He complied but was not pleased with the restraint. A low-level growl rumbled in his chest and his neck pulled forward in the collar.

She heard the footsteps crunching on the gravel in the driveway. Second thoughts raced through her mind. She stood to turn off the electricity and through the front window she saw Frank walking to the house. *He wants me dead. He wants me dead.*

She slumped back down on the sofa and held her breath. Sensing her fear, Romeo tensed from his ears to the tip of his tail and his growl grew louder. She heard the key slip into the knob and then an explosive noise, a thump on the porch and all the lights in the house flickered before turning off and the refrigerator drone stilled.

Still holding Romeo's collar, she eased up to the front window and pressing her face to the glass, she could see a bit of the porch and a stretch of Frank from his knees to the soles of his shoes. *I did it! I scared the bejeebers out of him!*

She led Romeo back to the utility panel to flip off the current again and saw that a circuit was blown. Just the same, to be safe, she switched off the main and let go of Romeo's collar. His nails slipped and scratched on the wood floor as he charged to the front door.

Emily removed the furniture blocking the way and detached the cables from the door before peering down through the window. He was still there. She disconnected everything from the outlet and refastened the plugs and the plate before looking out again. That's when she saw the pool of blood spreading around Frank's head.

She jerked open the door and stared down at her estranged husband. "Frank. Frank. Frank!!" She saw no movement in his chest. Stepping over his body, she kneeled at his side and started chest compressions. "Wake up, Frank! Dammit, Frank! Speak to me, Frank!"

She pressed on his chest again and again. No response. She kept it up as her arms grew heavy and her hands grew numb. "You must wake up, Frank!"

"Emily! Emily! Is that you? I saw Frank's car and I thought you might—Emily, is everything okay?"

"Nooooo!" Emily shrieked. "Help me, Mark!"

Mark raced to her side. "What happened? Oh my God, Emily!"

"Help! I can't keep this up much longer."

Mark slid his hands in to replace hers. "How long have you been doing this?"

"I don't know. I don't know."

Mark stopped and pressed two fingers to Frank's throat. "Emily, it's too late."

"No, no, it can't be. I didn't mean to kill him. I just wanted to scare him."

Emily reached forward to resume the chest compressions. Mark grabbed her hands. "Emily, it's too late. His skin is cool to the touch. Frank is gone."

"No. No. No."

"Yes. Now come with me. We'll sit on the bench, and you'll tell me what happened."

With one arm around her shoulders, Mark led her away from the porch and onto the bench nestled beneath an oak tree. "You sit here and don't move. I'll go inside and get a blanket and then we'll talk."

"But Romeo—"

"Don't worry. He and I are old friends," Mark said.

When he stepped into the house, the dog's hackles rose as he barred his teeth. When Romeo took a deep sniff, the signs of aggression were replaced by a wagging tail. Mark grabbed the throw off the sofa and threw it over Frank before snapping the lead onto Romeo and leading him out the back door and over to Emily.

Sitting down beside her, Mark said, "Honestly, Emily, I thought one day I'd come over here and find you dead on the floor. I never thought I'd be looking at Frank's body on your porch. I must say I'm shocked. Start at the beginning and tell me everything that happened."

Emily explained her afternoon adventure out to the cabin and the words Frank had said. Repeating them made her tremble.

"Oh, Emily, you should have called me last night. I would have slept on the sofa and stayed with you all day."

"Then, he could have shot you, too. He was capable of it, Mark."

"Okay. Then what?"

She detailed her plan and how she put it into action. "I just wanted to scare him, Mark. I swear to you. I didn't intend to kill him."

"I believe you, Emily. Now, we need to make sure no one else knows you did. Stay here. I will take care of you—of everything from now on."

Emily's brow furrowed. *Even in this situation that response felt over the top. What did that mean? Was I reading too much into his words?*

Mark studied the situation on the porch. "He looks like he hit his head on the railings when he fell back from the door. The blood pooled on the concrete is a bigger problem."

"Bleach. I have some bleach."

"No, when the police come out here, and they will, since you are still his wife, they will smell it and that would nail you to the wall. I've got paint that covers up stains and traps moisture. I'll paint the whole porch. All we need is a little bit of luck that they won't find the body before the paint dries."

"I'm confused, Mark. How could they not see it? It's in the middle of the porch. I need to call 9-1-1 right away."

"No, absolutely not." Mark strode across the lawn to where she sat and snatched the cell out of her hand. "I told you I will take care of you from now on. I've got a foolproof plan to get rid of the body."

"A foolproof plan? Already? How can you come up with that at the drop of a hat? This doesn't sound right, Mark."

"Emily, I've thought about it for years—ever since he outed me, and I lost my job as basketball coach at the high school. He did that. He told everyone and made-up stories about my interactions with the students. None of the kids came forward because nothing inappropriate ever happened. But the truth didn't matter—Frank just needed a good story to tell the school board and I was gone."

"So, you've been thinking about disposing of his body for years?"

"Yes. Years. Remember when he had brake failure coming down the mountain?"

Emily nodded.

"That was me. But it didn't work."

Emily's jaw dropped as she struggled to regain her equilibrium.

"Remember his food poisoning? Me, too. Damn, that was a failure, too. Now, you've made my day."

"I thought you didn't need to work because of your trust fund, yet you wanted to kill him because you lost your job?"

Mark kneeled beside her and took her hands in his as he gazed into her eyes. "It was more than that, Emily. More than anything I wanted you."

"What?' She struggled to release her hands, but he tightened his grip. She tried to rise but he pulled her down.

"By killing Frank, you made my dreams come true. We'll sell the cabin and this house, and you'll move into mine. With my trust fund income, you will never need to work again."

"But I like my job, Mark."

"You just think you do because you must work to support yourself. You are merely making the best of a bad situation. But now you don't need to work. I will take care of you forever. In fact, you will never need to leave the house. Anything you want, I can get delivered to our door. My trust fund is probably bigger than you suspected."

Emily's mind raced. *If a person acted crazy, you need to humor them while you look for escape.* "I think you better get busy getting the body out of sight. Someone could drop by."

Mark's eyes flashed and his brow lowered. "Are you expecting someone?"

"No, honestly, no."

"When people say 'honestly,' I get suspicious. He rose to his feet and loomed over her. "Are you expecting a delivery today?"

"No. But you never know. You have unexpected deliveries, too, don't you?"

His shoulders dropped. "I suppose so." He stared down at her. "Well, I guess you are right." He walked back to the porch. He looked back at her and asked, "Could you get me one of those green heavy duty trash bags? I don't want the blood to leak in his car when I take him away."

"Okay."

"Nothing flimsy—a heavy leaf bag would be best. I need to wrap his head."

Emily felt the bile rise into her throat. She swallowed a few times to make it subside. "Sure, Mark. Right back." She entered the back door and into the utility room where she located a bag and carried it out to her neighbor.

"Thanks," he said, pulling the blanket down from Frank's head. "Maybe you could search his pockets for his cell. We'll need to check his car, too. If he was coming here to kill you and he has any sense, he would have left it at home or his place or at work, but we need to be sure."

Emily took three steps backward, shaking her head.

"Of course, you can't do it. My dear, sweet Emily. Go back inside, stretch out and relax. I'll take care of everything for you. I always will."

His smirky smile made Emily want to puke. She wanted to run but forced herself to walk slowly to the back door. *Do I call 9-1-1 now or do I wait until he leaves with the body? If he catches me on the landline, what will he do? I don't know. I don't think he's predictable. Would Mark kill me if I defy him?"*

She fought the panicked anxiety rising in her chest. *I need to think.* She ran through her options. Nothing seemed right. She heard a loud thump and rushed to the front window. Mark had just dropped Frank's body into the car, slammed the rear hatch shut and trudged back to the house.

"Well, that's that," he said walking through the front door. "I moved the door mat over top of the blood pool in case someone comes with a package. I'll get rid of the body first and then I'll come back, clean up and paint the porch." He placed his hands on her upper arms. "You can stop worrying now, Emily. I've got everything under control. I'll fix you a cup of tea before I go. You need to find a book to read and crawl under the covers. I'll be in with your cup in a flash." He smiled at her again and her skin crawled.

She followed his orders out of fear. When Mark set the tea on her nightstand and planted a kiss on her forehead, she forced a smile. She listened until the tires-on-gravel sound gave way as Mark pulled out into the road. She worried he would turn around and come back—that it was all a trap. The clock ticked away the minutes. Romeo nudged her hand, and she went into action.

Down the hall and into the office, she picked up the landline receiver and prayed she would hear a dial tone. After an interminable split second, it arrived. She pressed 9-1-1.

"9-1-1. What is your emergency?"

"I accidentally killed my estranged husband."

"Is he still breathing?"

"No. And his body has been moved. You need to find my neighbor."

"Slow down, ma'am, and explain your situation with more detail."

"You need to hurry. You need to catch him. He is driving my husband's vehicle—a red Jeep Liberty with license plate HWP-219. My husband's body is in back of the car."

"What is your location, ma'am?"

"First, you need to alert officers to stop Mark Springer. He took my cell phone, so I could not call the police and my husband's body is in the back of the vehicle."

"Do you think he killed your husband?"

A sigh of exasperation burst through Emily's lips. "No ma'am. I did that. I will be waiting here at 1267 Warbler Lane. I will not go anywhere. I will give you my full cooperation. Just find that car. I'll stay on the line until you do. Just please hurry."

Emily put the phone on speaker and kneeled to scratch Romeo's chest and ears. "Sorry, old boy, I'll have to leave you for a while, maybe for a long time. As soon as I can, I'll call Laura. She'll take good care of you, and I'll never forget you." The sound of his wagging tail echoed as it thumped against the desk. Her tears fell on his head and soon she heard a siren coming down her country road. She was still alive, but her life as she knew it, was dead.

The Death Doula
Libby Hall

I can see why people think I killed my husband, Donny. I am a death doula. That means I am hired to sit with people as they die. I also help my clients and their families manage the practicalities of dying, from paperwork to wakes to delivering letters to long lost lovers. I've organized financial statements, opened safety deposit boxes, and arranged for all kinds of after-life ceremonies. I also study natural medicine and have often treated folks in town with natural remedies instead of over-the-counter medicines they can't afford. Since my doula job isn't covered by insurance, I can charge whatever I think the job is worth, balanced against what I think my client can pay.

For the record, I've never killed anyone by "helping things along," not even when it would have been the kindest thing I could do for them. I certainly didn't kill Mama Pierce or Donny.

Mama Pierce was 62 years old when she became my client. Her son Jemmy was the only family left to take care of her. Jemmy worked long hours at the paper mill by the river as a mill operator. He couldn't take off work to take care of her every day, and he needed to sleep at night.

When Mama Pierce learned she had end stage bone cancer, she called me. I was happy to take her on without charge. Mama Pierce had done me some kindnesses in the past when I was young and prone to making very bad decisions.

Jemmy was deeply religious and spent half his time at home on his knees, asking God to rid Mama of her pain. Pastor Jennings came by once a week to give Mama Pierce communion. I made myself scarce when he came. I don't much believe in God, and all that praying just makes me uncomfortable. In the days before she sank into unconsciousness, Mama Pierce fought to hold back her cries as the cancer triggered her nerves. I worked with hospice to stack her drugs to manage the pain as best I could, but sometimes it was a just too much, and Mama Pierce shrieked. On those days, when he was home, poor Jemmy held and rocked her. Most of the time it was just me.

When I stayed with Mama Pierce at night, I tended to her as quietly as I could. One night, her pain was so bad she screamed. The pain had to go somewhere, and I could see the scream made her feel a bit better. Unfortunately, it woke Jemmy up.

"Mama?" he called, rushing in. She was quietly moaning. I stood by the dresser putting away the meds.

"Can't you give her nothin'?" Jemmy asked.

"I'm sorry," I said. "You know I can't. They regulate all the drugs down to the last drop."

Something hard crept into his eyes that I didn't like. "You know what I mean."

I sighed. Just because I knew a lot about herbs and could make a good poultice didn't mean I would just brew up some hemlock and finish the job for the right price. I've had family members beg me while they weep, because they know their loved one wouldn't have wanted to linger that way. I've been told I'm cruel, letting them suffer when the hospice drugs aren't enough to dull the pain.

"Jemmy, your Mama's in a lot of pain, and we're doing the best we can. She's trying so hard to be brave for you, so go on back to bed and let her do what she needs to do to get through tonight."

Jemmy's shoulders fell. "Ain't there something you can do?" he begged.

I hesitated, then dug into my bag that I carried with me on the job. It had the notebooks I used to document everything for the hospice workers: medicines taken, dosage, time, appetite, food eaten, and so on. I also brought various homemade herbal teas. Sometimes they were helpful when a loved one was anxious, or when I needed something to keep me awake.

"Here," I said, taking a tea bag of chamomile and peppermint out. "I'll brew her some of this and see if she'll drink it." I didn't think she would, but it was enough to get Jemmy to bed. Tears ran down his cheeks while he worked his jaw. After a few seconds he straightened his shoulders and went back to his room.

The next day, Mama Pierce's body finally started to loosen its grip on life. Her breath hitched every now and then; sometimes there were long pauses between inhales and exhales as she eased her way from life to death. Jemmy had gone to work, and at lunchtime I called the mill to tell him he should come home. The foreman said Jemmy hadn't shown up. He had assumed Mama Pierce had passed.

All afternoon I held Mama Pierce's hand as I listened to her breathing slowly, and finally come to a stop. Still, no Jemmy.

I waited for him as long as I could before calling the police. As a last resort I called Jimbo's Bar, and finally found him. It wasn't the first time I'd had to call the bar to find a family member, or my husband, Donny for that matter.

Just as the funeral home was arriving to take Mama Pierce, Jemmy slammed open the door and staggered into the bedroom where I was tidying up.

"You bitch!" He screamed at me and lurched over to the bed. Mama Pierce looked like she was asleep, her mouth gently hanging open. He grabbed her hand, then dropped it like it was scalding hot, and turned to me.

"You said you would give her tea to make her sleep, not kill her! She wasn't ready. God wasn't ready, but you think you know better than God, don't you?" He took a step toward me. I backed toward the door. As he took another step, I spied an empty syringe carelessly left on the bedside table. I quickly grabbed it and hid it from view. It wasn't much of a weapon, but it might slow him down if he started swinging. Foolishly I tried to reason with him as I backed away, feeling my way out the bedroom door.

"Jemmy, don't do this. Your mama was sick and in pain. It was her time. She never woke up again after you went to bed. I didn't give her anything."

"Get out of this house, you demon!" He screamed, following me into the front room. "Get out and go back to hell where you belong!"

I fled through the open front door, out to my car. The hearse pulled in as I was leaving, followed by Pastor Jennings' Oldsmobile. I rolled down my window and briefly let them know what they were walking into. In the background I could hear Jemmy weeping.

*****

A week later I was in the grocery store when Donny's first wife Charlotte came round the aisle and nearly ran into my cart. Instinctively I reached up to touch my cheek. I'd done my makeup carefully before leaving the house and worn a mock turtleneck top to hide the fingerprint bruises Donny had left on my cheek and neck the night before. Charlotte took one look and nodded.

"Looks like we're due for a talk," she said. Our town was hardly a town, more like a village. Even so, Charlotte and I were just far enough apart in age that we had never really known each other, except for the fact that we both had married Donny Fowler. That day in the Food Lion, the six-year difference between us looked more like twenty. Charlotte was wire-thin and wearing a bandana around her balding head. Her skin and the whites of her eyes had a familiar, yellow tint.

"Hi Charlotte," I said, pretending to look for something while keeping the bruised half of my face turned away.

"He won't stop, you know," she said. Her voice sounded like it was being dragged across a cheese grater.

I pretended not to know what she was talking about. "Won't stop what?"

"That." Charlotte reached over and gently pressed the bruise on my cheek. "He won't stop. I don't think he can. That's why I left."

I didn't answer. There was nothing to say; I just hadn't gotten up the courage to leave yet. I had nowhere to go.

She shrugged. "Either way, that's not what we got to talk about. I want to hire you to help me die. That's what you do – help people die, right?"

I breathed a sigh of relief. I looked at her this time, really looked beyond the obvious signs of illness, the chemo, and the radiation. Charlotte had been a striking woman with high cheekbones, blond hair, and blue eyes. She and Donny married right out of high school and stayed married for ten years before she left him. That day, there were circles under her eyes and her cheekbones were origami planes. They had been divorced for four years by the time Donny and I met at Jimbo's. Never in a million years did I ever think I would be Charlotte's death doula. Donny only had venomous things to say about Charlotte, and she never gave me the time of day except to look at me sadly when we saw each other in town. I naively used to think she was jealous that she didn't have Donny anymore. Now, I know different.

Charlotte dove into her story right there in the baking aisle, telling me about her cancer, and that she just needed help getting things organized. Her sister Sara would be coming at the end to stay, and she wanted things tidied up so Sara wouldn't have to deal with it afterward. We agreed on a price, and that I would start the next day.

Her first task for me was to deliver a letter to Pastor Jennings. "You make sure this one only goes to him. Don't let that busybody secretary Mimi Dewar take it for him," she warned. "For his eyes only."

It wasn't the first time I'd delivered a confessional letter, and part of me wondered what secrets Charlotte hid that she needed to unload. For three weeks I helped Charlotte get her insurance claims together, sort through her hospital bills, get her will in order, and arrange for the furniture in the house to be sold after she was gone.

Twice a week Pastor Jennings came to see Charlotte, though I don't think she enjoyed it very much. To give them some space I ran errands or weeded the flowers in the front yard. She told me sometimes she pretended to be asleep while Pastor Jennings droned on, praying over her, and blessing her this way and that.

"Why do you let him come?" I asked.

"Oh, he's been trying to bring me back to the flock for years." Charlotte shrugged. "I'm just covering my bases."

For two days during my last week with her, I helped Charlotte write letters that I was to personally deliver. Most of them were apologies or thank you notes.

On my last day, when it was time for me to leave, Charlotte handed me one more envelope; this one had my name on it.

"I want you to put this somewhere nobody can get to it but you. Every woman needs some go money."

"Charlotte, I can't—"

She grabbed my hand and put the envelope in it. "I'm not taking it with me, and Sarah doesn't need it. Consider it a bonus."

I flushed and stammered "Thank you" before turning for the door.

"You got this, Lily!" Charlotte called as I left.

When Sara arrived, I stopped by to get her caught up. She paid me what was in the contract and thanked me for all the help. I stopped in to see Charlotte a couple of times after that, but Sara was doing a great job. Charlotte never mentioned Donny to me again.

*****

It was cold on the morning when the police came to our front door. I'd been up since six o'clock, restless after Donny staggered home late the night before, smelling like weed. I pretended to be asleep while he muttered and rummaged around for his sweatshirt. I heard the clink of a bourbon bottle and buried my head under the pillow, hoping he would leave. When Donny took the boat keys off the hook and went out the back door I sighed with relief. The boat motor started up and he took off. It was amazing how much bourbon that man could put away and still get up and fish. I'd forgotten it was striper season. These trips were going to happen every day Donny didn't have to work at the new hospital construction site.

Later, when I heard a car drive up, I peeked out the window and saw a county patrol car. I expected to see Donny in handcuffs in the back seat. Instead, Sheriff Tate and another officer I didn't recognize walked up to the front door and rang the bell.

"Lily, I have some questions I need to ask you," Sherriff Tate said. "Can we come in?" Numb, I nodded. Policeman at your door asking questions was never a good thing, if *Law and Order* had any truth to it.

"Did you see Donny this morning?" Sheriff Turner asked.

I shrugged. "He left pretty early to go fishing. Why?" I asked.

Sheriff Tate sighed. "We found his boat crashed onto the rocks at Kestrel Point."

I nodded. The Kestrel Point rocks aren't marked, but every local knows where they are located. Beyond the rocks, the lake's depth drops to about 60 feet where the original riverbed ran. God only knew what massive catfish lurked down there, hiding beside sunken trees and logs as they waited for their dinner to float by.

"Is he ok?" I asked, trying not to think about the stack of bills we had sitting on the counter. We couldn't afford medical bills on top of everything else. The extra money from my job was barely keeping us afloat as it was, no matter how much Donny hated it.

"I'm sorry, Lily, but we only found the boat. Donny's missing."

"Missing?"

Sherriff Tate nodded. "I wish I could tell you more."

Shaken and not sure how to respond, a spark of fear ignited in my chest. I absently touched the latest bruise under my eye. I hadn't put makeup on yet. No, I wasn't one bit sorry or surprised to hear that Donny had crashed his boat, but if he was going to do that, he'd better be hurt or dead. Missing was an unknown I couldn't control.

The other officer frowned "Is there anything you'd like to add, Ms. Fowler?"

I jerked my hand down. If they knew about Donny and the way he treated me, they'd probably think I did something to him. "No sir," I said.

The other man stared for a moment, then nodded. "We'll let you know if we find him."

"Is there something I can do?" I asked. I didn't want to, but I knew they'd expect me to ask.

Sherriff Tate shook his head. "It's better if you let us do our job. It's early yet. We'll find him."

Sheriff Tate and the detective took my statement and asked me more questions, but it was pretty clear they already knew he'd been at Jimbo's Bar. Apparently, several people said he'd had more than a few, and Pastor Jennings had helped him to his car. Even the good Pastor was known to have a drink or two now and again at Jimbo's. Donny always said he was just trying to drum up business.

"We'll let you know when we find him, Ms. Fowler," the other officer said.

I nodded, trying to look like a stunned, grieving wife. I must have pulled it off, because Sheriff Tate asked, "Is there anyone I can call, Lily?"

I shook my head. Both my parents were killed in a car crash seven years ago, and when I'd taken up with Donny, he slowly isolated me from my friends. Other than trips into town and when people needed my services, I hardly saw anyone.

Sheriff Tate blew out some air and shook his head. "All right then," he said. He and the officer got into the car and left.

They didn't find Donny's body right away. Between the man-sized catfish and the massive logs cluttering up the bottom of the riverbed, none of the rescue divers would stay down there very long. Most people knew Donny was an ugly drinker, but when he went missing people started looking at me sideways when I came into town. Over the next couple of weeks, my doula job requests started dropping off. While the adults were suspicious, the kids were downright scared of me. Several times I caught them sneaking around, daring each other to "touch" the witch's house.

Folks still came to me for natural medicine, though. It was a whole lot cheaper to get some "flu tea" from me than paying for Nyquil, and I could do a mean butterfly bandage if they couldn't afford stitches. Sometimes I even took care of pets.

When Laney Abel came by to get some of my anti-itch salve, she told me Sheriff Tate had been asking Pastor Jennings a lot of questions. Seems he had been talking a lot about 'God's will' and how the Devil was in our town, making things happen 'before their time.'

"And don't you know, Jemmy Pierce was standing right up there at the pulpit with him," Laney said. "He was cryin' and blabberin' on about how his Mama wasn't supposed to be gone so soon, and he was just sure the Devil had come in disguise to take her from us. 'Course, we all know it's a load of crap."

I was surprised to hear that Pastor Jennings allowed that kind of talk, much less allowing someone else sharing the spotlight, but then again, he loved theatrics. Personally, I think he allowed it because he thought my being a death doula was trampling on his territory.

The day after Laney came for her salve, Sherriff Tate stopped by again, the same officer trailing behind.

"Sherriff?" I asked, coming to the door.

"Lily this is Detective Moore."

In the living room Detective Moore started asking more questions. "Ma'am, what do you do with the medical equipment you use while you're with your patients?"

I was taken back by the question. I was meticulous, keeping records and leaving everything labeled and accounted for. "I don't use any medical equipment, other than dispensing pills, emptying bedpans and using wheelchairs," I said. "Hospice does anything more involved than that. Why?"

"There is a hypodermic needle missing from Mrs. Pierce's house. Do you happen to know where it is?"

I drew a blank for a moment, then remembered the needle I'd grabbed when Jemmy had come at me. I explained what had happened, then went to look for the needle. It wasn't in my bag or in my car, or anywhere else.

"But you did take it with you?" Detective Moore asked.

"I don't know what happened to it — I must have thrown it away."

Detective Moore frowned. "Well, if you locate it, please let us know immediately."

After he left, I ransacked the house again, but no luck. I knew hospice tracked their equipment so there could be no funny business with the drugs. I had never misplaced any medication or equipment before, and I didn't like the way Detective Moore was asking.

The next day, strange things began happening at my house. When I came back from the store, I found the shed to my herb house open. I kept it shut but never bothered to lock it because everyone knew Donny hated trespassers and that he had guns. Some of my bottles of dried herbs had been moved and replaced in the wrong places. I always label them and organize them by symptoms they relieved. All herbs can be harmful or deadly if prepared incorrectly or administered in the wrong dosage. Someone had been in there. Most likely it was the kids; one of them must have won huge bragging rights by getting into the shed.

In a locked wooden box under the table where I worked were the more dangerous herbs, the ones I used only for very limited, specific illnesses. I never used the ones in the box on people. Sometimes I was asked to help pets cross the rainbow bridge if they couldn't afford the vet or couldn't stand to put the beloved animal out of its misery themselves. Only then would I bring out the wooden box.

The next day Sara came by to tell me Charlotte was starting to go downhill and asked if I wanted to come see her. I drove out to Charlotte's house the next day, but she was already unconscious. Her cheekbones were sharp, her skin was gray, and her breathing was slow and labored. Sara let me sit alone with her for a bit. Since auditory processing is the last thing to go, I started talking, telling Charlotte all about what had been happening. Somehow it seemed like she was the only one who would understand.

When Sara came back into the room, she handed me an envelope.

"What's this?"

Sara shrugged. "Charlotte told me to tell you this is the last one. It's for Sheriff Tate, but you're not to give it to him until she's gone. I figured I may as well do it now before things get crazy."

I sighed, took the letter, and got to my feet. "Alright. You'll call me when it happens?"

Sara nodded. She looked exhausted.

I hadn't been home twenty minutes when Sheriff Tate and Detective Moore pulled into the driveway again. *What now?* I wondered.

When I answered the door, Sherriff Tate showed me a warrant and began searching the house. For what, I had no idea – he wouldn't say. Detective Moore went to the shed. When I looked inside, he was examining each of the bottles.

"Are these yours?" he asked.

I nodded.

"What do you use them for?"

I explained and made sure he knew how careful I was. "Has something happened? Is someone sick?" My stomach lurched at the thought of one of my teas making someone sick. I could only decide what to give based on the information folks shared with me. Detective Moore didn't answer. Instead, he silently placed each of the bottles in a bag and labeled it. I stared in disbelief. It had taken me years to collect and prepare their contents. They were heading out of the shed when Detective Moore spotted the box under the table.

My heart nearly stopped. The contents of those bottles would raise a lot of questions.

"What's this?" he asked, opening the lid.

Inside, the rest of my bottles were neatly lined up like little, deadly soldiers.

He lifted each one, read the label and raised his eyebrows. He looked at me for an explanation. I didn't bother. The less I said the better. Sheriff Tate removed the handcuffs from his belt. "I'm sorry Lily, but you're under arrest.

"For what?" I asked.

"The murder of Donny Fowler."

"What?" I gasped.

"We found his body two days ago. A bottle of bourbon was still in his pants pocket. When they opened it, it smelled weird, so they did an autopsy."

"But—"

Sherriff Tate cut me off and read me my rights as he firmly pressed my shoulders until I sank into the back seat of the car. Just before he shut the door, I remembered Charlotte's letter.

"Wait! I have something for you." I jerked my head toward the house. "There's a letter for you in my purse from Charlotte, Donny's first wife. Her sister Sara asked me to deliver it to you when she's passed. I guess you'd better take it now."

Sherriff Tate went back into the house, retrieved the letter, and threw it on the front seat.

*****

I couldn't make bail, so I was in jail for a while before they let me out and I learned what really happened. Turns out Donny didn't just take his anger out on me and Charlotte. Charlotte's letter to Sheriff Tate was the evidence they needed to find the real killer.

Dear Sheriff,

I don't know if it will do any good, but I have to speak up. I'm waiting to write after I've gone so you can't get me in trouble for knowing what he did and not saying anything. Not that it would matter anyway, but as the "good" Pastor says, "You gotta get right with God."

I found out Pastor Tate's daughter Penny was dating Donny while we were married. She was fifteen and he was twenty. When Donny got her pregnant, she told him, and he knocked her out. Penny came to me and told me everything. I guess she figured it was the best way to get him back. As you can imagine, I was shocked, but we were both scared of what Donny would do. You know his temper well enough. I had to admire Penny's guts, coming to me of all people. I took her to Richmond to have an abortion, and for my trouble Donny broke two of my ribs and gave me two black eyes. I don't know if he did anything to Penny — I didn't see her after that.

Since I'm dying, I've been trying to come clean on a lot of things. You should know I wrote Pastor Jennings a letter, telling him what happened. He was angry as a father can be, someone abusing his little girl like that. He's been coming around twice a week to try and save me, to bring me back to Christ. Sometimes I pretend to be asleep, so I don't have to talk to him. One time, and I know you only have my say-so, while I was pretending to be asleep so I wouldn't have to answer him, he told me he'd made sure I'd never run into Donny in the afterlife. He told me he knew Lily helped some of his parishioners from time to time by giving them her teas and powders, and he'd fixed up a nice cure for "that Devil, Donny."

I couldn't let on I'd heard, but when Donny went missing, I knew I had to say something. I'll save you some time. Pastor Jennings killed that son of a bitch. If you need proof, check the bottles in Lily's shed. He said he took the one that had hemlock in it, boiled it up and put it in the bourbon he gave Donny at Jimbo's. If you look, you'll find that empty bottle of hemlock somewhere on the side of the road between his house and Jimbo's.

I won't ask you to go easy on him because he must have wanted to make it look like Lily did it. But for the record, Donny deserved it. That man was mean as a snake and the world's a better place without him in it. I'm just sorry I won't get to enjoy it that way.

They did find my empty bottle of hemlock on the road near Jimbo's. Detective Moore also found the needle I'd taken from Mama Pierce's house in my shed, but in the end it didn't amount to anything; there wasn't any residue other than the meds she was supposed to have taken. When they interviewed Mimi Dewar, Pastor Jennings' secretary, she told them he'd gone into a rage the day I delivered Charlotte's letter. Poor Penny Jennings had to relive the worst time of her life, confirming what was in Charlotte's letter. Pastor Jennings' trial is coming up in a few weeks, and it promises to be the performance he's been practicing for.

Death in the Deep
Frances Aylor

It's not easy to say no to your best friend.

Even when she asks for something you absolutely, positively, without a doubt don't want to do. Like going on a long weekend to the island of Tortola with her and her husband Josh. His company had had a good year, and he wanted to celebrate by taking the top members of his staff on a weekend retreat. Brittany begged me to go along to entertain her while the rest of the group was tied up in meetings.

The only thing is, Josh used to be the love of my life. Until Brittany stole him from me.

Brittany and I had met him at a fraternity mixer ten years ago, during our senior year in college. He had a reputation as a womanizer, working his way through half the sororities on campus, leaving broken promises and broken hearts behind. Despite that, I was pulled in by his smile, warm and engaging, and by those blue eyes that focused on mine, making me feel that I was the most important person he'd ever met. Soon we were inseparable. Seeing him walk into a room made my heart beat a little faster.

Then one night I got back early to the apartment I shared with Brittany. Moaning noises came from her bedroom. I walked in on the two of them, tangled together in the blankets. I whirled around and ran out of the apartment. Brittany called out, "Nicole, wait, wait," as she chased after me, wrapping a sheet around her naked body.

I couldn't face her after what she had done. I avoided the apartment for weeks, sending a friend to gather my books and clothes, camping out with anyone who had a spare bed. Each night I cursed Josh and Brittany, but I was also angry at myself for being such a fool. Every woman on campus knew his reputation. Somehow I thought our relationship would be different.

To my surprise, the two of them got married shortly after graduation. I turned down Brittany's request to be a bridesmaid. Found the cheapest thing on their registry to send as a token gift. Skipped the wedding but hung out at the bar during their reception, downing vodka shots one after another while I flirted with every man who didn't have a woman hanging on his arm.

Now, years later, I am mostly past any physical longing for him. The three of us live in the same small town of Bridgewater. Josh and I still flirt a little at parties. Maybe our New Year's Eve kisses are a bit too friendly. But there is no lust anymore, none of that hot, aching longing that once had woken me up, night after night, causing me to pace frantically back and forth until the black passions of the night faded into the graying dawn.

I have buried deep inside me the anger and the jealousy that I once felt, convincing myself that Brittany is still my best friend. But tagging along on their Caribbean vacation was a huge ask. I couldn't see myself as odd man out while the two of them enjoyed long walks and romantic dinners. She insisted it wouldn't be like that. Josh would be tied up in conference rooms the entire weekend, while she and I lounged on the beach, reading racy novels and sipping fruity drinks.

She pleaded. She cajoled. And even though I wasn't totally convinced, and this trip seemed as appealing as a root canal, she finally wore me down, and I said yes.

*****

Tortola, in the British Virgin Islands, was an explosion of color: mountains covered with lush green vegetation; sandy beaches lined with palm trees; clear turquoise water. The island had been ravaged by hurricanes back in 2017, with fierce winds tearing down buildings and tossing yachts up onto the shore, but everyone had worked hard since then to restore the island to its former state. Now only a few roofless houses on the hillsides were evidence of that crippling devastation.

Our hotel was a sprawling, red-roofed structure wrapped with shaded decks. Josh stood at the check-in desk, passing out the agenda for the weekend. Meetings to discuss marketing strategy, new product development, and evaluating the competition were squeezed in between mountain biking, scuba diving, and a beach volleyball tournament.

I picked up my room key and turned to Brittany. "I thought you said the weekend would be endless meetings. Sounds like there's plenty of downtime. Tell me again why I'm here."

"I needed your opinion," she said.

"On what? Best trails for mountain biking? How to perfect a killer volleyball serve?"

"Something else. You'll see."

The two of us spent the afternoon on the beach, swimming in the warm water and then slathering on suntan lotion as cabana boys brought us fresh towels and fruity drinks.

Dinner was at a hilltop restaurant with creaking ceiling fans and expansive windows, their shutters folded back to expose panoramic views of the ocean. Josh pulled out a chair at one end of a long table. The others scrambled to sit near him, eager to have the ear of the boss. Brittany and I, the only non-employees, were relegated to the opposite end.

"Don't you want to sit near Josh?" I asked. "I'm sure someone will trade seats with you."

"No, it's fine. I don't need to sit in on boring conversations about work."

"If you're sure …"

"It's fine," she repeated, smoothing her napkin, checking everyone out. "You're much better company than any of those guys."

"Do you know all of them?"

"Most have been with the company for years." Brittany gestured toward a thin woman with severely plucked eyebrows and an angular face, her long dark hair gathered up into a messy bun. "That's Eileen. She heads up marketing. Josh thinks a lot of her." She sipped her wine.

"And the two guys down there who look like middle linebackers are Davis and Gerald. They're in product development."

"What about the two very cerebral guys sitting across from them? The ones who look like college professors?"

"That's Anthony and Fitz. They're both finance guys. Josh says each of them has more brains than the rest of the group put together."

I picked up my menu. "And the voluptuous blond at the end of the table, sitting next to Josh? The one whose boobs are falling out of her top?"

"That's Laura. Supposedly a social media expert."

"She looks young."

Brittany shrugged. "Just out of college. But Josh is pleased with her work. Said she was highly recommended."

Laura's shoulder brushed against Josh as she reached for her wine. "I'll bet that's not all he's pleased with," I said.

Josh tapped his glass to get everyone's attention. "We've had a good year, folks," he said, standing as he surveyed the group. "Not quite as good as I expected, but good, nonetheless. Revenues were up strongly. Earnings were a little soft, but I think we can fix that." He glanced at Anthony and Fitz. "I want you guys to take a deep dive into the numbers. See if we can tweak things a bit to improve our margins."

"You got it, boss," Anthony said, adjusting his glasses.

"Thanks. I have full confidence in you both." Josh shifted his gaze around the table, pinning each of them with those blue eyes that had once mesmerized me. "I'm so proud of this team. We're going to work during this retreat to figure out how to make next year even better. Tomorrow afternoon we'll focus on marketing. Eileen, you'll take point on that one."

"I'm ready," she said. "I've got a lot of good ideas to share with you folks."

"Excellent. But first we'll have some fun. Tomorrow morning we're going scuba diving, exploring the *RMS Rhone*. It sank over a hundred years ago during a hurricane and is one of the best dive sites around.

Any of you who don't want to join us can go hiking, hang out on the beach, or do whatever you want. Now let's enjoy dinner."

Josh ordered appetizers for the table and several bottles of wine. We were all pretty buzzed by the time our entrees arrived.

"OMG," Laura moaned in a wine-enhanced volume that carried to our end of the table. "Josh, you've got to try this lobster." She speared a piece with her fork and offered it to him.

He shook his head. "No, thanks. I'm more of a steak guy."

"No, you've got to try this." She leaned in close. "It's the best thing I've ever had in my mouth."

Josh laughed. "If it's that good, I guess I'll have to try it."

"Give me a break." Brittany glared at him as his lips edged the lobster off her fork. "Do they have to act like that right in front of me?"

"Brittany, relax," I said. "Josh would never cheat on you. He dated lots of women when we were in college, but you were the one he married."

Brittany picked up her wine glass. "Nicole, you are so naive. Josh cheated on me six months after our wedding. And he hasn't stopped since."

"I can't believe that." All these years I had convinced myself that Josh had finally found his soulmate, that his feelings for Brittany justified tossing me aside. "He loves you. You love him. You're the perfect couple."

She sipped her wine. "Don't think so."

"Then why do you stay with him?"

She sighed. "Because I love him. Because my world would be empty without him. And yet …"

"And yet?"

"I despise what he's done to me. How he's turned me into this jealous harpy who suspects every woman around him of being his lover. Unfortunately, most of the time I'm right." She turned to me. "And I know I did the same thing to you. Sleeping with him when I knew how much you cared for him. You must have hated me. Maybe you still do."

"It was a long time ago. Forgive and forget."

"You're a better person than I am."

"So, is this why you brought me here? To run interference for you between Josh and his latest girlfriend?"

"Something like that."

"What did you have in mind? Do you want me to slip some poison into her wine? Break her leg while she's playing volleyball?"

"They sound like great ideas."

"Okay, then," I laughed. "I'll think about it tonight. See what I can come up with. And by tomorrow, maybe I'll have figured out how to get even with both of them."

She grinned. "And that's why you're my best friend."

*****

Back in my room after dinner, I had just dropped off to sleep when a loud rumble of thunder rippled through the night. I stepped onto my balcony to check for an approaching storm. The wind had picked up, and dark clouds covered the moon.

Below me, I heard voices. "When do I get my money?" a woman asked.

"Be patient. It takes a while to make these things work."

"Oh, come on," she said. "You're the finance guy. Cooking the books should be easy for you."

A flash of lightning illuminated their faces. It was Laura and Anthony. As it started to rain, they moved farther underneath my balcony.

"Josh is getting suspicious," Anthony said. "You heard him talk about earnings being a little weak. How he wants Fitz and me to take a closer look at expenses."

"That's your problem, not mine. If you don't pay up, I'll tell him that you've been embezzling from the company. It won't end well for you."

"I'll tell him it was all your idea."

"Oh, please, who do you think he'll believe?" she said. "Some finance geek who he already suspects is not doing a good job for him? Or the gorgeous blond he's sleeping with?"

The rain came down harder, hammering against the roof, pinging through the downspouts. Anthony's words were garbled. "His wife already suspects …" The rest of his sentence was swept away by the wind.

I needed to get closer. A board creaked as I kneeled down to hear better.

"What was that?" Laura said. "Is somebody up there?"

I froze in place, hoping to hear more. But they scurried away as the rain pelted down.

*****

Brittany knocked on my door early the next morning. "Are you ready? We have time for a quick coffee before we leave for scuba."

I opened the door. "I'm not going. You know I don't like diving. I always start to hyperventilate when the water closes over my head."

"Concentrate on your breathing," she said. "Slow and steady. Inhale for four. Exhale for four. Over and over again. Like Darth Vader in *Star Wars*."

"As I recall, Darth Vader came to an untimely end."

"But not while he was scuba diving. And neither will you."

"That's easy for you to say." I sat down on the bed. "You've been diving forever. I've only done it a few times in open water. And I was terrified each time."

"So, today's a good day to conquer your fear. Now get your suit on and meet me downstairs. I'll grab a coffee for you."

"Wait. There's something I need to tell you first." I relayed the conversation I had overheard between Anthony and Laura.

She dropped down on the bed beside me. "I knew Laura was trouble. But I'm surprised about Anthony. He's worked for Josh a long time. Josh really depends on him."

"So, what are you going to do? Are you going to tell Josh?"

She frowned. "I'm not sure he'll believe me if I tell him Laura is in on it. He'll think I'm jealous. Making the whole thing up." She stood up. "Maybe you should tell him. After all, you're the one who heard their conversation."

"I'm not sure he'd be any more likely to believe me."

"Wait until we get back from the dive." She walked into the hallway. "And then you've got to tell him."

I reluctantly pulled on my bathing suit, knowing that Brittany would soon come back to get me if I didn't go downstairs. Several of our group were waiting in the lobby by the time I got there. "Hey, Nicole," Josh called out. "We thought you weren't coming."

Brittany put her arm around my shoulder. "I told you she'd be here. She was just running a little late."

"Sorry," I said. "Didn't mean to hold everyone up."

"Not a problem," Josh said. "Eileen has decided to stay here and work on her presentation. And Davis and Gerald are going mountain biking. But it looks like everyone else is here. You've all been diving before, right? You're all certified?"

Anthony, Fitz, and Laura nodded.

"Okay," Josh said. "Let's go. Captain Mitch is waiting for us."

We stopped by the dive shop to pick up our equipment and then headed to the boat. Captain Mitch was a stocky, dark-skinned man wearing a black baseball cap. He gestured toward a small model set up in the middle of the deck. "If you folks would gather round here, I'll show you where we'll be diving today. The *RMS Rhone* was a royal mail ship, over 310 feet long and 40 feet wide, thought to be unsinkable. Unfortunately, it sank during a hurricane in 1867 and split into several pieces." He pointed at the sections of the model. "We'll be diving first on the bow. It's in about 80 feet of water and has an open structure you can swim through. There's a lot of marine life down there, as well as healthy coral growing on the wreck. The storm we had last night has stirred up the bottom a bit, so visibility is not as clear as I would like it, but you should still have a great dive." He straightened the bill of his cap. "We'll be down there about 25 minutes or so, and then come up for a break. After that we'll dive down to the stern. You'll see the 15-foot bronze propeller, and a "lucky porthole" guaranteed to bring good fortune to all who rub it."

Brittany looked toward Laura, who had her hand on Josh's shoulder as they leaned down to study the model. "I could use some good fortune right about now."

"I need you guys to pair off," Captain Mitch said. "It's always important to dive with a buddy."

Brittany stepped toward Josh, but I grabbed her arm. "No way I'm getting in that water unless you're right there beside me."

"I don't want Josh to buddy with Laura," she said.

"Tough. You stick with me, or I won't dive."

"Fine," she muttered.

"I guess we finance guys should stick together," Fitz said. "Anthony, you okay with that? I know you've had a lot of diving experience."

"Sure."

Captain Mitch looked at Laura and Josh. "You two good to team up? Are you experienced divers?"

"I'm a newbie," Laura said, "but Josh has been diving since he was a kid. I know he'll look out for me."

"Was she really fluttering her eyelashes?" Brittany whispered in my ear. "I think I'm going to barf."

"Let's get ready then," Captain Mitch said. "Make sure you check your time and watch your air supply. Diving is safe – we haven't lost anyone yet – but you never know when things might get complicated." He gestured toward the sun-bronzed man beside him. "Fred will lead you down the mooring line to the wreck. When he says it's time to surface, take him seriously. You don't want to run out of air." Captain Mitch lined us up along the side of the boat. "Let's go over a few hand signals. It's good to be able to communicate with each other once you're underwater. First of all, once you all jump in and make sure your equipment is working, please put a hand on top of your head. When you're all ready to go down, Fred will give the signal to descend, a fist with his thumb pointing down. When you're ready to ascend, he'll make a fist with his thumb pointing up." He turned to Fred. "Anything else we should cover?"

Fred picked up his googles. "After we start back up, we'll take a three-minute safety stop. The purpose is to let your body slowly unload nitrogen, so you don't get the bends when you surface. The signal looks like this." He tapped the three middle fingers of one hand against the palm of the other. "And there are a few more signals you may be interested in." He touched the side of his hand to his forehead, with his fingers pointing upward. "This is the signal for a shark." Then he crossed his arms over his chest. "This one means danger. And this one…" he jerked his hand in a cutting motion across his throat, "this one means you are out of air. I hope no one needs to use it."

"That's probably enough, Fred," Captain Mitch laughed. "If we keep going, they'll be too scared to get in the water. Okay, folks, let's go."

We all jumped off the side of the boat, sinking below the water and then popping up to the surface, one after another. After everyone had put a hand on their head to indicate everything was okay, we let some air out of our buoyancy compensator devices and began to follow Fred toward the ocean floor.

Anthony and Fitz went down first, followed by Josh and Laura. I went down slowly, clinging to the mooring line. As usual, my breath came in fast gasps as I went deeper. I fought off a mini-panic attack as the phrase "if I am going to be drowned, if I am going to be drowned, if I am going to be drowned" kept repeating in my brain. Where had I heard it? Was it something I studied in college? A short story, perhaps? A poem? My heart was beating so fast I was sure it would jiggle my dive tank loose.

Brittany realized I was having trouble. She stuck by my side, slowly moving her hand away from her mouth and then back, over and over again in a very slow rhythm, until I matched my breathing to her movement. Inhale for a slow four-count. Exhale for four. Inhale for four. Exhale for four. I relaxed as my breathing finally came under control, air bubbles drifting slowly above me. I held out my fist, my thumb pointed down, as Captain Mitch had shown us. Brittany nodded, and we both started down toward the rest of our group.

My body felt weightless as I moved through the water, maneuvering around schools of brightly colored fish, yellow and blue and red. A giant turtle glided through the water, his front flippers moving in slow rhythm as his beady eyes focused on me. His head looked enormous as he drew closer. What did turtles eat, anyway? Fish? Seaweed? Humans? For a few minutes I was afraid he might take a chunk out of my arm, but he soon lost interest in me and drifted away.

Brittany was in front of me, steadily descending. I focused on following in her path while keeping an eye out for sharks and eels and other creatures of the deep. Finally, we were at the wreck. Captain Mitch had been right about the coral. It coated the wreck, inside and out, covering the long pieces of wood that were scattered on the bottom.

Colors were more muted at this depth. A school of tiny silver fish scattered as I swam through them. Sea creatures poked out of the debris, so unusual that I had no idea what they were. Something scurried past with skinny claws and long antennae – maybe a crab? Did those tentacles and bulging eyeballs belong to an octopus?

At first I stuck close to Brittany, still relying on her to help me with my breathing. But several other groups of divers were also swimming on the wreck, making it more challenging for us to stay together. As I grew more confident, I swam off on my own, enchanted by the peaceful, alien world that opened itself up to me.

Suddenly I realized that I didn't recognize any of the other divers near me. I swam through a large opening in the bow, moving to the opposite side of the wreck, looking for the rest of my group. Last night's storm had stirred up the seabed, limiting visibility, but I spotted Brittany several yards away. She put the side of her hand against her forehead, fingers pointing up, signaling that she had spotted a shark.

Laura, swimming near her, began to rip at her face mask and grab for her regulator, her feet kicking wildly. I didn't need any hand signals to see that she was panicking, her eyes wide and her fingers clawing at her throat. Had the shark gotten to her? Had she been bitten?

Anthony swam up beside her as her regulator came out of her mouth. She kept kicking, twisting away from him, her arms gyrating. He pulled his regulator free and forced it into her mouth, trying to get her lips to close around it. But her mouth opened, and I realized she was swallowing water, her body going limp. Anthony laid her on the seabed and began to pump her chest, an unsuccessful attempt at CPR.

Fred and Josh immediately moved in beside her, as well as other divers I didn't know, as it became obvious that this was an emergency. Fred pushed his regulator into her mouth, but there was no response. Her eyes were closed, and her arms drifted lifelessly in the current. Fred wrapped his arm around her waist and started swimming upward, his other hand giving us the ascent signal, with his fist tight and his thumb pointed upward. Josh and Brittany gathered the rest of our group together to follow him.

We swam back to the mooring line and started up toward the boat. When Fred gave us the signal, we leveled out for our three-minute safety stop, giving our bodies time to adjust to the changing depth. I clung to the mooring line, barnacles digging into my fingers. Laura floated above me, her legs dangling, and I searched for signs of injury, of a shark bite, of blood, but I couldn't spot anything.

We finally surfaced and swam to the boat. Captain Mitch grabbed Laura and pulled her aboard. He and Fred started CPR, pumping her chest, hoping to expel ocean water and start her breathing on her own. But we all knew it was too late. Laura was dead.

Fred started the boat, and Captain Mitch radioed ahead as we started for the dock. First responders met us there. They loaded Laura into an ambulance and drove away.

Two policemen in pale blue shirts and dark pants climbed onto the boat to question us, introducing themselves as Smith and Maduro. Smith appeared in his mid-forties and was apparently in charge, starting the interrogation.

We were all in shock, not knowing what to do, what to say. The swirling bottom had affected visibility enough so that no one seemed to know what had happened. "I spotted a shark," Brittany said. "And Laura immediately started to panic."

"Had she been drinking?" Maduro asked. "Even a few drinks the night before a dive can really mess you up the following day. Causes anxiety."

"We had all been drinking at dinner," Josh said. "And Laura wasn't an experienced diver. So yes, she might have panicked when she saw the shark."

"Tell me about this shark," Smith said. "How big was it? How close?"

We all glanced at each other, shaking our heads. "I didn't see a shark," Anthony said. "I only saw Laura, pulling at her face mask, kicking wildly. And I knew she was in trouble."

"It looked to me like she ran out of air," Fred told them. "I pushed my regulator into her mouth, but it was too late. I couldn't get her to latch on."

"So, faulty equipment, then?" Smith looked suspiciously at Captain Mitch.

"No," he said emphatically. "We checked all the equipment before they got into the water. Everything was working. No problems."

Smith's lip curled. "Well, we have a problem now, don't we?"

Captain Mitch turned toward Josh. "You were her dive buddy. You were supposed to stay beside her. What happened?"

Josh shook his head. "I don't know. We were swimming together, looking at the wreck, and then all of a sudden she wasn't there. I looked around for her and saw Brittany and Anthony beside her, and then Fred. They were all trying to get her to breathe, but it wasn't working. I swam over there, but there wasn't anything I could do. Fred grabbed her and started for the surface."

I kept thinking of Laura, her body flailing under the water. Suddenly I started to tremble, my shoulders shaking as I rubbed my hands against my arms. I was so cold. "Hey, she's going into shock," Fred said, stepping up beside me. He turned to Smith. "You need to get everyone into someplace warm and dry. We can answer all your questions then."

"Get the victim's equipment together, will you?" Smith said to his partner. "We'll need to have it tested."

They drove us to the hotel where we changed into dry clothes, but I was still cold. I didn't think I would ever be warm again. We gathered in the lobby, and they began to question us individually, taking us into a small office.

"I told them that Anthony was embezzling from the company," Brittany told me as she exited her interview. "And that Laura was blackmailing him. They want to talk to you next, to tell them about the conversation you overheard."

I stood by the window, staring at that beautiful turquoise water. So peaceful. So deadly. "Brittany, there wasn't a shark, was there?"

"Of course, there was. I saw it."

"But no one else did."

"Laura did." Brittany crossed her arms over her chest. "That's why she panicked."

I watched as a cabana boy handed two frosty drinks to a couple lounging on the beach. I could use a frosty drink myself, right now. Maybe two or three. "Or she panicked because someone cut off her air."

She hesitated. "Or it was an equipment malfunction."

I shook my head. "Everyone checked their equipment carefully before the dive. It's more likely that someone cut off her air."

"Like Anthony, you mean? That makes sense. He had a good motive. And he was the closest to her."

"No, Brittany. Anthony wasn't the closest. You were. And you had as much motive as he did. Laura was sleeping with Josh." I grabbed her hand. "Did you kill her?"

She jerked her hand free and stared at me, her eyes wide. "I can't believe you would ask me that." Not a confession. But not a denial, either.

I have known Brittany since college. She understands my thoughts, my fears, my goals for the future. She stayed with me when my mother was dying of cancer. She threw a big bash for me when I landed my dream job.

I know that she wants me to tell the police that I saw the shark. That Anthony had a strong motive to kill Laura. That he was the closest one to her when she started to panic, so he could have cut off her air.

Anthony's definitely guilty of something. Embezzling, for sure. Murder? Don't know about that one.

What I do know is that it's not easy to say no to your best friend. I turned away from Brittany and walked to the interview room.

Dearest Darkest
K. L. Murphy

This morning's argument had been the worst yet, her husband's indifference worse than any amount of vitriol or venom. Of course, that had only made Dawn madder, and she'd flung insults like grenades. With a shake of his head, he'd walked out, leaving her alone. Again. She remembered when they used to make up after fights. Now days passed before they spoke. When was the last time he'd wrapped her in a hug for no reason? Or they'd enjoyed a candlelit dinner? Dawn fell back against the chair and ran a shaky hand through her hair. When had they lost the desire to try?

With a weary sigh, she regarded her laptop. Like it or not, another deadline loomed, and her editor had a strict policy about running old columns.

"Let's keep it fresh," he always said, like she was plucking produce at a farmer's market and could control what kind of letters people sent, what kind of problems they had. Either way, it was going to be a long day. Taking a deep breath, she sat up, and started reading.

> *Dear Darkest Before the Dawn,*
>
> *My daughter insists on bringing her dogs and cats to our house for the holidays even though she knows I'm allergic. Her answer is to tell me to take a pill if I want to see her. Last year, I spent most of Christmas day isolated in my room, sneezing, and covered in hives. It took me days to get all the animal hair out of the house. This week, she called to tell me she got a new cat. That*

means two dogs and four cats in my small house! At this rate, when she comes, I'll be so sick, I won't see her anyway. I love my daughter, but I'm at a loss. What should I do?

Sincerely,

Sneezy Mom

Dawn tapped her fingers on the arm of the chair. She was tempted to slide this one into the "no answer" folder. Pets were a hot button for a lot of people, and she knew better than to call out dog and cat owners for loving their pets. She treated her own dog better than her husband, something he pointed out on a regular basis. Still.

She drafted a response.

Dear Sneezy Mom,

You've clearly raised a daughter to love and cherish animals which is a credit to you both, however, pet allergies can be a serious issue. Hopefully, her comment to "take a pill or else" is a lack of understanding about your suffering. Assuming she wants to see you as much as you want to see her, why not try arranging your holiday dinner at a restaurant? Or, if she is traveling to be with you, there are many wonderful hotels that have pet spas. Perhaps this could be a gift to your "grandpets"? If she refuses and you are unwilling to spend the holidays without her, you might consider speaking to your doctor before her arrival. Often, a physician can help alleviate some of the symptoms. Additionally, you could set up a "pet room" that limits your exposure. Fill it with dog toys and a litter box. Or, if the weather is mild, you could host your holiday dinner outside. A HEPA air filter might also give you some relief. As someone who has to have a "hypoallergenic" dog myself (the greatest dog ever!), I can sympathize with you both. Hopefully, one of these compromises will work for you and your family.

Best,

Dawn

Scanning the words she'd written, she thought she'd struck a reasonable balance, although she'd been unable to resist a tiny dig at the daughter. Dawn loved her dog, but she missed her mother every day. She'd leave Sadie home every holiday just to have a few more hours with mom. But sharp retorts and snap judgments came back to bite you in the advice business.

She'd never forget the way Ask Antonia was cancelled after she called out a woman who was on her third affair in as many years. Instead of reminding the woman these relationships were going nowhere and steering her toward counseling, she told the woman she had low self-esteem, and she should take a long look in the mirror. If she didn't like what she saw, instead of grabbing onto some other woman's husband, she should do something about it. Unfortunately, the woman did just that and "doing something" turned out to be swallowing a handful of pills. Many argued Antonia hadn't intended for the woman to attempt taking her own life, but Dawn wasn't so sure. Antonia's husband had recently left her for another woman. Either way, she was cancelled.

Dawn moved the letter and her response to the "maybe" file. She'd bring it up with her editor later.

The next few letters went straight to the delete file, too similar to other letters she'd answered in recent weeks. Readers wanted new heartbreak, new problems. They wanted train wrecks, like a printed version of reality TV, letters that made them feel better about their own lives. She clicked on the next one.

Dear Darkness Before the Dawn,

I'm in a difficult situation. There's a woman I can't get off my mind. What's the problem, you ask? She's married.

Dawn wrinkled her nose—Ask Antonia all over again—but she read on anyway.

> *I know, I know. Bad idea. But in my heart and soul, I know she's the one. Lest you think I'm crazy, I know this because we were together when we were young. We never actually broke up, but life happened, and we went in different directions. I did my best to move on, to build a new life, but I've recently been transferred back to Chicago and learned she still lives in the suburb we grew up in.*

Dawn paused. She, too, lived outside of Chicago.

> *I'm not the kind of man who believes in breaking up a marriage, not a good one anyway, but every minute of every day, I'm wondering about her. I have this overwhelming need to know if she's okay, if she's happy. If she is, of course, I would walk away. But what if she's not?*
>
> *Can you help me?*
>
> > *R.*

Dawn liked the simplicity and straightforward manner of that signature, although it seemed opposite from the kind of man who still pined for a teenaged romance. Surely, this was slush pile material, and yet, she hesitated. She read the letter a second time and a third before setting it aside. An hour passed and she was no closer to having a complete column. Without giving it too much thought, she plucked R.'s letter from the slush pile and typed out a brief response.

> *Dear R.,*
>
> *You seem to be a man of deep emotion and while I'm sure there is a wonderful woman out there for you, I cannot in good conscience encourage you to seek out a woman you know is married. If she is unhappy, this is something for her to determine on her own. If you find your feelings difficult to manage, you might consider speaking*

to a therapist.

She considered reminding him that she often told readers that obsessing over finding "the one" was the stuff of movies and romance novels. Instead, she wished him luck in life and love. She sent it to her editor, forgetting about it until the next one came two weeks later.

Dear Darkest Before the Dawn,

> *Thank you for answering my letter. I took your advice and have reached out to a therapist, but the reason I'm writing is because I've seen her. Don't worry, I didn't approach her, and I'm pretty sure she didn't see me. I don't know how it's possible, but she's even more beautiful. After seeing her, I'm more convinced than ever that we belong together. I'm not as pathetic as I sound. Ladies seem to like me. I've been engaged, but I broke it off before the wedding. Now I think I know why.*
>
> *I understand she's married, she has a life now, but it doesn't stop me from wondering. What if I'm right? What if we're meant to be together? Who are we to stop destiny? Circumstances tore us apart, but circumstances also brought us back together. Some would call that coincidence and others would call it fate. What say you Darkest Before the Dawn?*
>
> > *R.*

Rarely did Dawn get this kind of follow up letter, but this man and the intensity of his love intrigued her, even if she did find it somewhat adolescent.

Dear R.,

> *Your job brought you back to the same zip code. This is not to be confused with fate bringing you back "together." And if I were to subscribe to the*

concept of destiny, I would ask you, who are we to define anyone's destiny, including our own?

    Dawn

His response came the next week.

    Dear Darkest Before the Dawn,

That is certainly one way to look at it, a less hopeful way to be sure, but as I'm sure you'd agree, we are all entitled to our points of view.

Since you asked (or would if you could), I have not seen my love since my last letter. (For sake of ease, I'll refer to her as J. from now on.) Although I haven't seen her, I have discovered that all may not be wonderful in married land. No, I'm not stalking her. I ran into an old friend who happened to have a lot to say about our old crowd, including J. It hurts me to think her husband might not treasure her the way I do.

With each day, it gets harder not to let J. know how I feel. I'm doing what I can. I'm going to work. I'm meeting old friends and making new ones. I even had a date last week. Don't ask! The point is, I'm trying, but I worry it's not enough. We put our best faces forward, the ones we think everyone wants to see, but those aren't the same as the ones we see in the mirror, are they? And if that's true, why are so many of us hiding?

    R.

Dawn flinched at the reference to the mirror. Ask Antonia loomed large in her mind, and yet, R.'s question haunted her. *Why are so many of us hiding?*

She thought about the silence in her own house. Twice in the past week, her husband had spent the night in the guest room. She'd walked past the closed door without comment. Which one of them was hiding?

No one was more surprised than Dawn when her editor called the next day. "We're getting a lot of feedback on this thing you've got going with this R. guy." Expecting him to put a halt to the letter exchange, her fingers tightened over the phone. Instead, he directed her to the online readers' comments.

> *R., you should let J. know you're back in town.*
> *Maybe she's been waiting for you all this time.*

Or the opposite sentiment:

> *She hasn't been waiting around for you. She's married, you imbecile!*

But even those letters were eclipsed by more like this one:

> *I've been looking for a man as romantic as you,*
> *R. Message me.*

Dawn considered these responses an anomaly until she overheard a conversation in a local coffee shop.

"Have you been reading "Darkest Before the Dawn?" a woman at a nearby table asked.

Her friend set her cup down with a clink. "Oh, my God. Are you talking about R.? It's like that old movie, Sleepless in Seattle, where one of them is lonely and knows they should be with the other. Kismet or something." Her voice took on a conspiratorial tone. "Do you think she's reading the column? Does she know it's her?"

A third woman chimed in. "I hope not. I'd love to meet him myself." She leaned in closer, and Dawn had to strain to hear. "Sometimes I look around to see if I can spot him. I mean, what if he lives in Hinsdale? He could be here right now."

Dawn watched as each of the women looked around the coffee shop in search of R.

"I know he hasn't actually described himself, but he's definitely the tall, dark, and handsome type, don't you think?" The other women nodded, and she sat back again, letting out a heavy breath. "J.'s lucky—whoever she is. I mean, who wouldn't want a man to love you like that?"

Dawn resisted the urge to stare. Were they really crushing on a man who'd written a bunch of letters professing his love for a married woman he hadn't seen in twenty years? The idea seemed ridiculous, yet she couldn't deny what she'd heard, or the increased traffic in the chats. And so, at her editor's insistence, she kept writing.

Dear R.,

> *I'd like to think that the person we see in the mirror is the same person others see, although I understand that's not always the case. There can be many valid reasons for this, but I want you to know it's okay to let our best faces slip once in a while, too. We are all human.*

And because she now had a better understanding of what her female readers wanted to know; she added a suggestion about the woman.

As for J., I would again caution you not to seek her out. While I've no doubt the love you feel for her is powerful—love is surely a powerful thing—her reaction to seeing you may not be what you expect. She may be ambivalent about seeing an old boyfriend. She may harbor feelings of resentment or even anger toward you for leaving. Either way, I would encourage you to keep trying to build a life of your own without J. And as always, seek out counseling if you feel that things are getting difficult.

> *Best,*
>
> *Dawn*

His response arrived the day after the paper printed his letter.

Dear Darkest Before the Dawn,

> *I have news. I've seen J. again. Last night, I was on a date (see, I'm trying!), when she came into the same restaurant with her husband. I was so shocked I couldn't move, and thankfully, she was seated with her back to me. Anyway, I don't*

*think I'm wrong when I say my friend was right
that everything is not good between J. and her
husband. I could feel the tension from across
the room, and before they'd even gotten their
dinner, he stormed out, leaving her there. The
guy is a grade-A jerk if you ask me.*

Dawn touched a hand to her heart. The same thing had happened to her. In an effort to clear the air after their last standoff, she'd invited her husband to Millie's, neutral territory. But somewhere between the appetizer and entrée, their discussion went from tentative to testy to toxic. The similarity in her and J.'s situation made her sit back, wondering at yet another coincidence. Sweeping aside the thought, she returned to the letter.

*It was all I could do not to go over and console her,
but I didn't, of course. As I said, I was on a date of
my own, and I would never run out on a woman like
that. J. deserves better. So much better.*
*Thank you for trying to help me move on, but after
this, I'm not sure I can. No matter how many dates
I go on, no matter how hard I try to care, I can't
forget her.*
*As for seeking help, I will continue with my
sessions, but my therapist isn't helpful the way you
are. Maybe that surprises you, but I like the way you
don't minimize how I feel, like you understand that
this kind of love is not something to be taken lightly,
that it can give a person strength, that it can feed our
souls. It makes me know that you, too, have felt this
kind of love.*
> *Yours,*
> *R.*

She swallowed the lump in her throat. Had she though? Felt that kind of love? Once maybe, but that was a long time ago, and she'd been a kid, not unlike R. and J. These were things she didn't want to think about, and so she kept her response vague, reiterating the importance of respecting the boundaries of J.'s marriage and not giving up on a life for himself. She did her best to divert attention away from herself by adding:

> *You were young when you were with J. You're older now and presumably you've both grown up. People change and no doubt, J. has changed, too. I hope you will open your heart to the possibility that there may be another who could share your life with you.*
>
> *Best,*
>
> *Dawn*

His last letter and her response only brought out more women looking for "real" love and throwing themselves at R. in the online chats. That line about how he "would never run out on a woman like that" probably appealed to any woman—or man—who'd ever been stood up, walked out on, or snubbed. Many offered to be the one to share his life. It occurred to her that the guy on *The Bachelor* would kill to have this much interest. R. never responded in the chats which only fueled the fire.

A week passed without a new letter and the winter chill that dropped a foot of snow on the streets of Hinsdale settled inside Dawn's house. Her husband left before the sun rose and arrived home long after she'd gone to bed. Stubbornly, she matched his silence with her own. She found she cared less than she might have thought, her mind preoccupied with R. and his letters instead. She refreshed her inbox repeatedly and scoured the online chats. She skipped going to the gym. She missed book club. When another week passed without a letter, her head ached, and her stomach churned. Insomnia set in. Finally, a new letter arrived.

> *Dear Darkest Before the Dawn,*
>
> *J's husband is cheating. I saw him in his truck outside the Hinsdale Market (a local place) with a woman who wasn't J.*

Dawn stopped reading. The Hinsdale Market. It was on the same block as her husband's office building. There was a lot right next to it where he sometimes parked his truck.

> *I know I shouldn't have, but I followed him to an address that isn't his. He and the woman went inside, and he didn't come back out until very late.*

Dawn's breath caught in her throat and the words on the screen blurred. She saw it then. Her life was a mirror image of J.'s. They both lived in Hinsdale. Their marriages were in shambles. They were stuck. But J. had someone who loved her. What about her? What did she have? Wiping away a tear, her gaze returned to the screen.

> *Since I found out, I've wanted to confront him, to tell him what I think of him, but I won't because I know you wouldn't approve.*
>
> *J. and I had a bond, a plan to live our lives together. We were going to travel through Europe after college, get married, and live happily ever after. But our parents weren't encouraging. I know that sounds a little like Romeo and Juliet, but there we are, a real-life R. and J.*

Dawn's heart thudded in her chest. The initials R. and J. weren't for their real names but meant to be symbolic of their doomed high school romance. Memories of her own high school boyfriend flooded her brain. Jake Martin. They'd planned to travel, too, but he'd moved away before their final semester, and they'd lost touch sometime before their sophomore year of college. She remembered the way her father growled every time Jake came around and the way his mother looked her up and down as though she wanted to paint a scarlet A on her chest. Both sets of parents had been relieved when Mr. Martin was offered a better job three states away.

> *I wish I could tell J. how much I cherish her. I wish I could show her that I would never treat her the way her husband does. Harsh as this sounds, he doesn't deserve to walk the same*

*earth she does. Alas, I know what you would say.
J. needs to recognize this on her own. If only J.'s
husband were to disappear. Call me a dreamer. I
am who I am. A man waiting.*

    Yours always,

    R.

Dawn's hand flew to her mouth. She remembered now. That's what her father used to say about Jake. "He'll never be anything but a dreamer. Has his head in the clouds, Dawn. Take my word for it, you'll be better off without him." The room spun around her, nausea rising up in her throat. Could R. be Jake? She counted the number of coincidences, her eyes frantically searching through all the letters. The truck. The fight in the restaurant. *Call me a dreamer.* How had she missed it before now? But if she was J, that meant her husband was cheating. The truth felt like a bomb going off inside her. R. was Jake. She was J. And Jake had been writing to her the whole time, trying to tell her he still loved her. Her own long buried love came rushing back, filling her with a warmth she hadn't felt since she was young. How had she forgotten what true love was like?

Again, she couldn't sleep, but this time, it was Jake's letter that kept her awake. His words buzzed like neon in her brain. *If only J.'s husband were to disappear. If only J.'s husband were to disappear. If only J.'s husband were to disappear.*

In the cold light of morning, Dawn reread every word again. No, she wasn't wrong. Jake wanted to be with her. It's what she wanted to, wasn't it? To be unstuck. To be free of her cold and cheating husband. She could file for divorce, but financially, that could be a problem. Her husband's family had insisted on a pre-nup, one that gave her slightly more if she could prove infidelity but not nearly what she deserved. No. Divorce wouldn't work. *If only J.'s husband were to disappear.* Yes, a disappearance. But how?

Hours later and no closer to a solution, she typed a response to R.'s most recent letter.

    Dear R.,

    You are right that J. needs to learn about her

husband straying on her own. If and when she does,
what steps she takes after that will be up to her.

She looked down at the words. They were good. Exactly the kind of thing any counselor would say. She would not be like Ask Antonia.

> *While I can't promise that you and J. will be together*
> *as no one can predict the future, I can tell you there's*
> *nothing wrong with being a dreamer, for dreamers*
> *are the ones who inspire us to do what needs to be*
> *done.*
>
> *Best,*
> *Dawn*

Would Jake decode her message? She couldn't be sure, but she couldn't risk saying more. For the first time ever, she rued the paper's policy that all letters come through them, all contact information erased. She had no way to get in touch.

Over the next few days, she visited several libraries, using their internet access to research ways to get rid of her cheating husband. She considered poison or a hitman, but she didn't know how, and the risks were too high. Then it came to her. The truck. He loved that thing in spite of that big recall last year, the one about the starters exploding. He'd had it fixed, but what if the technician made a mistake? What if it hadn't been done right? She knew cars. After all, she'd worked in her uncle's auto shop every summer through high school and college. At yet another library, she studied the recall, the parts, and the wiring. The real problem wasn't unfixing the starter, but making sure it would explode the first time he hit the ignition. That took another two days to figure out.

During those days, there was only one new letter from R.

> *Dear Darkest,*
>
> *Somehow, I knew you'd understand me. Thank*
> *you for your faith, and I will take your advice to*
> *heart and allow J. to figure things out on her own.*
> *Until then, I'll keep dreaming.*
>
> *R.*

That was followed by more online comments.

Fingers crossed for you R.
If J. doesn't see your worth, know that I do, R. I'm
here for you. xxoo

Dawn laughed out loud. Romance wasn't dead among her readers, but it wasn't romance she was thinking of when she heard the garage door open and close that night. She glanced at the clock. Two a.m. A fight that morning meant he would spend another night in the guest room and, being a Friday, he'd sleep in. Even so, she didn't have much time. None of it went the way she'd planned, and she'd been forced to add an accelerant as insurance, but by six, she was finished. Leaving the house, she sent her husband a text.

Hitting hot yoga this morning, then breakfast
with Lisa, and some shopping. Catch you
later.

She considered adding a heart emoji but knew it might ring false. What if he'd been confiding in his girlfriend? Or his sister? What if she knew they barely spoke?

At yoga and breakfast, Dawn forced herself to act normal, to smile and nod even when she had no idea what was being said. Later, she wandered through the mall, checking her watch. His standard Saturday tee time meant he would leave the house at noon sharp. At five minutes to twelve, she sat in the food court staring at her phone. The minutes ticked by as shoppers filled the seats around her. 12:05. No call. 12:10. Her foot swung back and forth under the table. At twelve minutes past noon, her phone rang. It was her neighbor, Angie, sobbing that there'd been an explosion. Dawn didn't hear the rest. She hung up, walked out to her car, and drove home.

The funeral passed in a blur. For the first time ever, her editor published some of her old columns. "You need time to grieve," he said.

Friends and family came and went, and all the while, she waited. Did Jake know? And how would he contact her? She spent hours searching for him online but found nothing more than an old Facebook page that hadn't been updated in five years. She considered messaging but changed her mind. Some arson investigator was poking around, and her nosy sister-in-law was asking questions, insisting on a lawsuit. As if Dawn could let that happen.

Two weeks turned into a month. Hinsdale wasn't a big town, and she prowled the local restaurants and shops, searching for any sign of him. And then her editor called.

"Dawn, the letters are piling up. And there's a few from that lovelorn guy, too. R., right?"

She slapped a hand to her head. Of course. He'd write her a letter. The first had arrived in the days right after the explosion.

> *Dear Darkest,*
>
> *It seems that tragedy has struck, and J. has suffered a tremendous loss. You cannot imagine how difficult it is for me not to go to her, but I will resist.*

Tears sprang to Dawn's eyes. He wanted to be with her. She scrolled some more. The next letter was dated two weeks later.

> *Dear Darkest,*
>
> *Time is dragging for me as I wait for J. It seems that the recent loss in her life may have pushed J. further from me than before.*

The hair on the back of her neck prickled. This wasn't right. She wasn't further. She was closer. Jake was speaking in circles.

> *I know, I know. I'm supposed to be moving forward with my life.*
> *Still a dreamer.*
> *R.*

Her phone pinged. Another message from that arson investigator. Something in her gut churned, but he'd have to wait. She needed to read Jake's most recent letter.

> *Dear Darkest,*
>
> *You were right after all. Being back in my hometown wasn't the hand of fate leading me to J.*

but more like a two-lane, bumpy road taking me
toward a destiny I couldn't have foreseen.

Dread crawled up her skin. She didn't like the sound of this letter. Not one bit.

Who knew that all your advice to build my own
life, to move on from J. would be exactly what I
needed to hear?

Her breath came in quick, shallow spurts now.

Yes, you guessed it. I've met someone—someone
amazing! And from a blind date if you can believe
it.

This couldn't be happening. Head shaking, she mouthed, "No, no, no."

Oh, I almost forgot. I literally ran into J., practically
knocking her down at The Beanery. We got coffee
and reminisced for a while. What it made me realize
is that you were right all along. What J. and I had is
in the past. Thanks to you, I'm finally living in the
present.

Forever your fan,
Robert

Dawn sat frozen, hands curled like claws, struggling to understand. R. stood for Robert, not Romeo. R. wasn't Jake. She couldn't breathe. That meant she wasn't J. Her husband wasn't the man in the truck with the other woman.

Face flushed, her arm swung out like a scythe, sweeping everything from the desk. The lamp landed with a thump, pens flew across the room, and her laptop screen cracked and shattered. Throwing back her head, she screamed until her throat burned. Chest heaving, she caught sight of the blank screen, empty of words, and it hit her. She'd be vilified, worse than Ask Antonia. It was over. All over.

Batter, Batter, Swing!
Eleanor Cawood Jones

Delta Dawn DuBois rocked back on her heels to admire the elaborately decorated cake she'd just created, then carefully adjusted the topper. The groom and small dog were in the right place, but the bride was listing a little to port. Finally, it was perfect and, with a sigh of satisfaction, she slid her masterpiece to the back of the counter to sit safely until her husband Tim came home from coaching baseball and could help her box it.

She shook her head over the dog; did every couple in the town of Batts Belfry, Virginia, have to have a pet in their wedding anymore? And what was with vibrant green and pink as wedding colors? Maybe they were disco dancers. At least they'd chosen the vanilla mango flavor for both the wedding and groom's cakes. That showed some semblance of taste.

She began mixing the next batch of vanilla mango batter for yet another wedding (this one had two cats in it) and began once again to go over the to-do list she'd begun carrying around in her head.

#Full bar and ice bucket ready—check.

#Favorite evening dress cleaned and pressed—check.

#Disposable gloves—check.

#Knee length light raincoat—check.

#All-purpose cleaning wipes with bleach—check.

#Net bag of extra baseball bats and balls—check.

#Lighter fluid and matches—check.

#Location of remote dumpsters in the neighboring towns of Clark's Fancy and Jones Branch memorized—check.

#Tim's life insurance fully paid up—check.

Delta had been smart enough not to increase the size of Tim's policy; she'd watched enough Court TV to know how stupid *that* was. And she'd mentally designed her new business cards, expansion plan, and marketing campaign for Cakes by Dawn. That would be important to get going right away if she was going to go it alone. But, she thought, that should wait. Timing was everything. Nothing should look planned or suspicious.

Of course, she'd be so happy if she never had to put this to-do list into action. She'd had a relatively happy marriage and almost perfect life until recently. Not having kids had been a disappointment, but her growing and successful wedding and all-occasion cake business was thriving. Seems like everyone wanted a cake by a woman with the unlikely name of Delta Dawn DuBois from the small town named for its founding fathers, the Batts family.

Her customers thought it was a hoot, but Delta knew she was a talented baker, so that didn't bother her.

Tim's successful IT career had provided her with the financial means to start her business almost five years ago, and shortly afterwards she'd been doing well enough that she could leave her own boring banking job and set up full-time shop in her home. And she'd paid her husband back every penny of earnest money.

Paradise—well, for her, anyway. And she'd thought nothing of it when Tim was asked to coach baseball in Jones Branch. It was 40 minutes away, but it seemed there was shortage of adults willing to coach kids anymore, and Tim had coached in Batts Belfrey since before she met him at a Washington Nationals baseball game ten years ago.

She allowed her mind to drift back in time. It had been love at first pitch at that long ago game and, after a year of constant dating, they'd been married outside Nationals Stadium at the beer garden, which was a great venue for a baseball-themed wedding and a wonderful place for a party. She'd invented the vanilla mango cake for that occasion and never looked back.

They had baseball in common and had traveled to as many stadiums as they could to attend games, and discovered a whole community of folks doing the same thing. They spent their vacations on baseball stadium train tours, a memorable bus tour out west, and—her favorite—the East Coast cruise ship tour last summer where they squeezed in games from Boston to Florida, along with all the partying, dining, and tanning onboard ship.

She'd thought they rekindled their romance on that trip, but apparently the new spark in her handsome, dark-haired husband's blue eyes had nothing to do with her and everything to do with the group of baseball enthusiasts he'd met onboard who redefined the term "swing"—and not in a baseball connotation. While she'd been innocently sun tanning at the pool on Deck 7 with her best baseball friend Barbara from Washington State, Tim had apparently been spending time with his new friends behind closed cabin doors.

When they'd returned home six months ago, she'd thought her husband seemed restless and mentioned it to him.

"It's not like I don't still love you. You're my world," he'd answered.

She'd swallowed hard, put down her bowl and spoon, and joined him at the kitchen table.

"That's a hell of thing to say. I just asked why you're restless."

"I know that's what you asked. I've been trying to find a way to tell you."

She looked at her husband and steeled herself.

"Tim, what have you done?"

"I'm only forty-five, Delta. I'm still virile. I want to grab as much life as I can while I'm still young."

"Oh, my Lord, you're having an affair. Tim, how *could* you?"

And what did it say about her that her first thought was how this would affect her business? Would people still want to buy wedding cakes from a woman whose man was a dirty, rotten cheater? Would she have to pin a faded rose on her dresses and walk around town like her namesake from the old Tanya Tucker song? Should she leave him? This was a *disaster*.

"No, no, of course not."

"I thought we were happy, Tim. *Happy!*"

"Delta, honey, it's not like that. We *are* happy. Nothing has changed. I just need…more."

"Define *more*." She could hear the ice in her own voice and wished she hadn't left the wooden spoon on the sink so she could clobber him with it.

"It's not an affair. It's all anonymous. No strings, no attachments."

And while her mouth hung open—this was the Bible Belt, after all—Tim explained about the group of new baseball friends he'd met on the last cruise. Apparently the subculture of baseball stadium enthusiasts had a small, deeper subculture of swingers, and Tim had joined their lineup.

"It's all consenting adults and it's all private, and very safe. You know our love life has improved, Delta. And I'd like you to consider joining us on the new West Coast cruise this fall."

"I'll need some time to think it over," she managed to say.

What she'd meant was, she needed time to figure out what she was going to do, because no way was she going to get involved in something so, so…unseemly.

In the meantime, she moved out of their bedroom to the guest suite. Eventually, Tim quit asking her to move back in. Other than that, to all appearances their life together went on relatively normally. She didn't tell anyone about the situation, and she didn't think Tim had either.

And after almost six months, with the West Coast cruise looming, Delta found herself surprised how little she cared. She spent much of her time baking and seriously evaluating how her life would change if she left her husband.

In the end, she decided it was in her own best interest to reconcile, to Tim's delight. Maybe Tim would outgrow this new...hobby. She gritted her teeth and moved back into the master bedroom.

Divorce would hurt business, as well as her pride when the reasons became common knowledge. Batts Belfrey was growing, but it was still a small town. Your neighbor's business was automatically your business as well. She wondered if Tim could simply die conveniently of natural causes, and then was deeply ashamed.

They'd bought the tickets for the West Coast cruise months ago. She'd so looked forward to it, but now she just felt revulsion. The ship left in two weeks, and she still hadn't decided if she was going.

The phone rang and pulled her out of her thoughts. She looked down at the bowl in her hands. The batter was well and truly mixed, and she grabbed her cell phone.

"Baseball buddy!" It was her baseball bestie, Barbara, calling from Takoma. That was their standard greeting to each other. "Just bought us matching Seattle Mariners baseball jerseys for the first cruise game! I was gonna surprise you, but figured you'd want to prepare yourself mentally. I owe you one for making me wear that Nationals baseball cap last trip."

Delta forced a laugh. "I guess I can play along. But I hope you got a large size. Baking is great, but you get caught up in sampling your own products."

Barbara's honking laugh came down the line. "Got two larges. You think you have a solo license in cake sampling? Anyway, gotta go. It's time to hit the highway for work. See you in two weeks! Tally ho!"

She hung up and Delta's mind switched to the present day. It was Thursday afternoon and Tim was off to coach his baseball kids. Lately, he'd been coaching more and more—he said—and staying out later and later on Thursdays and on the weekends after games. He said he had some special needs kids he'd been spending extra time with. That part was believable; Tim had always had a generous heart.

But there was something subtly different about her husband lately. When he came home late at night, she had imagined she'd caught the scent of another woman's perfume on more than one occasion. And there was no doubt her husband was distracted. She thought today she'd show up at practice bearing cupcakes for the kids and parents, and maybe do some scouting to see if there were any parents Tim was paying special attention to.

She sighed. She missed the days when she'd floated happily on a pink cloud of matrimony, with no reason to suspect her beloved husband of anything amiss, and when the only swinging in their lives was at the batting cage.

She opened the refrigerator to take out the Tupperware containing the three dozen apple spice cupcakes she had made this morning, slathered with white cream cheese frosting and red and blue sprinkles. Baseball and apple pie. What better treat to enjoy to celebrate an afternoon of America's favorite sport?

"Okay, Delta Dawn," she said out loud. "Let's go see what your husband is up to."

*****

When she finally found her way to the Jones Branch kids' baseball field in the middle of nowhere, she discovered it wasn't a parent who had caught Tim's eye. It was a teacher. A very pretty, very blond, special-needs teacher in short shorts, who'd brought one of her pupils to baseball practice. She hung out by the dugout near Tim's net bag of bats, cheering for all the kids and making goo-goo eyes at her husband.

Tim made goo-goo eyes back—until he spotted Delta in the

198

bleachers a few minutes later chatting with his teacher friend, whose name turned out to be Rosie. It had been easy to sit by her and strike up a conversation, during which she learned Rosie's student was mildly autistic, he loved baseball, and Rosie often brought him to practices and games because his parents had busy careers and didn't always have time.

"They both work hard to provide extra tutoring and opportunities for Dave," she confided. "I figured it's the least I can do to make sure he gets to practice. That kid! He's got so many baseball stats memorized he's like a little walking encyclopedia."

"How about the coach? Do they get along?"

"Oh, the coach. Tim. He's a dream with that kid. In fact, he's a dream in general, if you know what I mean." She sighed with bliss and Delta fought an urge to retch.

"I know exactly what you mean, actually. But surely he's twice your age." Delta forced herself to giggle, and nudged Rosie companionably.

"Older men are just the best. So experienced!"

Delta turned her head and rolled her eyes. "Would you like a cupcake, Rosie?"

Big blue eyes looked innocently at her. "I'm watching my figure, but I'd love to take one for Dave. His parents don't let him have sugar very often, but what they don't know won't hurt them this once. Did you make these yourself?"

Despite herself, Delta found herself smiling at the younger woman. Impossible not to like her. Well, at least her husband had taste.

She struck up conversations with some of the parents in the bleachers, all strangers to her, before gathering up her Tupperware. She waved gaily at Tim on the way to the car, and nothing was ever said about her visit to the ballfield, other than him thanking her for taking time out of her busy day to treat the parents and kids to cupcakes.

"It's the least I can do to support you in your volunteer work," she simpered, then turned her back on him in their king-size bed. "It's so nice of you to stay out late to help those kids."

She thought she felt him squirm before she fell into a peaceful sleep, after realizing once again how little she cared anymore what her husband did.

*****

Delta was running out of time before the cruise and felt like the time was right to make a move. She believed her husband was serious about Rosie. A few times he'd acted like he had something serious to discuss with her, but never did. Still, she could sense a sea change.

She steeled herself. She had decided her husband's behavior would have a drastic effect on her business if it was ever found out. Tim had to go.

On Wednesday morning she once again went over her mental to-do list, and on Thursday morning she went to Tim's car before he left for the office and removed his net bag of balls and bats. It was practice day again, and she knew he'd go straight from work to the ballfield. She hid the bag in the guest room. This would give her a reason to head to the ballfield that evening if anyone she knew saw her. A loving wife taking his baseball essentials to her coach husband after he accidentally left them at home. How thoughtful!

Next, she made sure her favorite cocktail dress was pressed and hanging up, ready to put on that evening.

She double checked that all her cleaning supplies, gloves, matches, lighter fluid, and her raincoat were packed in the Tumi backpack her husband had given her for their anniversary and put that in the back seat of her car. She went to the grocery store to get fresh flowers—her husband preferred roses for their special occasions—and put them on the bar.

And that's when she stopped short.

Some of the bottles were missing from the bar. What was that about? Two cut crystal glasses and matching tray, the ice bucket, the tall, elegant bottle of Galliano, the Absolut Vodka, all gone. And the orange juice was absent from the bar fridge. She recognized the missing ingredients as the components of Tim's favorite drink, a Harvey Wallbanger.

What the what? She could only assume Tim had packed them up for a reason. Some sort of celebration? Her heart sank. She'd really need to move quickly.

She moved the spare ice bucket and orange juice in the kitchen to the bar, but she'd worry about rearranging the bottles later. She had cakes to bake and an evening delivery. By that time, she'd be ready to head to Jones Branch and the ballfield to confront her husband and his late-night "coaching."

"Coaching after hours, indeed." Delta said aloud. She snorted. How stupid did men think women were, anyway?

"We always know," she said to her reflection in the bar mirror. "Always."

She stopped momentarily to dictate a text to her baseball BFF, Barbara. "Can't wait to see you on the cruise! So nice for Tim and me to have something to look forward to after our hard work this year. Go Mariners, ha!"

She hit send, and a few seconds later, Barbara sent back a thumbs up and a smiley emoji.

Delta heard Tim leave and took the bag of bats and balls out to her own car in the garage, along with the Tumi backpack. Then she headed for the kitchen to bake.

This would be a busy day indeed.

*****

After joking and laughing with the bride-to-be who accepted the cake delivery that evening just after sunset, Delta headed for the ballfield. She had time during the drive to prepare herself for what was next.

She reminded herself that she was the victim here; that Tim

was a cheater, and that her entire career and financial future in this town depended on her good name. Nobody would want a wedding cake from a divorcee who couldn't even keep her spouse at home, she told herself. But a widow whose marriage had been ideal? Who wouldn't want to support Cakes by Dawn in that scenario?

By tomorrow, the whole town—heck, the whole county—would love her. Even those who had never heard of Delta Dawn DuBois before the tragedy at the baseball field.

She flipped off the lights as she approached the small parking lot. Her hybrid made little noise and she didn't see anyone. There was only one car at the field, Tim's black Mercedes SUV. With any luck, she'd find him packing up the bases and other equipment and getting ready to leave. She wondered where he planned to meet Rosie, because surely that was his agenda.

Things were quiet when she got out of the car with Tim's net bag of bats and her own backpack. She left her driver's door open and paused to put on her long raincoat and gloves. September evenings in Virginia were chilly and, even if someone saw her, her outfit wouldn't seem unusual. She took a sturdy Louisville Slugger wooden bat out of the bag, hefted it, and took a deep breath.

She was surprised to hear the crack of a bat hitting balls as she walked silently around the dugout and approached the field. She saw Tim tossing balls into the air and hitting them.

He turned around and saw her approaching but kept tossing balls and smacking them into the outfield.

"I guess I'm a little late, but you left your extra baseball supplies at home. I ran late with the cake delivery. Sorry I didn't get them to you sooner. I thought maybe you had late practice, so I came on by."

"No late practice tonight," Tim said. He turned his back on her and tossed another ball into the air. "Delta, I know you suspect what I've been up to. You're a smart woman."

Smack! Another ball went into the outfield.

"That cruise last year? That meant nothing," Tim continued. "But Rosie. Rosie is different. I'm leaving you, Delta. I'm proposing to Rosie tonight. She wants the whole nine yards, the house, the white picket fence, kids, everything. And I'm going to give it to her."

Delta felt her blood rushing to her head. "Tell me, Tim. Does Rosie even know you're married? Does she know you can't have kids of your own? And does she know about your penchant for swinging? Or are you saving those little details for later?"

"She's meeting me back here at the field for drinks just as soon as she delivers Dave back to his parents. I told her last week about my wife and our lousy marriage, and she was quite sympathetic. The rest I can worry about later. I told her I was serious about her. I've got flowers and drinks in the car and I'm going to get down on one knee right here on the ballfield."

He looked at Delta, pure fury in his eyes. "If you gave a flip about anything but that stupid cake business of yours, you might have noticed years ago that our marriage was in trouble. But no, you had to get the fondant right, get the roses straight on the edges, put the stupid toppers in place. That was more interesting to you than I was. You're a worse than useless wife. I'm glad I couldn't have kids with you. Less to leave behind."

Delta couldn't believe what she was hearing. "You encouraged me in the business. You loved the income! Don't justify your cheating ways by blaming me! I'm the victim here!"

Tim's voice was cold. "I'm well rid of you, Delta. And don't think you're getting one penny of my retirement, either. I'll find myself a good lawyer."

He turned his back on her again—he knew she hated being ignored when they argued—and tossed another ball in the air, swung, and missed. He grabbed another ball out of the basket and continued to ignore her.

"I'm well rid of you, too, Tim." Delta raised her bat, stepped closer to him, and closed her eyes.

Smack! The sound of Tim's bat hitting the ball into the outfield.

Thwump! And a grunt.

Then stillness.

Delta opened her eyes, still holding the bat, and stared right into Rosie's eyes.

Rosie stepped back from her and dropped a tall bottle of Galliano onto home plate next to Tim's still form.

"He just lied to you. He never told me he was married. He never told me he couldn't have kids. I can't believe I fell for his song and dance. He was married to the nice lady with the cupcakes, and he never even told me!"

She looked down at Delta's husband. "I came back and was waiting by Tim's car and thought I'd make myself a drink. I don't even know what this stuff is. I was just holding the bottle and admiring it. I heard voices and came over and heard how he was talking to you. What a monster! And I took a swing and I'm not even sorry. This isn't the first time I've had to defend myself from a verbally abusive man."

They looked at each other.

"I should have known," Rosie said. "He didn't want me to tell anyone we were seeing each other until we decided if we were serious. No phone calls, no public dates, just late nights at the ballpark dugout. He called it romantic. I was about to call it quits if he didn't step it up, but he told me tonight would be our special night, that he was serious, that everything would be different from here on out. He said he couldn't wait to make it official and introduce me to all his friends. And boy, it's different, all right."

Delta was studying Tim's lifeless form and obviously fatal injury. She knew the chief of police in Jones Branch was known to be lazy and probably wouldn't look too hard for a murder weapon. Baseball field, bat at hand. Intentional, or a tragic accident from someone swinging a bat at the wrong time? She could almost sense Chief Brown figuring out the easiest explanation and course of action.

"You know, Rosie, my favorite bartender, Rolando, at Lazy Bob's Sports Bar once told me the shape of a Galliano bottle reminds him of a bat, and that the handle stays sticky like resin. Now I know what he means, I guess."

"I'm not sure what that has to do with anything, but I guess now you're going to call the police. I'm not sorry. I'm going to tell them I was defending you, that he threatened you with a bat and that I was afraid for your life. But I'm not going to admit I was involved with this rat."

"I have a better idea, Rosie. Let's not call the police. Let's instead have you take off those clothes and shoes and wrap them in my raincoat. I'll give you some lighter fluid and matches and you go straight to the dumpster on Route 27 at the mini mart. It's closed at this hour and there aren't any cameras there. You're going to burn everything, including the coat, and toss it all in the dumpster. It's in the middle of nowhere and no one will see you. Then you're going to drive home in your panties and bra, take a long, hot shower, and forget this ever happened."

Rosie seemed to notice the bat in Delta's hand for the first time. She took in the raincoat and backpack.

"You see, Rosie, I'm going to be expanding the cake business in a month or so, after a proper period of grieving. I'll need some help. I'll pay well if you want to help part-time. I can't imagine a special-education teacher makes a tremendous salary. And I've just decided that ten percent of profits will go towards helping battered women. Maybe you could run that aspect of the business as well."

"You came here to do what I just did. You thought it all through." For the first time, Rosie seemed shocked.

"Maybe I did and maybe I didn't. But if you do what I say, there's a good chance you'll be spending your life in the classroom and making beautiful cakes for happy people and not rotting away in some jail cell for a crime of passion and justifiable homicide. I'd tell you to think it over, but we don't really have the luxury of time, do we."

Rosie looked at her. "Give me the raincoat. Turn it inside out when you take it off. And I'd better take your shoes, too."

"First, take some of these wipes and help me clean off this bottle. I'm taking it with me. Then I'm stopping by Tim's car and taking everything else home that doesn't look like it belongs in a middle-of-nowhere ballfield."

*****

Delta had cleaned and replaced all Tim's favorite drink supplies at the bar, showered, put on makeup, and donned her favorite dress by the time she called the police for a welfare check on her dear husband, who hadn't returned home from ball practice to celebrate the anniversary of their first date. She told the dispatcher she couldn't imagine what would keep him from their private little celebration, and he wasn't answering his cell phone.

She was worried, she said. So worried.

She mixed a couple of Harvey Wallbangers and left them on the crystal tray on the bar, so they would be nice and watery by the time the police came to break the bad news to her, like they'd been sitting there for some time in anticipation of her beloved husband's return home.

She wondered when Tim had started resenting her, what had happened to the sweet man she married, and she figured she would have no problems manifesting tears and shock once the police spoke to her. They did have some good years in their marriage, after all.

Poor Tim.

And while she waited for a knock at the door, she readjusted the roses on the bar, then turned on some romantic Frank Sinatra tunes and sang along, all the while wondering how soon she could order the business cards and begin placing ads for Cakes by Dawn as part of her new marketing campaign. Probably pretty soon, she decided. She had to support herself. People would understand.

*****

After a short and inconclusive investigation by the laziest sheriff in a dozen counties, Delta was planning a proper funeral service for Tim a few weeks later, right in the middle of baking. She popped a strawberry cheesecake in the oven and was washing her hands when the phone rang. Lazy Bob's Sports Bar was on the caller ID.

Delta raised an eyebrow and answered. "Hello, this is Delta!"

"Delta, Rolando here. The bar would like to send some flowers as a tribute to Tim's funeral, since you both are such loyal customers during baseball season. We're all just so sorry about what happened."

"That's so thoughtful, Rolando. So very, very thoughtful."

"What kind of flowers would you like? What was Tim's favorite? The boss wants to know."

"Anything but roses would be nice, Rolando. Anything but roses."

There was a pause.

"Delta, are you alone?" Rolando's voice had dropped to a whisper.

"Yes. You?"

"I am. Delta, how long do you think before we can be seen in public together?"

"I've been thinking about that. I'll start coming back to the bar soon. I'll be lonely. I'll need some sympathy and conversation. It's only natural I'd want to start spending time with such a kind and sympathetic man as my favorite bartender."

"True. Start slow. I'm thinking maybe six months."

"I don't know if I want to wait that long, Rolando. I'm thinking maybe four months."

"It's going to be hard to stay away from you till then, Delta."

"It's got to be done, Rolando. Like many things in life. I'll miss you, too. Better not call again anytime soon."

"I'll see you soon, Delta."

"You will indeed, Rolando. You'll see. The months will fly by and soon we'll be together. And now I've got to hang up because I have a new assistant stopping by any minute now. She doesn't know the first thing about baking, but she does know all about baseball and seems willing to follow instructions, so I'm looking forward to working with her."

"I admire your dedication to your business, Delta. I hope she's a quick learner."

"Oh, I have a feeling she is, Rolando. I really do."

She hung up and smiled to herself. The future was looking very bright indeed.

Ripped by Love
Leah St. James

"My husband wasn't the man many thought he was."

Abbie Johnson inhaled until the urge to cry passed, her eyes steady on her sister standing behind the pulpit. Somehow Claire managed to look beautiful—even dignified—while sniffling and wiping away the tears racing down her cheeks.

"Although Roger dealt with people every day, he wasn't really a people person," Claire continued. When several in the pews chuckled quietly, her lips turned up in a watery smile. "He was an entrepreneur, an expert at what he did, and very competitive. He traveled to business conferences and gave speeches around the world. But one-on-one…not so great. Many saw him as aloof, stiff. Even my closest friends and family wondered what I saw in him."

Claire's gaze met Abbie's, and a silent message passed between them. Claire was right. When she was first introduced to Roger, Abbie had been less than impressed. The guy might have hailed from the British royal family—some cousin x-number of times removed—and been filthy rich, courtesy of that ancestral wealth. It was also true that he was tall, lean, and too blasted handsome for his own good. People who enjoyed dry, snarky humor even considered him witty. And thanks to an international upbringing, he spoke with that vaguely European accent that made some American women lose their panties.

But Abbie had always sensed a chill that the wit, money, and pretty face failed to warm. In the year and a half since they'd first met, nothing had persuaded her to fully like, or trust, her sister's husband.

But Claire had loved the man. She'd trusted him. And Abbie loved Claire, so she kept her mouth shut and her eyes open.

"But once my friends got to know Roger, they discovered what I already knew. Inside, he was a different man." Claire cleared her throat and looked over the several hundred who packed the church. "I won't argue that it took Roger time to warm up to some people, and they to him—except for the occasional woman." She stopped as if she'd surprised herself with her comment, and a few nervous chuckles broke out.

"I think it was more that his brain never shut off. He saw the world in terms of monetary transactions." She glanced up, frowning. "He once told me he dreamed about mergers and acquisitions." A hoarse, weeping noise slipped from her throat. "I never understood the thrill, but then, I stopped balancing my checkbook the day I married him."

The line got a laugh from the attendees. Most knew Claire was a financial genius, thanks to their father. He'd taught them well, leaving them each financially set for life, and Claire had aggressively increased her portfolio over the years.

In fact, Claire had met Roger through a women's investment club. He'd given a presentation, the two had clicked, and were married less than six months later.

Claire shrugged at the laughter. "He knew I didn't need the help, but he spoiled me rotten. Every day, up to that last perfect day."

She stopped again to stare into the distance. "It was our first wedding anniversary. We'd planned to celebrate at my family's cottage at the Virginia Beach oceanfront. Roger told me not to plan a thing. He had it all worked out, which wasn't surprising. He had planning notebooks for everything. But the romance…" Her voice trailed off, and for a moment the atmosphere seemed to weep.

"He took my breath away. He'd arranged for bouquets of white roses throughout the cottage. It smelled like an English garden. Lights glittered around the deck and wrapped the railings down to the beach. There, we dined under a tent, our meal a replica of the menu from our wedding reception."

Abbie's mind retreated to that day. Roger had contacted her a month before the anniversary saying he wanted to surprise Claire for their special day. She'd been shocked, but she was happy to help, and he'd needed a lot.

It was Abbie who ordered the flowers and set up the twinkling lights. She who arranged for the catering and selected the menu, down to the wine list.

"A white velvet jeweler's box sat on my plate. It was tied with a blue satin ribbon." Claire touched one of the sapphire drop earrings she wore—each a genuine two-carat sapphire in a marquise cut, bordered by quarter-carat diamonds. Abbie had selected them as well. "These were his last gift to me."

She choked on the final words, then turned away.

Abbie hopped from her seat and rushed to her sister's side. "Claire, you don't have to do this."

"You're wrong. I do have to do this…for Roger." Claire sniffed and waved her hands in front of her face. "I'm fine. I'm okay." She swiped her hands under her eyes and tried to smile at the congregation. "Roger is probably yelling at me right now from … Heaven." She glanced up as she said it, her face crumpling. "He wasn't always comfortable with emotions."

Abbie stared into Claire's eyes and saw the resolve behind the pain. That resolve had seen her sister through the ten days since Roger's death. Ten days since he'd fallen victim to the vicious current that ripped him out to sea and tossed him aside, dead. With a gentle squeeze to Claire's shoulder, she returned to her seat.

When Claire finished, she dropped into the pew and grabbed Abbie's hand. Two years earlier, they had sat in this same pew mourning the loss of their parents—their dad from a stroke, their mom a few days later from a broken heart.

Shoving the memory aside, Abbie focused on the pastor's final words of comfort, to have faith and find peace in believing it wasn't the end for Roger, but a beginning of a new and glorious life eternal.

Claire whispered "Amen" along with the congregation, and the service ended.

Together they rode in the limo behind the hearse to the cemetery. After the pastor's prayers of commitment, Claire was the first to throw a handful of dirt on his casket before it made its descent into the Earth.

"I loved you so, Roger," she murmured as she dribbled the soil. "Ashes to ashes, dust to dust. I commend you now to your eternal home." She leaned over the casket, murmuring a message meant only for his spirit, wherever it was.

As they left the cemetery, Abbie tried to find words of comfort.

You'll learn to love again? Maybe. But that was no solace at this time.

I'll be there for you? True, but as close as they were, *she* wouldn't be warming Claire's sheets at night.

Time will heal the pain? An expression used by people who'd never experienced sudden, devastating loss.

Finally, they arrived at Claire's home, an old country estate in Virginia's Loudon County. Catering staff had set up a post-funeral repast, enough to feed a pro football team, which was good since half the congregation had chosen to attend. People spilled from the house onto the patio and lavishly landscaped yard beyond where summertime blossoms scented the air.

A woman stood by herself near the patio door. A beautiful honey-blond, she wore a simple black sheath dress and black pumps, and she held a wine glass filled near to the brim. Her gaze was fixed on Claire, not with the sympathy of the other guests, but with a calculation. Before she could stop herself, Abbie strode forward and extended her hand to the woman.

"Hello, I'm Claire's sister, Abbie. Have we met?"

The woman gave a polite smile and clasped Abbie's hand. "Nice to meet you. I'm Janet Murphy." She shook her head and made a *hmming* noise. "Such a shame about Roger, isn't it? So young and fit. And to die in such a horrible way." She shuddered. "I can't even imagine watching someone I love being pulled out to sea like that, knowing you're powerless to help."

"It's been a terrible shock to everyone, but most of all to Claire. She's always been a strong swimmer. She was a lifeguard in high school."

"Really?" The woman's eyes widened. "And she couldn't save him?"

"She was watching from the shore, but by the time she ran in, he was…gone."

A hurricane had been brewing near Bermuda, churning up the mid-Atlantic waves. Despite the city's red-flag warnings up and down the beach, Roger had raced into the waves. Claire had warned him about the currents, about the lack of lifeguards on duty, but he'd ignored her concerns. Now he was dead.

"How awful," Murphy murmured. "I can't imagine what she must be feeling." She caught Abbie's gaze, like she expected her to share Claire's most private emotions.

But Abbie had no intention of revealing Claire's thoughts during those first few days—the shock, the survivor's guilt, and more that Abbie would never comprehend.

"It's been difficult," Abbie murmured as her gaze landed on Claire, stoically exchanging hugs and handshakes from the stragglers who claimed to be close to Roger.

Apparently noticing the same thing, Murphy said, "I wonder how long she can stand there. I'd have gone up to bed by now. With a big glass of wine." A wry laugh slipped out. "Sorry if that was inappropriate."

Abbie found herself smiling. "I was thinking the same thing." She narrowed her gaze on the woman. "So how did you say you know Roger?"

She took a sip from her glass. "I didn't."

Abbie was about to launch an interrogation when Claire joined them.

"Hello," she said to Murphy. "Thank you for coming."

Abbie made a quick introduction, and the two shook hands as Murphy shared condolences.

"How did you know my husband?" There was an unexpected edge to Claire's voice. She'd never been the jealous type, but then what wife wouldn't wonder how her now-dead husband knew a beautiful woman who showed up unexpectedly at his wake?

Murphy's mouth firmed into a thin, straight line, and she inhaled until her chest expanded. "We need to talk. Can we go somewhere private?"

Claire stilled and grabbed onto Abbie's arm.

Abbie glared at Murphy. "What's this about?"

"It's between me and your sister."

Hugging Abbie's arm, Claire said, "Anything you have to say to me, you can say in front of Abbie. We'll use the office."

Claire led the way. When the door closed behind them, she stopped at the antique Cherrywood desk that took up a third of the wall space, then pivoted and dropped onto the sofa in the sitting area, dragging Abbie next to her. She waved Murphy to the opposing chair. "Now, what is it you have to say to me?"

The woman slipped her hand into the pocket of her sheath and withdrew a small black case. She opened it to reveal a gold badge and a card that identified her as a detective with the Virginia State Police.

Claire's face blanked as the color leeched from her skin, but she met the investigator's gaze. "Obviously you're not here as a personal friend."

"No, I'm not. I've been cleared to inform you that your husband was the subject of an active investigation for identity theft and conspiracy to commit fraud."

Abbie jerked, willing her expression to stay calm.

At the same time, Claire screeched, "Roger?!" Her eyebrows shot into her forehead, and she pushed to her feet. "That's not possible. He didn't have the personality." Moving like an old, frail woman, she shuffled to the small bar at the side of the room and pulled a bottled Perrier from the fridge under the bar. She guzzled it, her eyes on the detective, finally asking, "What kind of identity theft?"

"Evidence points to a ten-year spree of conning women out of their personal information—logins, passwords, real estate records, things like that. With that information, he would set up credit accounts in their names, get into their banking records, change ownership of valuable property. Over the last decade, we believe he's stolen upwards of eighty million dollars in cash and property. Most of his victims never knew what hit them until it was too late." She paused, as if debating, then said, "We believe you were his latest mark."

Claire squeaked, her hand on her throat, then dropped to the floor with a thud.

Abbie rushed to her side, elbowing the detective out of the way. "Call 911."

Later, after the EMTs packed up, Claire lay in her bed, pale, and weeping. Abbie sat beside her, holding her hand, while Detective Murphy stood in the doorway, watching.

"I've called her personal physician." Abbie stood and approached the detective. "She's not usually so fragile, but this has been a trying day."

Murphy pushed away from the door and handed Abbie a business card. "I'll give her a day or two, but I will need to speak with her. I need to wrap up this investigation."

"Why? He's dead."

"Yes, but there could be more victims, and we need to find where he hid the proceeds of his criminal activities."

"Probably in an offshore account. I doubt it was here if he was planning to steal from Claire."

"I'm inclined to agree, but I have a responsibility to those victims to recover what we can."

She turned to leave, but Abbie stopped her with a hand on her arm. "Can you tell me, what was his real name?"

Murphy's eyes flickered, then she shrugged. "Robert Atkins, born in Canada. He had dual citizenship with the U.K."

"So, his marriage to Claire wasn't legal."

"No." Murphy shook her head. "In fact, he is legally married to a woman in London. They have three kids, one of them less than a year old."

Abbie snorted. "Busy man. Maybe that's where you'll find his stash."

*****

After she left, with Claire sleeping soundly, Abbie crept downstairs to call her husband. He answered on the third ring.

"How'd it go, sweetheart? Are you doing okay? How's Claire?"

Tears leaked from the corners of Abbie's eyes, and she swiped at them angrily. "It was a funeral. Everything went like clockwork. Claire is sleeping, but she learned some disturbing news about Roger today." She explained what Murphy had told them.

Jeff grunted. "So, you were right about him all along."

"Being right doesn't feel good in this case. The news really threw her. She's already so vulnerable, and I'm afraid she'll…"

"Do something stupid?" He'd said it softly, maybe fearful of raising that specter, but it was already raised.

"Maybe. I'd like to stay for a few days if you don't mind. I took the week off from work, just in case."

As a forensic accountant with the state's Bureau of Criminal Investigation, Abbie had been working on a task force to investigate a suspected money laundering ring. Her boss hadn't been thrilled when she'd asked for the leave, but she convinced him that evidence wouldn't disappear in the time she'd be gone. Fingers crossed, anyway.

Her husband was even less happy. After a beat, he said, "The boys and I can manage, but they miss their mom."

"I miss them, too. And you." A pang zinged through her heart. It hadn't been easy to leave her husband and young sons to be with Claire for the past few days, but that's what sisters did. They stuck with each other.

After disconnecting the call, she checked on Claire—still sleeping, looking waif-like in the king-sized bed—then made her way downstairs to the office. There, she closed the door and stood listening for a few moments, for what she wasn't sure. Aside from the occasional hum of the HVAC, the house was graveyard quiet. Too far back from the roadway for any traffic noise. Too far from other properties for neighborhood noise. Too creepily quiet for her own liking.

Shivering, she took a seat behind the big desk. Armed with a fresh pair of disposable gloves from the kitchen, she began a methodical search of the desk and file cabinets. Con men usually didn't leave evidence lying around, but if there was any, Abbie wanted to find it before Janet Murphy showed up with a search warrant.

After finding nothing relevant in the filing cabinets or desk file drawers, she dropped to her knees and wriggled under the desk. Using her phone's flashlight, she examined the interior frame. *There.* Like many antiques, the desk had multiple small compartments, some obvious and some not so obvious. This one had a cubbyhole hidden at the back wall.

With one gentle push, the spring latch disengaged, allowing a small door to open. Abbie shoved her hand into the opening until her fingers touched something soft. She withdrew a black leather notebook, five by seven inches and two inches thick, bound with a leather string. She settled on the floor, under the desk, and stared at the book.

"What are you doing?"

Abbie jerked, smacking her head on the top of the desk frame, then peeked around the edge. Claire stood in the doorway, arms folded over her chest, wearing a silky robe, fuzzy slippers, and a deep frown.

Abbie crawled forward and pushed to her feet. "Claire, you should be resting."

"I was, but clearly, I should have been down here."

Abbie's shoulders fell and she stepped forward, the book in her hand. "I know this looks bad."

"It is bad, Abbie." She held out her hand. "What have you got there?"

Abbie started to pass her the notebook, then pulled her arm back. "You should wear gloves. Otherwise, your fingerprints—"

"Don't be ridiculous." Claire grabbed the book and started leafing through the pages.

"I've been looking for evidence of Roger's...activities before the detective comes back with a warrant, hopefully get rid of her, quickly." When Claire continued to glare, Abbie added, "You should know exactly what you're dealing with before you talk to her."

Fortunately, Claire wasn't prone to anger, and rarely held a grudge. She tipped her head toward a worktable to the side of the room. "Let's see what we find."

She placed the book on the table and pulled her hands back, as if suddenly afraid of contamination. "You do it," she said, nudging Abbie's shoulder with her own.

After another nod from Claire, Abbie picked up the book and turned it in her hands. "There are three tabbed sections, labeled: Planning, Active, and Completed. She glanced at Claire. "If nothing else, the man was methodical and organized. He had a running pipeline of victims. And its paper, not digital, so couldn't be easily found. Smart."

Claire made a rude noise and waved her hand to continue.

"I think we should start with the 'Completed' section. I'll cross check against the federal databank—"

"No, start with 'Active.'" Claire's chin trembled, but she firmed her lips and nodded. "Do it."

The first page held a chronological list of names. A column to the right listed a date. Behind it were three sheets with individual names, itemizing personal information for each—birth dates, social security numbers, logins and more. Claire's sheet was on the top. "It looks like he was working on…"

Her voice caught in her throat, but Claire picked up the thought. "He was working on three of us simultaneously—me, a woman from St. Louis, and another from San Diego." She snorted. "All the business conferences were nothing more than covers for his cons."

"I'm so sorry, Claire." Clearing her throat, Abbie flipped to the "Completed" section. Again, the first page was a listing of his past victims. She skimmed the names, and flipped through the pages, stopping on each victim.

"It looks like he transferred the sheet with the individual's personal information from section to section as he moved them from one stage to the next, adding information he needed along the way." She pointed to a string of numbers on one. "This looks like account information where the stolen monies might have been funneled."

Claire leaned in and pointed to a different section. "These look like names of storage companies. Maybe they're his accounts at facilities where he stored the physical property."

Her eyes on the last page, Abbie snapped the book closed. "We need to give this to Janet Murphy. It'll take time, but hopefully the funds and property can be returned to his victims."

Claire sighed, and a tear slipped down her cheek. "I cannot believe he fooled me, and for so long."

Abbie hugged Claire tightly, then she pushed back to catch her gaze. "I know this is hard, but maybe Roger's death was meant to be. If he hadn't died, you would have lost everything. The man was slick."

"Meant to be?" Claire inhaled and exhaled on a shudder. "Maybe. If fate hadn't stepped in, he would have taken everything from me."

The next day, Detective Murphy stopped by to follow up. Claire gave her the notebook and allowed her to look through their personal financial records as well, although Abbie had cautioned her to ask for a warrant. It wouldn't matter. Truth would be out, either way.

"Thank you for your cooperation," Murphy said as she headed out the door. "I'll be in touch if we need anything else."

*****

Two weeks later, Abbie pulled into Claire's private roadway, pausing at the entrance to gather her thoughts. In the days since Roger's funeral, life had resumed in a new normal. She and Claire talked frequently, got together when they could, and tried to forget the devastation of Roger's wrongdoings. So, when Claire called an hour earlier needing her, Abbie jumped in the car, praying the investigator hadn't dug up more dirt.

She eased the car down the drive, through the entrance gates, and into the circular driveway in front of the estate. A plain black sedan screaming *Government Issue* sat several feet ahead. Sweat erupted on Abbie's scalp.

She tried to breathe normally as she climbed the front steps and waited patiently for the door to open, but an unease roiled in her gut. There was only one reason she could think of for an official visit—Janet Murphy had discovered the truth.

Claire pulled the door open. "Abbie, thank God you're here. Detective—"

"I figured. What does she want?"

Murphy stepped from behind the door. "Just a few things to clear up with your sister." Her gaze jumped from Claire to Abbie and spit pooled in Abbie's mouth.

"What do you need to clear up?" Abbie asked, keeping her voice nonchalant, as if Murphy were there for a social call.

"Let's have a seat."

Claire led the way, this time to the kitchen where she grabbed mugs and pointed them toward the coffee maker.

Once they settled at the table, she lifted then dropped her hands. "So, what is it now?"

Murphy gave them a pained half-smile. "I was looking at the medical examiner's report of your husband's—I'm sorry, Robert Atkins' death."

Claire planted an icy gaze on the detective. "He was stupid and went swimming in rough seas. Mother Nature did the rest."

"But he'd been drinking prior to that. A lot. His blood alcohol was three times the legal limit."

"We were celebrating what I thought was our wedding anniversary." She crossed her arms in front of herself, and Abbie wondered if it was to hide the fact that her chest was rising and falling at the rate of a marathon runner.

Abbie interrupted to pull the focus from Claire. "Certainly, you can't think there's anything suspicious, Detective Murphy."

Murphy gave her a side eye. "You're in law enforcement, aren't you?"

Abbie lifted her shoulder. "I'm a forensic accountant."

"And with your expertise, you didn't see anything interesting in that notebook you and Ms. Delaney turned over to me?"

Abbie kept her eyes level on the other woman. "You'll have to define 'interesting.'"

"How about the fact that your parents, William and Eleanor Delaney, were earlier victims?" Murphy met Abbie's gaze. "He went from them to your sister. It looks to me like he was deep in their con when he set his sights on her. Certainly, you couldn't have missed their names in the book."

Abbie froze for a beat too long, and Claire jumped in.

"So, we both got taken by the bastard. I guess the apple didn't fall far from the tree." She jabbed a finger at Murphy. "Our dad was suffering from the early stages of dementia. He never would have let Roger con him out of money otherwise. He was too smart." She sniffed back threatening tears. "Suddenly they were penniless. After years of careful saving and investing, it was gone. *Poof!*"

Murphy let the comment sit before asking, "So when did you discover that your so-called husband had conned your parents out of their life savings?"

"She didn't." Abbie interrupted. "I found the notebook and saw their names."

"And yet you turned it over to me, knowing there was evidence that could implicate your sister—or maybe you—in Atkins' death?"

"We have nothing to hide. His death was accidental, whether he drank too much or not. If I were you, I'd take it as a win, a gift to get as much of that stolen fifty million back for the people he scammed, and let it rest. If any of the money comes back to me and my sister to compensate for our parents, good."

Murphy's eyes narrowed, and she tilted her head, studying them, as if trying to figure out which, if either of them, had orchestrated the man's death. "I've heard worse advice." She stood and gave them a closed-mouth smile. "You won't be hearing from me again, ladies. Thank you for your time."

After she left, Claire pulled Abbie into a hug. "Thank God. I thought she was going to arrest one of us."

"I sweated it there for a minute, but I think we'll be okay."

Claire stared into Abbie's face. "It doesn't matter, but I have to know. The alcohol level. Roger was half drunk by the time I got there. How? And why? I know you were there. I know it was you who set everything up at the beach. He didn't have it in him."

Abbie stilled, then shrugged. "You're right. He asked for my help, and when I met with him a few days earlier, I saw the book lying on the desk. I admit I snooped. I nearly died when I saw our parents' names in there. I realized Dad hadn't lost the money; he'd been swindled. I wanted to tell you, but you were so happy. I had to get you out of that marriage." She shook her head, remembering her panic. "That day at the cottage, I encouraged Roger to have more than a few glasses of wine to loosen up before you got there—hoping he'd fall asleep so I could talk to you."

"And then we had more." Claire chuckled and lifted her coffee mug in a toast. "So that's why he went under so easily."

Abby felt her eyes pop wide. "I'm sorry?"

"I discovered the book before you did," Claire said. "That last week was torture, trying to pretend that I didn't know what a creep he was. I think I deserve an Oscar for my performance at the funeral, and with Detective Murphy."

"What are you saying, Claire?"

"I'm saying, I appreciate your trying to save me, but I had it covered."

Abbie was afraid to ask what she meant but had to wait only a few moments before Claire continued. "I pictured it so clearly in my mind. He loved the ocean but wasn't a strong swimmer. I'd lure him in, and once there, I'd wait for a big breaker and hold him under. Then the storm happened with the rip current. It was rough that day. So rough I didn't want to go in. My plans were ruined. But Roger was so wasted, he was irrational. The waves were a challenge. I told him I'd be right behind him, then watched from the shore as the current caught him. In the end, all I had to do was watch him die."

A chill zipped down Abbie's spine. "I thought you tried to save him."

Claire smirked. "Oh, I went in and got knocked around enough to make it look good for the cops."

Abbie sipped on her coffee, trying to let the fact settle that she'd inadvertently helped a man to his death. Or that her sister had done even more. "Do you feel guilty?" she finally asked.

Claire quirked an eyebrow. "Why should I? His betrayal killed our parents. He tried to con me. He deserved what he got." Then she shrugged. "Roger really wasn't the man people thought he was."

Stalked by Her Past
Sheryl Jordan

The early morning sun rose just above the horizon, painting the sky in hues of pink and orange mixing with gray clouds. Brianna left her house after double checking the lock on the front door. Walking down the sidewalk she heard shuffling across the street.

What was that? I don't see anything. A quick glance revealed nothing out of order, but a shiver ran down her spine and she picked up the pace.

Oh crap, there it is again. Run!

Running as fast as she could down the block, she reached her sister and brother-in-law's house in record time.

Bam! Bam! She pounded the heavy brass knocker against the door.

"Are you trying to tear the door down banging on it like that?" Brittney asked, swinging the door open as her identical twin sister rushed through the entryway.

The two women faced each other in a mirror pose. Huge brown eyes and coca skin matched perfectly. Only the facial expressions differed as Brianna gasped for breath and concern etched a frown on Brittney's.

"What's going on?" Damien ran to the foyer.

"Someone was following me." Brianna's heart pounded like a drum in her chest.

Damien walked down the sidewalk, checking both directions, and turning with a shrug.

"No one's out there, but the neighbor's dog." He stepped into the foyer and closed the door.

"He probably started chasing me when I ran past their house like a mad woman," Brianna said.

"Glad you're okay. I've got to finish getting ready for work." Damien headed upstairs.

"Why do you think someone is following you?" Brittney hugged her identical twin sister and led her into the kitchen.

"I heard footsteps or a shuffling sound on the sidewalk across the street, but when I stopped to look around, nobody was there. I took off running," Brianna said.

"Sit down and have some water." Brittney grabbed a bottle of water from the refrigerator. "Why are you looking at your phone like that?"

"I keep getting friend requests from this guy, but he has no profile and only pictures from the internet. I denied his previous requests, but he just keeps sending them."

"Sounds like you have a secret admire." Brittney sipped her coffee.

"More like a stalker!" Brianna reached for an apple from the fruit bowl on the counter.

"Who's a stalker?" Damien asked as he came back into the kitchen. He gave a sheepish grin as he rummaged for a bottle of water from the refrigerator. "Forgot my hydration."

"She keeps getting friend requests from a strange man on her social media," Brittney explained.

"It's probably nothing. People get friend requests from people they don't know all the time," Damien said.

"I feel like I'm being followed and watched, but I never see anyone out of the ordinary around." Brianna shivered as she took a bite of the apple.

"When did this start?" Damien frowned.

"Last week when I was on campus walking to my car," Brianna said. "I thought I was being paranoid. It's happened before just like what happened a few minutes ago. I got the same eerie feeling, then heard shuffling."

"Stay aware of your surroundings. If this continues, I'll have the firm's investigator tail you for a couple of days," Damien said. "After what happened to you in college, we want to be extra careful."

"Thank you, Damien." Brianna exhaled a sigh of relief.

"Thanks, babe." Brittney blew her husband a kiss. "I love you."

"I love you too. You ladies be careful today." Damien kissed Brittney's forehead.

"Let's get going, sis. A good workout and shopping will help relieve some of the anxiety you're feeling," Brittney said.

*****

While the twins were stretching to warm up before their workout, a man looking at his cell phone walked right into Brianna.

"I'm sorry," the man said, still looking at his phone.

"Maybe you should pay attention to where you're going instead of to your phone." Brianna snapped.

"You're right." He glanced at the women. "Hot damn! You two are gorgeous!"

"Again, I apologize. Enjoy your workout." He smiled and walked towards the weight benches on the other side of the gym.

"Girl, that man is fine!" Brittney said.

"He's all right." Brianna shrugged. Her gaze remained on the stranger as he began bench pressing at least 150 pounds of weights.

"Tell me you didn't notice his luscious lips surrounding his bright smile? Or his dark curly hair and brown eyes with thick, long lashes?" Brittney stared in the same direction as her sister.

"Yeah, not to mention those dimples, his muscular physique, and nice butt," Brianna added. She tapped her sister on the shoulder. "What are you doing looking? You have that nice hunk of husband at home, remember?"

"I'm just looking."

The man glanced at the twins before moving to another apparatus.

"I think he has his eye on you. You should talk to him." Brittney playfully nudged her sister.

"I'm here to workout, not meet men." Brianna gave a prissy huff as she headed toward the treadmill.

"You're watching him, not working out. Let's forget him and get to work."

After an hour workout, the sisters went to the locker room to shower and change, with no further sightings of the man they'd seen earlier.

"I'll wait for you at the juice bar." Brittney finished dressing before Brianna.

"Okay, I'll be there in a few minutes." Brianna said.

"More like thirty," Brittney grumbled.

"Whatever, sis."

Brittney ordered her favorite protein drink and sat down at an empty table and scrolled through her phone.

The man from earlier approached her. "Excuse me, do you mind if I join you?"

"Um, sure," Brittney said, startled.

"Now look who's so focused on her phone." The man smiled.

"At least I'm sitting down, not walking around bumping into people," Brittney said, giggling.

"Ah, you got jokes," the man said as they both laughed. "I'm Antwon Monroe."

"I'm Brittney."

"It's a pleasure to meet you, Brittney." He gazed at her.

Brianna approached the table.

Antwon introduced himself and extended his hand, half standing as she sat down. "You two must be twins. You have the most perfect facial structures."

"Thank you." She accepted his handshake. *Damn, his hands are even fine, strong yet silky soft.*

"Have you worked out here before?" Antwon flicked his gaze between the two sisters before dropping to the ring fingers of their left hands.

"We come here a couple of times a week. What about you?" Brianna's interest was piqued when she saw he had no wedding ring, then deflated when she realized not all men wore their rings during a workout.

"This is my second week coming here. I just moved to the area to start my new job," Antwon said.

"Congratulations and welcome to the area," Brittney said. "What type of work do you do?"

"I'm a plastic surgeon. I start in a couple of weeks but came early to get familiar with the area," he said.

"My sister Brianna is in her last year of med school specializing in pediatrics."

"That's awesome. Once I became a surgeon, I did most work reconstructing birth defects in children. Now I also do pro bono surgeries on disfigured trauma patients."

"That's a noble practice to be in," Brianna said. "I have a long way to go before I can think about doing things like that for those in need." Antwon nodded. "I believe in helping others have a better life when they are dealing with circumstances beyond their control."

"It sounds like you've been in the field for a while," Brianna said.

"It's been seven years now," Antwon said.

"No way. Did you start med school when you were fifteen?" Brittney interjected. "You look like you're in your early to mid-twenties."

"You're too kind. Close. I began college at sixteen, graduated in three years and started medical school," Antwon said.

"Have you had a chance to look around town? Why don't I show you around the area this week? I'm on a two-week break from school," Brianna said.

"I would love it," Antwon said.

"Are you married?" Brittney asked in her usual to-the-point style. Brianna kicked her leg under the table.

"Ow!" The injured sister glared at her twin.

"No, I'm not married, never have been. I also don't have any children in case you're wondering," Antwon laughed at the exchange between the women.

"I had to ask. You know people play the game all the time," Brittney said.

"I'm not that type of person," Antwon said, placing a hand over his chest.

"Okay then, let me get your number so we can plan a tour of the area," Brianna said.

They exchanged numbers and walked to the parking lot together. The sisters got into Brittany's silver Mercedes as Antwon headed to a red sports car.

"Do you see that man by the bushes staring at us?" Brianna's voice shook.

"Where?" Brittany asked as she started the engine.

"By the bushes next to the—"

"No one's there now. Maybe he was just walking to his own car." Brittney pulled out of the parking space.

"I swear I saw him. After Antwon left, he stood there watching us," Brianna said. "Something about him seems familiar."

"Well, I don't see him now. We'll keep a lookout from now on until we figure out what is going on."

Neither woman saw when the man stepped onto the sidewalk, watching them drive off.

*****

The twins spent several hours at the mall shopping and talking about Antwon.

"When are you going to call him?" Brittney asked while they stood in line at their favorite clothing store.

"Later tonight after dinner," Brianna said.

"He seems nice and cares about people."

"Yeah, he's handsome too. I could look into those eyes all day. If I think long enough, I can even imagine him touching my body." Brianna smiled.

"Girl, you're a hot mess!" Brittney shook her head.

Buzz. Buzz. Brianna rummaged through her purse to grab her phone and check the incoming caller ID. "Hey, Patrice," she greeted their longtime friend from high school and later her college roommate.

"I know its last minute, but do you and Brittney want to meet for lunch at the Soul Food restaurant by the mall?" Patrice asked.

"Yes, we're at the mall now looking at clothes. What time will you be here?" Brianna asked.

"In about an hour."

"Okay, we have one more stop to make, then we'll get a table. See ya soon."

"What's going on?" Brittney asked.

"Patrice wants to meet for lunch in an hour," Brianna said as she slipped her phone back into the bag.

"Perfect timing. We'll still have time to pick up mom and dad's anniversary present." "Yep. It'll be nice seeing Patrice again," Brianna said.

After leaving the clothing store, the sisters headed to the photography studio to pick up their parents' present.

"I think—" Brianna paused and lowered her voice. "The man watching us at the gym is by the sneaker store."

Brittney looked towards the store, as a man wearing a gray jogging suit turned and walked away.

"Let's follow him," Brittney said, running towards him, Brianna not far behind her. Moments later, they stopped and looked around after losing sight of him among the racks.

"He must have gone out the side door. He could have gone anywhere," Brianna said,

"Are you sure it was the same guy you saw at the gym?" Brittney asked.

"I'm not sure now, but he was about the same build and height. And their clothes look similar. I guess I didn't get that good a look at him at the gym because he was further away."

"Maybe it was just a coincidence. There are a lot of people here today," Brittney said.

"That's true," Brianna said. "Let's get the present and get out of here."

✶✶✶✶✶

The women arrived at the restaurant before Patrice and selected a table. The waitress took their drink order and left. Patrice arrived about five minutes later.

"Hi, you guys!" Patrice hugged them in turn.

"It's been too long. How have you been?" Brittney asked.

"Doing well," Patrice said. "What about you two?"

"I'm doing well. Brianna, on the other hand, is not so good."

"Let's order, then I want to hear everything." Patrice beckoned the waitress to their table.

After they placed their orders, the sisters told Patrice everything that happened over the past week.

"Look at you, a stalker, and a potential lover all in one week." Patrice winked at Brianna.

"I hope it's just my imagination about the stalker. On the other hand, I want to start dating again since it's been a while," Brianna said. "Antwon seems like a good man. He made a good first impression anyway."

"Just take it slow, see what happens," Brittney advised.

"Yes, considering your history with men. Remember when you thought you were head over heels in love with Bryson in high school?" Patrice asked.

"Until she found out he was dating that girl from a private school. He was such a jerk. When he got her pregnant, he tried to deny he ever slept with her," Brittney said.

"That poor girl was devastated. I dropped him after all that drama." Brianna took a huge swig of her drink as if to wash away the memory.

"What about Ryan Johnson from college?" Patrice asked.

"Now he was pure psycho. I still want to beat his ass for what he did to you," Brittney said.

"He sure was cray-cray. We dated for six months, and he started being possessive and needy. I couldn't deal with him anymore. When I broke up with him, he was shattered."

"He started showing up at the dorm all the time to walk you to classes and work. He even sent you flowers. I told him to leave you alone the time he came by the dorm when you twins went home for the weekend. He was so mad at me," Patrice said.

"And, Sis, I remember the time he thought I was you and begged me to let him take me out to dinner and give him another chance. I told him I wasn't you, but he insisted I was. When my then-boyfriend Damien came up to us and kissed me in front of him, he started crying, I couldn't believe it. I showed him my student I.D. to prove I wasn't you so he would stop crying." Brittney shook her head. "He was so embarrassed. I didn't see him around campus much after that."

"I didn't either until the night I was leaving work late at the restaurant on campus and someone grabbed me from behind. He started choking and punching me in my head and back. I heard him say, 'I'm sorry, I just want you to love me' before I passed out. My co-worker said she saw someone standing over me when she was leaving, and he ran off. She called the police, and they took me to the hospital. I didn't see his face, but I know it was him," Brianna said. "I remember that night like it was yesterday."

"You stayed in the hospital for three days. Mom and Dad were furious the police never arrested him," Brittney said.

"Neither of us was able to identify him even though I heard his voice. They never found any evidence he was there. The security cameras only showed a figure who appeared to be male matching his weight and height committing the crime. He made sure his face was covered and never turned towards the camera," Brianna said.

Patrice leaned forward and frowned. "I didn't tell you this at the time, but I was afraid you were going to marry Ryan and something bad would happen to you. All I could think of is first comes love, then murder."

"Oh my gosh, Patrice, that's morbid." Brittney lowered her voice. "But I had that same thought once. I wonder what he's doing now?"

"I heard after graduation, he was in an accident and had to have multiple surgeries and extensive plastic surgery," Patrice said.

"Karma's a bitch! I promised myself if I ever see him again, I'd get my revenge," Brianna said. "He got his anyway."

"What if he's the man stalking you?" Patrice asked. "You probably wouldn't recognize him after all the plastic surgery."

"Oh. No, now that worries me." Brianna's eyes widened in horror.

"Look, let's just enjoy lunch, keep our eyes open, and talk about this later," her twin said. "We still need to pick up groceries for our Italian dinner tonight."

*****

The twins sipped wine while Brittney prepared lasagna. The aroma of bell peppers, onions, and oregano filling the air. Brianna was busy chopping cucumber, tomatoes, and lettuce for the salad. Listening to old-school R&B music, they sang and performed popular dance moves from the past. Damien returned from work as Brittney took the lasagna from the oven.

"Hello, my love," Damien said and kissed his wife.

"Hey, babe!" Brittney set the hot dish on a silicone trivet.

"Hi, Brianna," Damien said as he swiped a cucumber from the salad.

"Hey, there."

"Dinner will be ready in ten minutes." Brittney put garlic bread in the oven.

"Great, I'm starving and it smells good," Damien said. "I'll be back as soon as I change."

After he joined the women at the dinner table, they blessed the food and began eating.

"How was work?" Brianna asked.

"It was fine. We took in several new clients," Damien said. "How was your day?"

"Interesting to say the least," Brittney said.

"Interesting how?" Damien raised an eyebrow.

The twins shared the events of their day as they ate.

"I don't think you should be this guy's personal tour guide without getting to know him first," Damien said. "How do you know he's even a doctor?"

"What if you meet him first?" Brianna asked. "We can all meet for breakfast tomorrow if you guys don't have any plans."

"I don't have any meetings until the afternoon so I can go at nine." Damien checked his phone's calendar and nodded confirmation.

"I didn't plan anything all week while I'm off work, so that works for me," Brittany said.

"Wonderful, I'll call him when I get home and text you later," Brianna said.

Brittney and Damien walked Brianna home. They ensured all the windows and doors were locked and the house secured.

"Are you sure you want to stay here tonight? Brittney asked.

"I'll be fine. You're only a few houses away," Brianna said.

"I know, but I don't want you here alone. You're welcome to stay with us until Mom and Dad come home," Brittney said.

"I'll be fine. I'll set the alarm as soon as I lock the door. You have the security app on your phone, as well," Brianna said.

"Okay, I love you, Sis."

The twins hugged.

"I love you too. Good night!" Brianna closed and locked the door behind them and set the alarm.

She poured a glass of wine and went to her bedroom, changed into her favorite pajamas, and climbed into bed.

Okay, here it goes. Scrolling to Antwon's number in her phone, she pushed the call button.

"Hey, Brianna," Antwon said.

"Hi, are you busy?"

"No, just watching TV." He turned the television down. "How was your day?"

"After the gym, we went shopping, met a friend for lunch, and I just got home from having dinner with Brittney and her husband."

"You had a full day," Antwon said.

"Yeah, it was fun to spend time with her," Brianna said, leaving out the parts about thinking someone was stalking her.

"After I worked out, I went to the office to introduce myself to the rest of the staff. I'm meeting the other surgeons at the hospital next week for a grand tour.”

“Cool. Would you like to join me, Brittney, and her husband for breakfast tomorrow morning?” Brianna asked.

“Sure. What time and where?”

“At nine. There’s a café a few blocks from the gym. I’ll text you the name and address.” She would also text Brittney letting her know he said yes to breakfast.

“Got the text,” Antwon said.

They talked a while longer, getting to know each other a little more until they both yawned and laughed.

“Time to go. I enjoyed chatting with you and I’m looking forward to seeing you tomorrow,” Brianna said.

“Likewise. Meeting you has been the highlight of my day,” Antwon said.

“Goodnight, Doctor Monroe,” Brianna said.

“Goodnight, beautiful lady.”

*****

Buzz. Buzz.

“Hey, Brittney,” Brianna said into her phone.

“Good morning, Sis. Do you mind picking me up for breakfast?” Brittney asked.

“Sure, I can pick you up. What’s going on?”

“Damien got called to the office about an hour ago. He’ll meet us there,” Brittney said.

“Okay, I’ll be there in a few minutes.”

“Thanks! See you then,” Brittney said.

Driving to the café, Brianna told Brittney about her conversation with Antwon the night before.

“His voice is so deep and soothing. I could have talked to him for hours nonstop,” Brianna said, gushing like a young schoolgirl in love for the first time.

“Sounds like you two are hitting it off,” Brittney said.

“Yeah, I hope he is as wonderful as he seems.”

“I always hoped you would meet and fall in love with someone who is kind, gentle and treats you right," Brittany said. "You deserve a lifetime of love."

Brianna parked next to Damien's car. They could see he was on a phone call, so Brittney motioned they would go get a table.

Antwon was already seated at a booth near a window facing the parking lot. He smiled when the hostess walked them to the table.

"Good morning, ladies."

They took a seat and Damien joined them shortly after. He shook hands with Antwon. They ordered breakfast and their conversation flowed easily. Damien and Antwon discovered they shared common interests in sports and community service.

After they ate, Damien invited Antwon to watch an upcoming football game and cookout at their house the following weekend. "Brittney and Brianna put on a good football feast."

"Sounds good." Antwon's phone rang and he excused himself to answer it. Brianna went to the restroom.

"By the way, Bri, I checked the home security videos of yours and your parents' house this morning. Yours was fine, but the camera picked up a man standing directly across the street watching their house last night. His face was partially covered by the hoodie he had on. I saved the video to my phone and met with one of my private detective friends this morning who owes me a few favors," Damien said.

"Why didn't you tell me?" Brittney asked.

"I wanted to see what the investigator thought. The man in the video is shorter and a bit heavier than Antwon. I checked him out on the internet and sent his name to the PI. He came back clean, and his bio matches everything he shared with us."

"So, someone really is stalking Brianna. I thought she was having anxiety attacks remembering what happened in college," Brittney said.

"It's real," Damien said hugging his wife. "I have Jackie following her as we speak. That's why I didn't object to her taking Antwon out to explore the city."

"I know she can protect herself from an attacker now, but I still worry."

"Yes, we'll keep her safe," Damien, said rubbing his wife's back.

*****

Brianna showed Antwon around the city for the rest of the week. She took him to museums, fine restaurants, and theatres. They enjoyed each other's company. Their relationship grew quickly, as they spent every waking moment together. She introduced him to her parents, who liked and welcomed him as her friend. Their relationship became intimate after spending so much time together. Brianna told Antwon about her past with her ex-boyfriend and how she felt someone was following her sometimes.

"I care about you and want you to know what's going on," Brianna said, lying in bed after a morning of steamy sex with Antwon.

"I'm glad you told me. I haven't noticed anyone following us though. Have you?" Antwon asked.

"No, I haven't lately, but I've been so distracted by you that I haven't noticed much of anything else."

"Good, maybe no one was following you. You may be experiencing post-traumatic stress," Antwon said, wrapping his arms around her protectively.

"I don't know. Whatever it is I want it to stop." Brianna said, hugging him tight.

"I will be here for you if it doesn't. I can get used to waking up next to you each morning." Antwon stroked her long curly hair and kissed her neck.

"Yeah, too bad we go back to work and school next week. I loved every moment we've shared these past weeks together." Brianna snuggled her head on his chest.

"Yes, it's been nice," Antwon said, deep in thought. "What was your ex's name?"

It can't be the same Ryan.

"I need to shower and have some breakfast. I'm famished after all the blissful exercise," Antwon said picking Brianna up from the bed and carrying her to the shower of his ensuite bedroom.

*****

"That was a good movie," Brittney said as they entered Antwon's home as the evening sun began to set.

"Thanks for having us over for dinner," Damien said.

"We thought it would be nice to get together before I start work and Brianna returns to school," Antwon said.

"Yes, our schedules will be pretty busy," Brianna said.

"Make yourselves at home. There's wine and liquor over here. I'm going out back to light the grill." Antwon turned on music which piped throughout the house and outside by the grilling area. He grabbed grilling utensils and went out the patio door.

Damien made himself a whiskey sour and joined Antwon outside.

"Man, you have a very nice house." Damien sat in the outdoor kitchen by the pool and wooded area beyond the property.

"Thanks, I fell in love with the place when I first looked at it," Antwon said.

"So how are things going between you and Brianna?" Damien asked.

"Great, we have a lot in common and similar goals. She has a wonderful personality, and loves her family and friends. Not to mention her striking beauty."

"Yeah, Brianna and Brittney are so much alike. Not just being identical twins, but their personalities are similar," Damien said.

"I've noticed that too," Antwon said. "They have a close relationship."

"They've always been that way. They even went to the same college," Damien said.

"Brianna told me a little about her college days. She shared what her ex-boyfriend did to her," Antwon said. "She thinks someone is following her."

"She must really like you because she doesn't share her past with people. Very few know about it." Damien stopped as the women brought the steaks and their drinks out.

"Here you go, babe." Brianna handed Antwon the meat tray and set his drink on the table.

Antwon put the lean beef on the grill and gulped his drink. He and Damien continued grilling the meat while Brianna and Brittney went back inside to check on the baked potatoes and get more wine.

"The salad is already made, and the potatoes should be done in about…" Brittney paused and pointed. "There's someone by the front door," she whispered as the doorknob jiggled.

"Let's get the guys," Brianna whispered as they made their way to the back door.

Bam! Bam! Bam!

The front door burst open just as Brianna opened the back door. The twins ran outside.

"Where are they?" Brittney asked looking around. She sees the two men on the far side of the yard, going into the pool house.

"Guys!" Brianna screamed upon seeing a man walking towards them.

No time to run. Time to fight!

"I've got you now," the man said, looking in confusion from one twin to the other.

"Let's get this bastard!" Brianna yelled.

The man grabbed Brittney's arm. She moved from his grasp and kicked him in the groin.

"Argh!" the man cried out in excruciating pain. Bending over he grabbed his privates.

"Wrong twin, idiot!" Brittney yelled as Brianna kneed him in the face, then elbowed him in the kidneys, and the man crumpled to the ground. Brianna turned him over and punched him repeatedly in the face.

Antwon and Damien run from the pool house to pull Brianna off the man.

"What the hell happened?" Antwon asked, holding the man's shoulder.

"It's him, the man who's been following me." Brianna's voice ended in sobs.

"How do you know this is the same man?" Damien asked while Brittney called the police.

"He said 'I got you now' just before trying to grab Brittney. He thought she was me. I recognized his voice. It's Ryan Johnson," Brianna said, kicking him in the face for good measure.

"He's my brother," Antwon said, looking at the man on the ground.

*****

While waiting for the police to arrive, Brianna, Brittney, and Damien questioned Antwon.

"What do you mean he's your brother?" Brianna demanded.

"He's my half-brother. We have the same father, but different mothers. I hadn't seen him since he was a kid until after he was in an accident."

"Did you know he was stalking Brianna this whole time?" Damien asked.

"No, I didn't. I got suspicious after she told me what happened to her in college. My dad told me Ryan had been in an accident after he graduated from college and needed multiple surgeries. I performed the final surgery to make the scarring less visible. I hadn't seen him nor spoken to him since," Antwon said.

"I couldn't handle your rejection, Brianna." Ryan's voice was muffled as he pressed his head to the ground. "I lost it when I saw you leaving your job on campus. I love you, Brianna! I attacked you because I wanted you back. Then momma died. After graduation I was depressed. I got drunk and crashed my car into a streetlight. I had lost both women I ever loved within a year. Momma didn't get to see me graduate. It was too much for me." Ryan sobbed. He struggled to his feet, but Antwon held him in a firm grasp.

"Why are you stalking me?" Brianna asked, pointing a long grilling fork at him.

"I still love you and want you back. After years of counseling, I can show you how much I've changed. I found out you were in medical school, and I started following you," Ryan said, his eyes darting around like a madman.

"Apparently, the counseling didn't work," Antwon said.

"You betrayed me!" Ryan reached for his belt and lunged at Brianna with a knife in his hand. The police arrived to see his body fly into the grilling fork she held, stabbing him in his chest.

"Oh, my God!" Brianna screamed, letting go of the fork. "What have I done?"

"Everybody freeze," an officer shouted.

Another officer rushed to Ryan, feeling his wrist for a pulse. He called for an ambulance.

One officer handcuffed Brianna as the fourth questioned the others.

"We're taking Ms. Oliver to the station for questioning. You all need to come down as well," the officer said.

"Don't say a word until I get there," Damien said. "Which precinct are you taking her to?"

The officer gave Damien the information. The ambulance arrived and took Ryan away. Antwon turned the grill off and locked up the house.

*****

Damien contacted one of his partners at the law firm to meet them at the station. They all made individual statements which eventually collaborated with Brianna's statement.

Ryan went into cardiac arrest and died on the way to the hospital. They released Brianna and her attorney advised her the district attorney would review the case.

The foursome drove to Brittney and Damien's home. Damien made them much needed drinks.

"I'm sorry, babe," Antwon said.

"It wasn't your fault. You barely knew your brother and certainly didn't know he was my deranged ex-boyfriend and stalker." Brianna patted his knee.

"They say it's a small world and this shows how small it really is," Damien said. "I'm glad you have closure now."

"Yes, I do. We kicked his ass. I didn't want him to die though," Brianna said solemnly.

"I still think if you'd married him, you'd have been the one going to the morgue," Brittney warned.

"Maybe. But I do have someone new and safe in my life now." Brianna smiled at Antwon.

"You still want to date me?" He responded in surprise and relief.

"Absolutely." Brianna kissed Antwon.

Veiled Threats
Allie Marie

Phoebe Parker opened the door of her bridal veil boutique, intending to hike to the curbside mailbox but she nearly stumbled over the unexpected package sitting just outside the door.

"What the…" She picked up the package, studying the return label with a wary eye. A glittery wedding veil watermarked the label that read *Veiled Obscura: Always a perfect choice!*

She'd never ordered merchandise from that shop before. Wrapped in heavy gold paper, the box bore neither a return address nor the full address of her actual business.

Hmmm, no postmark or stamps—someone must have delivered this in person. Frowning, she let her gaze roam over the fine calligraphy on a gold-framed white delivery label.

> TO: Clarabella Conrad, Bride-to-Be
> C/O Phoebe Parker, owner of:
> Heads or Veils: Your One-Stop Wedding Headdress
> Shop

Mail forgotten, she went inside and gently shook the ten-inch square parcel.

Just the right size for a wedding headpiece!

"Please, please, please let this be something Clarabella wants," Phoebe prayed out loud as she set the box on the counter. Her fingers itched to open the mysterious box but since it was addressed to

Clarabella in care of the shop, she resisted.

Only heaven knew how many different styles Phoebe had offered to the bridezilla, from sparkly rhinestone tiaras to feathery Vegas toppers, from pearl-studded combs to flower crowns, from silk top hats to dainty fascinators to cowgirl hats. Snoods. Birdcage veils. Even fascinators.

Nothing had suited the finicky bride-to-be.

She fluffed a trailing floral-and-ribbon cascade on a display dummy's head, then straightened a tiara on another. Heads or Veils had started small with traditional wedding headpieces but had expanded because of Phoebe's inimitable ability to find toppers for any unique— or challenging—tastes.

She plopped onto a white and gold brocade chair and let her mind drift to the day three weeks earlier when that ill-fated phone call came in. Her memory recalled every tiny detail.

Busy with a sale, she could not answer her cell phone until the third ring.

"Heads or…" Before she could finish, Darcy's rushed voice overrode Phoebe's customary store greeting.

"Hey, Pheeb, are you available today?"

"Darcy? Are you okay?"

"Yes, but I'm sending a bride-to-be to you for a headpiece. I'm one of her bridesmaids. You should see the hideous dresses she picked out for us, but never mind that right now. She's got her dress and veil, going for a mermaid theme but not finding a suitable topper. She can be a little difficult, but you have such a wide variety of pieces. I'm sure she'll find something at Heads or Veils."

"Um. Darcy—why do I sense you're not telling me everything?"

A moment of silence passed before Darcy spoke. "Bridezilla—er, Clarabella—likes nothing more than to be the center of attention. She's chosen a satin strapless mermaid gown, covered in iridescent pearls and beads that shimmer like water as she walks, but she wants her wedding veil to be her crowning glory. Her *pièce de resistance*." She added a guttural, "*Ooh la la.*"

"You do know the French don't really talk like that, don't you?" Phoebe smiled. Darcy was a not-always-accurate Francophile.

"*Sacrebleu!* Anyway, back to my story. Once the diva had settled on the dress and veil, she could not find a headpiece that suited her, giving the previous bridal shop owner considerable grief. Due to the dress alterations, the contract had required her to pay for the gown in advance, but when Clarabella became increasingly difficult, the shop owner canceled the rest of the contract, leaving the bride-to-be to stomp out, dress underarm, in a petulant huff."

"And I should take her on now because…?"

"Let me finish before you say no. A second bridal shop owner had similar experiences and refused to offer a contract, telling Clarabella to leave the shop. Our witchy bride refused and only left when the police were called in and advised her she could be charged with trespassing if she did not leave. But she's driving everyone crazy about this stupid veil piece and I know you can help her."

"Oh, Darcy, I don't need this kind of drama."

"Please, pretty please, as a favor to me."

A sigh escaped before Phoebe answered. "Oh, all right, send her over. Tell her to come in at two o'clock. What's her name and phone number?"

"Clarabella Conrad."

"Who the hell names their kid Clarabella?" Phoebe scribbled the name and phone number. "Tell her to come at two."

So—fifteen minutes after one, Clarabella Conrad sashayed into the shop, dressed to the nines in a pink silk dress and matching stilettos, and carrying a sea-green box with a white bow nestled under her arm.

"Hello, I'm…" Phoebe began.

Clarabella cut her off. "Did Darcy tell you I was coming?"

"Oh, you must be Clarabella. I thought you weren't coming until two, but it's nice to meet you." She extended her hand to the prospective bride, who ignored it and brushed past her to pick up a pillbox hat before tossing it to the side and removing a pearl-crusted cap from a tiered stand. She set it askew and whirled on her heel to face Phoebe.

"My gown has pearls and beads. I'll show you a picture in a minute. I just wanted to be sure there would be something here I might like. You do seem to have an extensive inventory despite being in this rinky-dink strip mall. Here's my veil." She plopped the box on the countertop.

Phoebe bit her tongue. She'd worked hard to build her business to be able to move into a suitable building and wanted to kick Clarabella out. But she also knew she could probably find what this woman was looking for and tack on an extra twenty-five percent for being such a— bridezilla.

Clarabella removed tissues to unearth a cathedral tulle veil from the box. The scalloped border was trimmed in lace, and each scallop contained a lacy seashell encrusted with pearls and white and green-blue sequins.

"My veil is traditional enough, but I wanted a headpiece that would shine the spotlight on *me* as the bride. I've planned everything around this veil. My gown is perfect, this veil is perfect, but now I need the topper to be perfect! Darcy assures me that if you don't have it here, you can help me find what I want."

"I'll do my best," Phoebe promised.

Thirty-nine headpieces later, she wasn't close to discovering what would satisfy the woman and had no more inventory to offer.

"Well, I don't see a thing in here that I like," Clarabella whined. "But you do have some nice pieces."

"I have a new shipment coming in soon. I can let you know when I have the inventory ready."

Clarabella narrowed her eyes as she tapped her chin with a perfect pink fingernail. "I suppose you have the best opportunity to find something. I'll stop by soon."

Twirling on a sharp heel, she flounced out the way she had entered.

Phoebe then spent the better part of a half hour straightening tilted tiaras and disheveled display stands. When the new delivery came in, she knew she still had not found a suitable headdress. For three weeks, she perused every catalog in search of something—anything that might suit the bride.

Until the strange box had arrived! Phoebe snapped her attention back to the present and jumped to her feet. Her gaze drifted to the strange box, narrowing her eyes in suspicious study.

Maybe, just maybe.

She roamed her fingertips across the package edge just as her phone pinged with an incoming text. Her phone screen brightened, revealing Darcy's number. With a sense of dread, she read the message.

> **Heads up! Can't talk but Bridezilla is dragging the whole bridal party over to your shop to help her decide on a veil topper TODAY! We're just leaving the wedding wine tasting at the OBX Wine Shop, and she really acted out there. Says Wesley is cheating on her, and she plans to find the beyotch and tear her hair out. Look out for drama!**

Phoebe typed back.

> **Oh, crap! Darcy Ainsley, you are so going to pay for unleashing Clarabella on me. How do you put up with her? And poor Lainey! I hope she made it through the day.**

PING! Darcy's response was immediate.

> **She did, but the scene was ugly. Do you have any non-alcoholic wine or fake Champagne on hand? Let her think she's getting the real thing. Six of us are coming—five of whom want to kill her and two of those want it to be a long, slow death.**

She signed off with a kissy face icon.

Heaving a sigh, Phoebe clicked the end call button and shoved the phone into her pocket. *"Poor Lainey"* was right. Just weeks earlier, her friend Lainey Gentry's OBX Wine Shop had been the scene of a murder where an unfortunate bridesmaid was stabbed with a corkscrew. Upon hearing the news, Phoebe had worried that Darcy had been the victim until she learned the incident involved a different wedding group. Lainey was even once considered a suspect and was just getting back on her feet after the incident had scared away business.

The wine reminded Phoebe to make a note to order a few specific bottles for a meeting with another wedding party next week, organized by a much sweeter bride-to-be than the disaster about to darken her doorstep. She jotted a list and set it by her laptop, then pulled two bottles of non-alcoholic sparkling champagne from the wine cooler.

Car doors slammed outside the shop.

The shop door swung open with a bang. Clarabella, waving an empty wineglass in one hand and sweeping the other in an arch, used a foot to kick the door open as she made her grand entrance into the Heads or Veils shop. Over one shoulder of a turquoise t-shirt, she wore a white sash with "Bride" emblazoned in gold letters.

"We're hee-eere!" Her nasal singsong stretched the word to two syllables as her scowling entourage followed. Darcy and three of the attendants wore white tee-shirts under bubble gum pink sashes with "Bridesmaid" in white letters, except for one tall brunette, whose darker rose satin sash displayed "Maid of Honor." She wore the tight-lipped look of a person whose patience was at an end.

"Welcome, ladies!" Phoebe forced a bright smile on her face and motioned to chairs scattered around the shop. "Please have a seat. Would anyone like a drink?"

Clarabella gave an expectant wiggle of her wrist to indicate her empty glass and began perusing the countertops. Two of the women glared in her direction as they found seats. Two others rolled their eyes and took a few steps away to stand at one of the counters. None looked at the merchandise.

"This is the same stuff you already showed me," Clarabella slurred as she turned in a petulant circle and leaned against the glass case. Two bright red botches dotted her cheeks. With disdain, she flicked her fingers at a small tiara, sending it skittering across the counter. One of the bridesmaids, a petite blond with bouncing curls, caught the crown before it hit the floor and set it out of Clarabella's reach.

"Nice catch, Ellen," Darcy muttered.

Tamping down her annoyance, Phoebe turned to pour the mock champagne, unable to prevent a sigh from escaping her lips. She had a room full of potential customers and no one noticed a hat or topper on her shelves. *Why did this 'Zilla have to come along and ruin a good thing in her shop*?

She arranged glasses on a tray, glad she'd opted for plastic stemware instead of glass. Her gut feeling told her a plastic stem might be less lethal than glass in the possible and imminent homicide of a maniac bride...by either disgruntled bridesmaids or a battle-worn shopkeeper.

"Can I help?" Darcy said. She walked to Phoebe's side and lowered her voice. "This is mock champagne, I hope?"

"It is. It's top-notch though. She'll never know the difference," Phoebe whispered back. "She's had enough. Her cheeks are already flushed."

"The flushing bride," Darcy added. Both women smothered their giggles.

"Drinkie, winkie, please," Clarabella called with another wave of the glass, which slipped from her grip. The same little blond showed further amazing reflexive prowess as she caught the glass before it reached the floor.

"Clarabella, you've just about plucked my last nerve." A fuming Darcy stormed past Phoebe, took the bride by the arm, and led her to a delicate brocade chair. "Sit your arse there and don't move."

She poured some of the non-alcoholic champagne in the plastic goblet and handed it to the bride-to-be, who drained it in one swallow and held it out for more. As Darcy poured another glass, she sloshed it over the rim, spilling the drink onto Clarabella, who burst into tears.

"You're so mean! How can you do this to me? I bet you're the one shleeping with Wesley."

"In his dreams," Darcy said as she stalked off. "And you're drunk."

The little blond patted the bride's hand. "Now, Clarabella, that's the second time today you accused someone of sleeping with Wesley."

"Maybe, Ellen. But I think he's been shleeping with somebubby…" Clarabella reached for the tip of her sash to blow her nose but stopped. Tears dried instantly as her eyes widened and she pointed. "Priddy!"

Phoebe's gaze followed the direction of Clarabella's fingertip toward the mysterious package.

"Oh, I almost forgot. This package arrived a while ago." The shopkeeper retrieved the gold-foil box and carried it over to the bride. "It's addressed to you…"

Clarabella snatched the box from her hands and tore into the wrapping without looking at the label. "What is it? What is it?"

Phoebe shrugged. "I don't know."

"Oooooh! What's in here?" Clarabella squealed as she removed layer after layer of gold and white tissue paper. "Who sent this?"

With another lift of her shoulder and holding her palms up, Phoebe answered again, "I don't know. It came from a shop with no info…"

"Oh, my!" Clarabella removed an odd white-gold tiara covered with pearls and aquamarine stones and held it over her head. Resembling the crown on the Statue of Liberty, each ray emanating from the base contained a thin glass tube filled with glitter. She shook the crown, sending the sparkles into a twirl.

Ellen squinted and drew the crown closer to her face. "Look, there's a switch inside the rim."

Clarabella fumbled for a few seconds until her thumb flipped the switch Ellen had indicated. Twinkling fairy lights danced amidst the pearls and stones and tiny bubbles twirled the glitter like a snow globe turned upside.

Inwardly, Phoebe winced. Although beautifully handcrafted, the glittering light points and bubbling water were over the top. She wondered why she put up with this client and glanced at Darcy, who rolled her eyes skyward.

"We used to have Christmas lights with bubbling water like that," a plump girl interjected. "There was a base like an ornament with the water going up the tube of glass."

"Shush, Lettie," Clarabella demanded. She raised her hands and hovered the crown over her head. "I love it. What do you all think?"

Her dutiful minions oohed and aahed as Clarabella sent the crown around for each to inspect.

"That's beautiful. I wish you had your veil with you to see how they look together," Ellen said with a sigh.

"It's perfect. Gives the aura of an enchanted undersea princess," Lettie gushed.

"You mean the undersea *queen*!" Clarabella snapped as she snatched the crown back.

Phoebe shuddered in distaste. Of all the variety of tiara, hats, and other headgear in her shop, she had nothing as garish as this crown. Just bend the pointed tips, add bells, and the crown could turn into a jester's hat of pearls, rhinestones, and water tubes.

Picturing Clarabella the Bridezilla walking down the aisle, jingle-belling amidst glistening bling and lace, with water tubes bubbling glitter, nearly sent her into giggles. So engrossed was she in the visual image that she didn't realize the bride and her matron of honor were in a heated discussion.

"I said it t looks like the Statue of Liberty in electric overdrive," Maid of Honor Marsha said in a raised voice.

"I heard you the first time, you shnot. I mean you snot!" Clarabella screamed. "How dare you!"

Marsha straightened from where she had leaned on a display case and ripped the banner from her shoulders. "That's it. I'm done, Clarabella. Find yourself a new MOH. And I hope Wesley finds a new bride."

"You come back here, you bitch," Clarabella slurred. "I'll bet *you're* the one whoosh been sleeping with Wesley behind my back."

The MOH shot the bird over her shoulder as she exited the boutique.

"I'm outta here." The plump bridesmaid jumped from her chair and followed suit.

"Why is everyone being mean to me?"

Ellen said, "Aw, honey, you just have the jitters today. None of us are sleeping with Wesley, and you know Wesley and Marsha haven't been a thing for years. They broke up long before they left the mission in South America, and that was over two years ago."

"But they ubes...to be...engazed, Ellen," Clarabella wailed, hiccupping in between her mangled words. Her inebriation back in force, she blew her nose on the end of her sash.

"Look, we need to get you home," Ellen cautioned.

"Nope. Not until I decide if I want this headpiece or not. Is there a full-length mirror around here?"

Holding back a sigh, Phoebe led the prospective bride to a dressing room off the main room. A long, thin mirror hung on the outside of the door.

Clarabella turned her head from side to side, squinting and leaning closer to the glass. "I don't have my glasshes on, but this looks good. I'll take it." She turned on her heels and danced into the dressing room, where a variety of mirrors lined the walls. She preened, losing her balance. The crown slid to one side.

"Oops." The bridesmaid named Ellen helped her to a chair just inside the door to the dressing room. Several mirrors lined the walls.

"Thish ish it, girlsh. I love thish crown! I need a drink to shelebrate."

"You've had enough," Ellen said. She straightened the crown on Clarabella's head and pushed it firmly in place. She pushed the button and turned off the bubbling, twinkling headpiece. "Just relax for a minute. You've had a long day."

"Okay, shweetie. You're sush a good friend. You can be my new MOH." Clarabella settled in the brocade wing chair, yawned, and fell asleep.

When Phoebe and Ellen returned to the main room, Darcy shook her head. "Ohmigosh, she was getting on my nerves." "Let's all have one last sip and chill out before we wake the 'Zilla and get her home."

Phoebe refilled the champagne glasses. As the wedding party discussed the antics of the bride, she lined tissue paper inside a pink and white box emblazoned with her store emblem. She would place the headpiece inside once the bride woke up.

Darcy stood. "I'm getting tired. All right, girls, shall we wake her now?"

"Yes!" the other bridesmaids said in unison. Ellen and Lettie stood on either side and shook the sleeping bride. Clarabella's head tilted forward, the crown askew but still on her head.

"Come on, Bridey girl, wake up!" Darcy called from across the room.

Alarmed, Ellen leaned close and shouted, "Clarabella, Clarabella!"

"She's not breathing!" A panicked Lettie stepped back, waving her hands as if to indicate she wanted nothing to do with the scene.

Darcy ran forward and pushed the frantic bridesmaid to one side. She felt for a pulse. She yelled, "Oh, my God, call an ambulance, Phoebe! Or a hearse. I think she's dead."

Soon sirens wailed outside. Uniformed police arrived first, followed moments later by the ambulance crew. The paramedics worked for several minutes but could not detect a pulse.

"I knew she was dead," Ellen wailed. A flurry of confusion arose as the officers shuffled the remaining women into the main parlor and away from the body.

They gathered in the smaller waiting room.

"We're going to need a statement from each of you. Who owns this shop?" a tall, burly officer asked.

Phoebe raised her hand.

"Where can we talk? I will need to interview each of you separately."

"You can use my office through that door beside the one leading to the dressing room where—Clarabella is."

"I'll talk to you first." He pointed at Phoebe and nodded toward the office. She led the way. Over his shoulder, he told a second uniformed officer to begin gathering pertinent witness names and information.

He perched on a white and gold brocade wingchair as Phoebe sat at her desk. He introduced himself as Officer Barnard, and then asked for preliminary information from Phoebe as to her full name, address, and contact information. He wrote as she talked.

"What happened here?"

"I don't know, Officer. Clarabella brought her wedding party here to find the final accessory to her wedding veil. She seemed to be very high-strung today. She'd been drinking before she got here, and we only served her non-alcoholic champagne, so as not to make matters worse. She was having a little conflict with some of her bridal attendants, but I think it might have stemmed from her being inebriated. Then I remembered a package had come for her today and she opened it to find an elaborate tiara. She tried it on and liked it. Of course, there was discussion about it. That caused some words between the bride and maid of honor, who walked out, followed by one of the bridesmaids. After a while she got quiet, and we all thought she'd fallen asleep. It wasn't until Ellen and Lettie, two of the bridesmaids, tried to wake her so they could leave, that she didn't respond. We realized she was frozen in place and unresponsive."

"Frozen?"

"Not in the literal sense of temperature, but in her movement. Paralyzed like."

"Other than the package, was anything else suspicious?"

"No, not really. I thought she had ordered the headpiece, since she came to the shop without an appointment. But she seemed surprised it was here when she saw the box."

"Where is the crown and the box?"

"The crown was still on her head. I'm sure they removed it to treat her, but it's in the room where the bod…where Clarabella is. The box should be on the counter. No, wait, it's over there." Phoebe pointed to the floor where the box had been knocked off the counter.

"Who else was here when the victim was trying on this head thing?"

"It's a veil topper."

"Okay, whatever it's called."

Phoebe pondered. "The maid of honor already left. All I know about her is her name is Marsha. I don't know the name of the girl who followed her out the door. She and Clarabella had some words. The others are still here. Bridesmaids. One is my friend Darcy. One is Ellen, and one is Lettie."

"Fine. I'll speak to each of them. If you don't mind, don't touch anything in your shop until the forensics team has completed their job." He paused and added, "Oh, and don't leave. I may have more questions to ask."

"I can't leave. This is my shop." It was her turn to pause before she asked, "Am I a suspect?"

The officer shrugged. "That'll be up to the detectives. Right now, this is a suspicious death. Everyone present is a suspect at the moment."

Phoebe returned to the main room. The medical examiner was on the scene. One by one, Officer Barnard interviewed the remaining bridesmaids.

To pass the time, Phoebe prepared orders and invoices.

Attendants from a local funeral home arrived and waited until the medical examiner released the body to their custody. Ellen broke into fresh sobs as the attendants brought in the gurney and again when they wheeled back through the doors. A sheet covered the body bag. Officer Barnard exchanged some words with the other uniformed officer.

Ellen glared at Phoebe. "This is all your fault. That headpiece killed Clarabella!"

"You don't know that," Darcy snapped.

"I didn't order that headpiece," Phoebe protested.

"Maybe Marsha did it," Lettie interjected. "She and Clarabella have been arguing like cats and dogs lately. She stomped out in a tiff. Maybe she knew something would happen and didn't want to be here when it did."

"Look, we can't go around accusing people without evidence," Darcy said.

Officer Barnard stepped back to the group of women and pointed at Ellen. She burst into a fresh round of tears when he asked her to come to the office for her interview. She pointed at Phoebe. "Arrest her. She's responsible! That crown killed the bride."

"Just let us do our investigation, Miss," the officer said as he followed her into the office and closed the door.

Phoebe chewed on a fingernail as she glanced toward her office. "Ohmigod, she's trying to blame me! I never even touched that gaudy crown."

"Oh, dear." Lettie stood and put a hand to her mouth. "The rest of us did. We all passed that around before she put it on."

"Look, everyone! Let's just stop speculating, get in there, and give our interview. Let the po-po do their job." Darcy sliced her hands through the air in a crisscross motion to indicate stop.

Phoebe's stomach roiled. What if she couldn't disprove Ellen's accusations?

*****

As the days passed, that thought filled her every waking moment. The police had combed through her shop several times before allowing her to remove the crime scene tape and resume normal business. The detectives assigned to the case contacted her two more times for further questioning. Although her fingerprints were found on the outside of the package, they had not found hers anywhere on the crown itself.

For a while, Darcy was a suspect due to the rather incriminating texts she'd sent to Phoebe on the day of the homicide, as was Marsha the MOH, who'd sent texts to friends saying she could just kill Clarabella. Phoebe and Darcy had attended the funeral services, remaining a discreet distance from the mourners.

For the first few days, gawkers strode past her shop or peered in through the windows. To make matters worse, two of her clients canceled their orders when word got around about the suspicious death inside Heads or Veils.

Life had almost returned to normal when she got a call from the police. She had just ended the ten-minute conversation when Darcy came into the shop.

"Hi, Darcy. I just got off the phone with the detectives. Guess what? The police have arrested Clarabella's killer. You'll never guess who."

"Who? How? Who? Marsha? Don't tell me Wesley the Weasel did it." Darcy's words rushed together as her breath hitched.

"No, it was Ellen! The last one I would have suspected. She was the one who sent that mysterious package with that dreadful headpiece. Do you remember what she did? After Clarabella opened the box and tried on the crown, Ellen was the one who 'noticed' the on-off switch that operated those bubbling lights in the crown?"

"Yes. I can't believe this. She was so concerned about Clarabella, so helpful. Hurry up and tell me what she did."

"It was blowdart poison! She rigged one of those glass tubes like a syringe. When the crown slipped down on Clarabella's head, she used the opportunity to inject the poison."

"You're kidding me! Where did she get the poison?"

"Oddly enough, the poison did come from the fiancé Wesley. It's curare and was used by indigenous people in blowdarts and as a form of anesthesia. While in South America on his missions, Wesley extracted the toxins as part of an experiment and brought home a vial with some of the residual paste. When they began their affair, he told Ellen about his experiments with the vial and its effects but never thought any more of it. Then she got the idea to create the headpiece and her medical training enabled her to adapt one of the tubes with the syringe laced with the poison. Then she sent it to your shop. When Ellen straightened the crown and fiddled with the on/off switch, she pushed the plunger, sending the needle into Clarabella's scalp. Apparently, the Bridezilla may have been too drunk to feel the prick of the needle. The poison entered her system, rendering her paralyzed. Within minutes, she suffocated when her respiratory muscles could not function."

"Did Wesley help her do this?"

"No. Even though he and Ellen had been in an affair, he still wanted to marry Clarabella. Ellen thought she'd have a better chance if she could get Clarabella out of the picture. When Wesley found out what she'd done, he immediately reported her to the police. She was already under suspicion because of her constant references to the crown during her interview. The autopsy showed the wound where the needle poked her scalp. Although the toxicology reports will take longer to confirm the exact poison, she confessed to everything, even to trying to throw suspicion on me."

"So, all the time she was gushing and admiring the bride-to-be's wedding veil and crown, she was planning to do her in. She thought she had the perfect cover by sending the rigged crown to you and it would cause the suspicion to fall on you?"

"Yes," Phoebe concluded. "I guess you could say it was a case of 'Veiled Threats' after all."

First Comes Love, Then Comes Murder

Teresa Inge grew up reading Nancy Drew mysteries. She is a member of Sisters in Crime, Short Mystery Fiction Society, Virginia Writer's Club, and Hampton Roads Writers. Teresa is an author in over a dozen anthologies including *Virginia is for Mysteries, Mutt Mysteries, Coastal Crimes, and Promophobia,* an Agatha award-winning collection. By day, Teresa works for a global financial firm as an assistant, corporate reporter, and notary administrator. When not writing, Teresa can be found showing her 1955 Thunderbird at car shows. She resides in Southeastern Virgina and can be reached on social media and her website www.teresainge.com

Heather Weidner has been a cop's kid, technical writer, editor, college professor, software tester, and IT manager. She writes the Pearly Girls Mysteries, the Delanie Fitzgerald Mysteries, The Jules Keene Glamping Mysteries, and The Mermaid Bay Christmas Shoppe Mysteries.

Her short stories appear in the *Virginia is for Mysteries* series, *50 Shades of Cabernet, Deadly Southern Charm,* and *Murder by the Glass,* and she has non-fiction pieces in *Promophobia* and *The Secret Ingredient: A Mystery Writers' Cookbook.*

Originally from Virginia Beach, Heather has been a mystery fan since Scooby-Doo and Nancy Drew. She lives in Central Virginia with her husband and a pair of Jack Russell terriers. You can find more about Heather and her books at http://HeatherWeidner.com.

Judge Debra H. Goldstein is the author of Kensington's Sarah Blair mystery series, *Should Have Played Poker* and IPPY Award-winning *Maze in Blue*. Her novels and short stories, which have appeared in numerous periodicals and anthologies, have been named Agatha, Anthony, Derringer, Claymore, and Silver Falchion finalists and received Silver Falchion, Bethlehem Writers Roundtable, and Alabama Writers awards. She serves on the national board of Sisters in Crime and previously was a national board member of Mystery Writers of America and president of the Guppy and SEMWA chapters. Find out more about Debra at https://www.DebraHGoldstein.com.

Grace Topping is a *USA Today* bestselling author and Agatha Award finalist. A recovering technical writer and IT project manager, she was accustomed to writing lean, boring documents. Let loose to write fiction, she is now creating murder mysteries and killing off characters who remind her of some of the people she dealt with during her career. Grace is the former vice president of the Chesapeake Chapter of Sisters in Crime, a member of the Guppy Chapter steering committee, and a member of Mystery Writers of America. She lives with her husband in Northern Virginia.

Ellen Butler is the international bestselling author of the Karina Cardinal mystery series. Her experiences working on Capitol Hill and at a medical association in Washington, D.C. inspired the mystery-action series. Critics call the Karina Cardinal mysteries, "intelligent escapism" and "electrifying yet light-hearted and humorous." Butler also writes historical spy fiction. Her WWII spy novel, *The Brass Compass*, won a 2022 Speak Up Talk Radio Firebird Book Award. The second book in the duology, *Operation Blackbird: A Cold War Spy Novel*, is inspired by true events and won a Next Generation Indie Book Award gold medal for historical fiction. Reviewers are calling it "riveting," and, "a thrilling adventure."

Kristin Kisska is a native of Virginia, where she currently resides with her family and their moody tabby, Boom. She holds a BS in commerce from the University of Virginia and an MBA from Northwestern University. She is the author of a dozen short stories published in anthologies and her debut novel, *The Hint of Light.* Kristin loves hearing from friends and readers at www.KristinKisska.com.

Shawn Reilly Simmons is the author of nine novels in the Red Carpet Catering mystery series featuring Penelope Sutherland, chef-owner of a movie set catering company. She's also written over twenty short stories which have been published in various anthologies. Shawn has been nominated for the Agatha Award three times and has won twice. She's also an Anthony Award winner in the Best Anthology category as an editor. In addition to her own writing, Shawn is President and Managing Editor at Level Best Books, a crime fiction press with a roster of roughly two hundred authors. She hosts a weekly podcast, *Five Compelling Questions with Shawn,* where she chats with writers across all genres about writing. Shawn is also a co-host of the YouTube series *We Are What We Read,* which features authors highlighting books that have inspired and influenced them and their careers. She is a member of Sisters in Crime, Mystery Writers of America, the International Thriller Writers, and the Crime Writers' Association in the UK, and a founding member of The Dames of Detection. Shawn served on the Board of Malice Domestic for over twenty years (2002-2023), where she welcomed hundreds of mystery writers and fans to the Washington, D.C. area each spring to celebrate the genre of Traditional Mystery and Agatha Christie. In 2027, Shawn will co-Chair Bouchercon, Mystery Most Monumental, in Washington, D.C. She lives in historic downtown Frederick, Maryland, with her husband, son, and Dino, their very huggable French Bulldog.

Marilyn Levinson A former Spanish teacher, Marilyn Levinson writes mysteries, romantic suspense, and novels for kids. Her books have received many accolades. As Allison Brook she writes the Haunted

Library series. *Death Overdue*, the first in the series, was an Agatha nominee for Best Contemporary Novel in 2018. *Out of Circulation*, the eighth book in the series will be published in August 2024. Other mysteries include the Golden Age of Mystery Book Club series and the Twin Lakes series.

Her juvenile novel, *Rufus and Magic Run Amok*, was an International Reading Association-Children's Book Council Children's Choice and has recently come out in a new edition. *And Don't Bring Jeremy* was a nominee for six state awards. Her YA horror, *The Devil's Pawn*, will be out in a new edition in 2024.

Marilyn lives on Long Island, where many of her books take place. She loves traveling, reading, doing crossword puzzles and Sudoku, chatting on FaceTime with her grandkids, and playing with her kittens, Romeo and Juliet.

Sandra Murphy lives in St Louis with Ozzie the Almost-Westie dog and Louie the tuxedo cat. She spends much of her time communing with her imaginary friends who tell her their stories. Unlike guests who eventually leave, imaginary friends stay forever with an endless number of tales to share. Sandra also writes magazine articles, edits a newsletter, and may someday hear a story that will reach book length.

Mary Dutta is the winner of the New England Crime Bake Al Blanchard Award for her short story "The Wonderworker," which appears in Masthead: Best New England Crime Stories. Her work can also be found in numerous anthologies including the Anthony-nominated Land of 10,000 Thrills: Bouchercon Anthology 2022 and Malice Domestic 16: Mystery Most Diabolical. She is a member of Sisters in Crime and the Short Mystery Fiction Society. Visit her at marydutta.com and enjoy her blog at Writers Who Kill.

Maggie King is the author of the Hazel Rose Book Group mysteries. Her short stories appear in the *Virginia is for Mysteries series*, *50 Shades of Cabernet*, *Deadly Southern Charm*, *Death by Cupcake*, and *Murder by the Glass*. Maggie is a member of James River Writers, Short

Mystery Fiction Society, and is a founding member of Sisters in Crime Central Virginia. She manages the Sisters in Crime Instagram accounts at the chapter and national levels. Maggie graduated from Rochester Institute of Technology and has worked as a software developer, retail sales manager, and customer service supervisor. She lives in Richmond, Virginia.

Diane Fanning is the author of 15 true crime books, and 11 mystery novels and has been featured in 3 anthology collections. She has been a consultant for 48 hours and been on numerous other television shows including 20/20, the Today Show, and Deadly Women. She lives in Bedford, Virginia, with her husband and a Sheltie named Emmitt Otter.

Libby Hall is relatively new to the publishing scene. She has had short stories published in the Murder by the Glass and Southern Deadly Charm anthologies and is currently working on a Southern fiction novel. To keep her sanity, she writes a humor blog, Subourbonmom.blog, where she shares her (unsolicited) thoughts on everything from the pitfalls of middle age to port-o-john etiquette and why chardonnay is the perfect workout substitute. Libby is a long-time member of the James River Writers Group and Sisters in Crime.

Frances Aylor is an avid traveler who has paraglided in Switzerland, climbed the Great Wall of China, gone white-water rafting in Costa Rica, and fished for piranha in the Amazon. She is a member of Sisters in Crime and International Thriller Writers. Formerly an investment analyst, she now focuses on her writing and has published two mysteries and several short stories. She won the Rising Star award from Ingram Spark for her thriller *Money Grab*, and was first runner-up for the 2021 Claymore Award for *Choosing Guilt*.

K.L. Murphy is the award-nominated author of *Her Sister's Death*, a 2023 Silver Falchion Finalist for Best Mystery, as well as the Detective Cancini Mystery Series: *A Guilty Mind, Stay of Execution*, and *The Last Sin*. She is also the author of *Last Girl Missing*, the first in a new series featuring Detective Callie Forde (coming in 2024). You can find more of her short stories in *Deadly Southern Charm* and *Murder by the Glass*. From Richmond, VA, K.L. is a member of Mystery Writers of America, International Thriller Writers, Sisters in Crime, and James River Writers.

Eleanor Cawood Jones, inspired by *Ellery Queen's Mystery Magazine* at a young age, grabbed a #2 pencil and began writing mysteries starring her stuffed animals. Her more recent stories include "The Importance of Being Urnest" (*Black Cat Weekly*), "Bon Bon Voyage: Gone with the Tide" (*Murder at Sea*), and 2021 Derringer Award-winning "The Great Bedbug Incident and the Invitation of Doom" (*Chesapeake Crimes: Invitation to Murder*). A former newspaper reporter and recovered marketing director, Eleanor now works at an international airport. When not traveling or writing, she's rearranging furniture and trying to figure out how the neighbor's cat moved in.

Leah St. James writes stories of good and evil, the mysteries of life, and the enduring power of love. Her published works span the genres from romantic suspense, mystery, and police procedurals to women's fiction and even a children's fairy tale.

A member of Sisters in Crime, Central Virginia Chapter, and the Alliance of Independent Authors, Leah is a native of the Central Jersey Shore but now lives in Richmond, Virginia, with her husband. Together they have two wonderful sons, two amazing daughters-in-law, and several fun and rambunctious grand critters.

Sheryl Jordan was born in Portugal, and raised in Minnesota. She has a bachelor's degree in criminal justice. She is a member of the Sisters in Crime National Chapter and the Mysteries by the Sea Chapter Secretary. Sheryl is the author of Manipulation, Money, and Murder, a fictional novel based on actual events. She has contributed short stories in Coastal Crimes Mysteries by the Sea (Mama Saundra's Shenanigans) and Virginia is for Mysteries Volume III (The Lady Ginger) anthologies. Sheryl enjoys spending time with family, watching football and basketball, and writing mysteries.

Allie Marie is an Award-winning author who grew up in Virginia, where her favorite childhood pastime was reading Nancy Drew and Trixie Belden mysteries which led to a career in law enforcement in the US as well as overseas.

After retirement, Allie embarked on a quest to fulfill a long-time dream—to write mysteries and crime thrillers. Ancestry research, however, inspired The True Colors Series, a paranormal mystery series with modern local settings and colonial history that has garnered multiple awards, followed by a spinoff collection, The True Spirits Trilogy. Her standalone historical mystery, *Return to Afton Square*, bridges the two series. She has contributed short stories in various genres to several anthologies.

Those other planned mystery stories? They still patiently wait for their turn.

Besides family, her passions are traveling anywhere, any time, and camping with her husband Jack.